MUCKY STREAK

Squeaky Clean Mysteries, Book 7

By Christy Barritt

CHRISTY BARRITT

Mucky Streak: A Novel
Copyright 2014 by Christy Barritt

Published by River Heights Press

Cover design by The Killion Group

Seek justice,
Love mercy,
Walk humbly
With our God.
~Micah 6:8

CHRISTY BARRITT

CHAPTER 1

I brushed away my discomfort, instead trying to appear sophisticated and coolly in control. I felt neither of those things. My life at the moment felt about as frazzled as my curly red hair.

I brushed a piece of the thus stated hair behind my ear, sucked in a measured breath, and extended my hand. "Mr. Mercer."

"Ms. St. Claire. I'm glad you could meet with me." Garrett Mercer grinned, the ever-present sparkle still in his eyes as he circled from behind his desk and took my hand. His grip lingered a little too long.

As I pulled my hand back, his eyes remained smiling in a way that made me think he was more Irish than British. The man liked getting a reaction from me. I knew that much from my last encounter with him.

Garrett owned a company called Global Coffee Initiative that not only sold organic, free trade coffee, but also donated a good portion of the proceeds to build water wells for the less fortunate around the world. He was a textbook entrepreneur/prodigy, and he had a killer accent.

I lowered myself into the chair across from him and crossed my legs, trying to maintain an aura of professionalism. Lack of sleep and stress made common courtesies feel a little more challenging. I wished for a moment that I had the unruffled composure of the woman who'd just deposited me in Garrett's office. I was pretty sure she was Garrett's assistant—a neat and prim little blonde named Lyndsey. She probably wasn't just his assistant, if I had to guess based on the glance they'd exchanged. Then again, all of Garrett's employees looked like they'd just stepped out of an Abercrombie & Fitch catalog.

I cleared my throat. "Your phone call certainly made me curious."

He'd left a message two days ago, asking me to call him about a possible job. I had no idea what kind of job someone like the wealthy, world changer Garrett Mercer might want to hire a crime scene cleaner like me for.

I didn't know the man that well, other than the fact I'd met him during my last investigation. One of his employees had been a suspect, and Garrett and I had chatted a couple of times. After the case was closed, I figured Garrett would be gone from my life for good. Yet, here I sat.

Garrett leaned against his desk, his ankles crossed and his arms now resting to his side. "Anything I can do to get you thinking about me."

He winked. The man was charming. I'd give him that. Probably one of the many qualities that helped him build his successful enterprise in the coffee world, and landed him on several "most desired," "most beautiful," "most interesting" and any-other-positive-superlative-you-might-want-to-include lists. He had this certain kind of demeanor that made women clamor for a chance to be around him. That made employees eager to please him. That made the media swoon.

But not me. I was immune to the man's charms. I was . . . wait for it . . . I was all professional.

Barely holding it together was more like it.

What I really wanted to do was take a nap. Maybe escape to the Bahamas for a while. Maybe lose myself in a musical. None of those things were an option.

Instead, in the overhead music of my mind, I continued to blare "Stronger" by Kelly Clarkson. That's right—I was determined that all these hard times were just going to make me more of a fighter.

Garrett studied me for a minute, not even trying to hide his curiosity. "You look tired. Can I get you some coffee? Maybe one of our new flavors like maple bacon or autumn harvest?"

Normally, I might refuse. But I could really use some coffee to chase away my chills and my crankiness. Escaping the man's scrutiny for a moment also sounded delightful. "Actually, that sounds great. Just regular coffee, please. Two sugars and one cream."

"I've got it."

I should look tired. I'd been working myself to the bone. When I wasn't working, I was taking Riley, my fiancé, to therapy as he tried to recover from a brain injury. I had to admit that everything—being abducted by a serial killer and almost dying, my busy schedule, the stress, the shock of life's unexpected curveball—was catching up with me. I was just plain exhausted. My joy was slipping away, and life was beginning to feel like a chore.

It's just a phase, I reminded myself. I could get through this. As long as I had God and Riley by my side, I could handle anything. In theory, I easily believed that. It was much more difficult to put into practice, though.

I glanced around the office as I sat there waiting for Garrett to return. Garrett's company headquarters was located in an old warehouse turned office space. The floors were still cement, only sealed and polished. Open space, windows, and skylights made the area feel big and exuded a very urban, modern, and repurposed vibe.

Very much like Garrett.

Tall, sturdy, and stylishly underdressed, the man was considerate of the environment, responsible, and wealthy. Apparently, he'd nearly flunked out of college, only to turn his life around and create the successful business he had today. That's what my best friend Sierra had told me, at least. I tried not to ask too many questions or appear too interested when Garrett and I spoke.

I glanced around at his office. Minimalist decorations. Large picture windows. An enormous aquarium with crazy looking fish inside. Pictures of him surrounded by kids with dirty faces but big smiles and barren landscapes behind them.

Gerard Butler, I decided. That's who the man reminded me of.

A moment later, I heard him in the hallway. He murmured something and a woman giggled incessantly. I glanced behind me. Lyndsey. His "assistant."

He handed me a cup, made from recycled paper—of course. Our hands brushed, and I'd bet anything it was no accident. Garrett was a touchy feely kind of guy. He liked getting what he wanted.

"So, I'm sure you're wondering why I asked you to meet with me." He settled back in his normal position, leaning against his desk like he was posing for some random *GQ* photographer. He wore jeans that probably cost more than I made at one job site and a lush beige sweater that zipped up to his neck.

I took a sip of my coffee and let the warmth spread through me. "I am curious as to why you wanted to meet with me."

"I'll get right to the point, then. I heard about your work in the Milton Jones case. By all accounts, you were brilliant and brave. Your work helped to take a serial killer off the streets, and we're all safer because of it."

"What can I say? It's all in a day's work." I didn't mention that I'd almost died and that I was still having nightmares—night terrors were more like it—about the ordeal. I cringed whenever I saw a swamp or an old cabin or when thunder shook the walls of my apartment. Each caused strong memories to swell so fiercely that I could hardly breathe.

Milton Jones had probably made some lists himself—as one of the most horrific serial killers that America had seen this decade. Maybe in the past two decades. I wasn't sure. Thankfully, he wouldn't be a problem for anyone else anymore.

"I understand that you worked for the medical examiner for a while." He took a sip of his coffee, but his eyes stayed on me, watching my every expression.

"You've done your research."

"I'm nothing if not thorough." That smirk—it was becoming all too familiar—tugged at his lips.

I had no doubt that the man was as smart as a whip . . . or as sly as a fox. I wasn't sure which one yet. "What's all of that have to do with this meeting? You want details on how I tracked Jones down? Because, honestly, I have a million other things I need to be doing. No offense."

Reporters had been knocking down my door, trying to get the inside scoop. Even a few national broadcasts had contacted me. I had mixed feelings on sharing my side of the story . . . mostly because my side of the story included almost losing the love of my life. I was so grateful Riley was alive, but so much had changed since he'd suffered from a gunshot wound to the head.

Though the doctors expected a full recovery for Riley, I was trying to accept the fact that things would never be the same. I was trying to be okay with that. It was easier said than done, though.

Like most things in life.

"No offense taken." Garrett leaned closer. "No, I didn't bring you here to waste your time. I want to hire you, actually."

I raised an eyebrow. "Hire me? You have a crime scene you want me to clean? Something you want to tell me? Let me guess: Entrepreneur by day, serial killer by night?" I wouldn't have said it so lightly except I knew it wasn't true. Well, I was pretty sure it wasn't.

"No, I don't need you to clean for me." His grin slipped some, and he straightened the sleeves of his sweater. "I'd like to hire you as a P.I., Gabby."

This was a new one for me. Sure, I'd solved a few crimes. But no one had ever *hired* me to do that. No, it was just because I was nosy and pushy and loved justice too much for my own good. "A private investigator?"

"Yes. A private investigator. Just one more confirmation that you're good. Nothing gets past you." He winked.

I scowled again. "Funny."

"All right, enough playing, right? Yes, I want to hire you to look into a case. Law enforcement would call it a cold case. It will require some travel, but I promise to compensate you well."

Compensation sounded good. Especially since I'd just overdrawn my checking account by more than three hundred dollars. "I'm listening."

He stiffened and rubbed his chin. Instead of gushing out some story in the gregarious way I'd become accustomed to when it came to Garrett, he stood. He went to the other side of his desk and sat, a somber new expression on his face.

"There's a part of my life that most people don't know about. I try to keep it quiet because, quite frankly, it's painful."

He had my attention now. I supposed in my mind I pictured people like Garrett to have everything handed to them on a silver platter; to live charmed lives void of pain and heartache. I should know better than that by now.

"My family moved here from England when I was fourteen. My dad worked for a consumer products company, then moved on to a start-up before being offered a job with a pharmacy company in Washington, D.C. My mum and sister and I came along for the ride. Begrudgingly, I might add."

I shifted, intrigued by his story already. "Okay."

"We moved again three years later when a pharmaceutical company in Cincinnati offered my father an even more prestigious position. When I was 19, I came home from college for the weekend. I was late arriving. I'd decided to stay for a party the night before, so I came home on Saturday instead of Friday night as planned."

I waited to hear what happened next.

His face tensed, as if the memories were painful. "Quite truthfully, my mum and dad had been quite argumentative the past several times I'd seen them, and I would have rather not been around them. They insisted they had something to speak with me about, however."

"Go on."

"When I walked into my house that morning, I found my family." He paused and rubbed his throat. "They'd all been shot in the head execution style."

I sucked in a deep breath, the horror of the event washing over me. "That's terrible."

"To say the least. My life changed from that day forward. Tragedy does that to you." He shifted, tugging at his pant leg now, a small tell as to how painful this was to him. "This is where I would like for you to come in. You see, the police never found the person responsible for my family's death. I won't have a moment of peace in my life until the person who murdered them is behind bars."

"Where are the police at with this? Have they completely given up?"

"They say that they've followed every lead, and that every lead has dried up. They've got nothing."

"I know it's hard to get closure without all of the answers. Any of the answers, for that matter."

"You've got that right." He held up a folder stuffed with papers. "I was able to get my hands on the police reports. I have all the information on who they interviewed, who their suspects were, what evidence they found."

I stared at the papers like a kid salivating for cotton candy at the circus. I wasn't delighting in his pain; I was salivating at the chance for justice to be served, for answers to be found, for lives to be restored.

He pressed his lips together. "Are you interested in taking this on?"

I paused, trying to think through my response. Putting my brain into gear before my mouth engaged was my new resolution, and no, it wasn't New Year's. Big life changes could cause a person to rethink things. "What makes you think I can figure this out if seasoned investigators can't?"

"Something tells me you're different, Gabby. You're spunky and determined. I have a feeling people open up to you more easily than they'd ever open up to one of those crusty old detectives."

"I'm flattered." I actually *was* flattered, despite how sarcastic my words might have sounded.

"I'm serious." Garrett's eyes met mine, all teasing

gone. "What do you think?"

The offer was tempting. Very tempting. But I didn't know if I could take it on right now. I had my hands full with my crime scene cleaning business and trying to help my fiancé. Taking Riley back and forth to therapy as he recovered from his brain injury seemed like a full-time job. Plus, I was cooking for him, cleaning his apartment, buying his groceries, and even doing his laundry. Small, molehill-sized tasks had turned into giant mountains for him.

"I'm not sure what to say," I finally said. "To be honest, I have a lot going on in my life right now."

He nodded toward my engagement ring. "When's the wedding?"

I realized I'd been absently twisting and turning the jewelry on my finger, remembering the events that had played out over the past couple of months. I frowned. "I'm not sure."

Garrett quirked an eyebrow and tilted his head compassionately. "That doesn't sound good."

My heart squeezed at his words. I wouldn't let Garrett Mercer get the best of me. Things were fine between Riley and me. "It's a long story."

He stared at me again, and I wondered what was going on behind those green eyes. "I see. I won't pry. Just promise me you'll think about taking this job. Take these files. They contain the basic information. Look them through."

"I will. I'll be in touch." I glanced at my watch. "But I should run now. I have another appointment."

"I understand. But you should know that I'm not a very patient man." He leveled his gaze. "I need an answer in a week."

"I can do that." I took the file from him, and something stirred inside me. Something I hadn't felt in the last couple of months. Something I hadn't felt since Milton Jones.

The longing to find answers. The excitement of a new mystery. The adrenaline surge of facing an engaging challenge.

Garrett stood to walk me to the door. His hand went to my lower back to guide me across the room and, just as it happened last time, a jolt of electricity shot through me. I wasn't sure why the man had this effect on me, but he did. And the fact had me steamed.

He seemed to realize this, too, based on the sparkle in his eyes. Maybe he could feel my skin tighten. Maybe he could hear the quick intake of my breath. I wasn't sure.

But I didn't like that, either.

"Good day, Gabby. Help yourself to another cup of coffee on the way out."

I walked toward the reception area, hating the uncertain feeling in my gut. I hated the pull between two opposing desires: investigating an intriguing case or being a good, responsible fiancé. It appeared I couldn't be or do both.

It didn't matter right now, though. I had to pick up Riley from therapy.

CHAPTER 2

Ten minutes later, I sat in the parking lot of the hospital. Traffic had been miraculously light, so I'd gotten here earlier than I anticipated. Instead of going inside to wait, I decided to peruse the papers Garrett had given me.

The paper on top of the file appeared to be the most recent article about his family's murders. The article was glossy, from a magazine. A nice magazine. I glanced at the bottom of the page. *Time* magazine.

Wow. This *had* been a big story.

The headline read, "Murder at the Mercer House." As I skimmed the article, my gut clenched at the details.

Garrett's dad, mom, and sister were all shot point blank. Nothing was stolen from the house, and nothing had been left except for a couple of footprints. It was almost as if a ghost had come in, done the deed, and disappeared.

The police had no motives and no real suspects.

Apparently, some suspected a contractor hired to renovate the Mercer's bathrooms who'd been seen flirting with Elizabeth Mercer, the mother. The contractor had a criminal history and no alibi. But the authorities also had no proof that he'd been to the house on the night of the murders, nothing to tie him to the scene.

Another man named Arnold James was also suspected. He'd killed another family in Missouri, had stolen nothing, and left very little evidence. There certainly seemed to be similarities in the cases, but nothing that truly connected James with the Mercers. The man was now in prison, serving a lifetime sentence, so confessing to the murder of the Mercer family wouldn't have added any real time to his stay behind bars, yet he still claimed his innocence.

Some speculated it was a copycat crime, one meant to mirror Arnold James' pattern of murder. The problem was, even if it was a copycat crime, they had no suspects for the copycat perpetrator.

There seemed to be absolutely nothing to go on when it came to finding the killer.

Which would make one interesting investigation.

I glanced up at the time on the console of my van and gasped. I was three minutes late meeting Riley.

I threw the folder into my passenger seat, grabbed my purse, and dashed through the parking lot. In my haste, I darted in front of an oncoming car. The smell of burning rubber quickly assaulted my senses and deepened my guilt.

I tapped the hood, waved, and tried to ignore the driver shaking his fist out the window at me. I knew Riley would be fine for a few minutes without me. But a small part of me feared leaving him alone for too long. I feared he might wander or forget who was picking him up.

I was so thankful to have Riley in my life. The past couple of months had been hard, though. Despite the fact that he was recovering physically from his brain injury, he was still having trouble with his memory. The doctor wasn't sure how quickly those issues would resolve. In my mind, there was a possibility they would never resolve.

Honestly, I just wanted my old Riley back. I felt selfish, but every night, that's what I prayed for. Over and over again. To the point of tears.

And I had moments of hope. I had moments when I

saw glimpses of my old Riley. His humor came out. His protective instinct showed. His intelligence became clear.

But then he had other moments of looking vacant. Of not remembering certain moments in our history. Of looking like he couldn't find the words.

Those were the heartbreaking moments. The moments when I realized that Riley may have survived the gunshot wound, but he still had a lot more to survive.

I tore inside the building, bypassed the elevator and climbed two flights of stairs. I was breathless by the time I reached the Neurology Wing.

Riley was in the waiting room. He stood when I walked in.

Good. He hadn't wandered out. Hadn't forgotten I was coming. Hadn't panicked.

I rushed toward him and kissed his cheek. "Sorry I'm late."

"It's okay," he insisted.

I studied his face a moment. His blue eyes were gloriously beautiful and clear. He had thick, dark hair and nicely proportioned, even features.

Really, Riley looked the same. If someone saw him and didn't know what had happened, they'd have no idea. They wouldn't know the trauma his brain had been through. They'd have no clue that the once successful attorney had put his law firm on hiatus and assigned his cases to other attorneys. They wouldn't guess how frustrated he became sometimes because his life had been turned upside down.

Today, there was something new in his gaze. Almost . . . an apology? I couldn't be sure. I decided I was imagining things.

We started walking back down the hall. "How'd it go?"

He shrugged. "My therapist said I'm making progress."

"That's great. It's going to take time. But it will happen." I reached down and grabbed his hand. He used to be the one who grabbed my hand, but I wasn't complaining. Not really. At least, I was trying not to complain.

"That's what everyone says." Riley frowned. My old Riley was a fighter, a crusader. He'd been athletic and sure of himself.

It's going to take some time. But it will happen. My own words echoed in my head. Maybe my problem was just that I was impatient.

We climbed on the elevator, squeezing between three senior citizens, two nurses, and a family with a small child. The ride down felt awkward and tight. There was no need to attempt a conversation.

We stepped off and began walking toward my van. I pulled my canvas jacket closer. Winter seemed ready to stake its claim on the area, even though it was only early November.

As we walked, I sensed a new heaviness about Riley. I wanted him to tell me what it was, though. That was one of the things the therapist said to do. Not to push too hard. To let him deal with things on his terms.

"Did you get any work done today?" Riley asked, changing the subject.

"I worked a little while this morning. Chad and I are renovating fire damage at a house. Can you believe it? It was Chad's idea. He mentioned something about wanting to expand our company outside of crime scene cleaning."

"What do you think about that?"

I shrugged. "I guess it makes sense. Expanding would give us more opportunities, though there's a part of me that's still holding back. Regardless, I spent all morning learning how to properly use a nail gun."

He smiled. "I'm sure you'll master it in no time."

"I just hope I master it without accidentally killing someone first."

"Didn't you say you had a meeting with someone, also?" Riley asked.

"As a matter of fact, I did." I told him about Garrett's job offer, probably delving into too many details. But it was something to talk about. Something that wasn't life changing or a sad reminder in our own lives of what could have been. The topic seemed like safe territory.

Riley looked down at me, that same heaviness still present in his eyes. "You should go for it."

I shrugged. In times past, I would have been tempted to say yes to the challenge of officially investigating a case. But things had changed. "It's a tempting offer, but I probably won't accept it."

"Why not? It's because of me, isn't it?"

I paused right there in the parking lot and laid my hand on his chest.

"Of course it's not because of you." I shook my head, realizing that the words I'd intended to be soothing might actually sound like apathy. "I mean, yes, you do play a part in my decision."

Riley looked confused.

What did I mean? "I'm just trying to say that I want to be there for you. This isn't a good time."

He squeezed my arm. "You've already made a lot of sacrifices, Gabby. It's starting to wear you down. I can see it in your eyes."

I shook my head and looked away, afraid he'd see too much truth in my gaze. "That's not true."

He let out a sigh but said nothing. Slowly, almost unwillingly, we started walking again. We took several paces in silence until we reached the garage.

"You'd need to go to Cincinnati if you took the case, wouldn't you?" Riley pulled away from me and stuffed his hands inside his jacket pockets, his steps slowing.

My eyes widened. "You've heard of the case."

I was amazed at what he remembered and didn't remember. For instance, he couldn't remember when we'd almost been killed while tracking down an escaped serial killer whom Riley had put behind bars back when he was a prosecutor in L.A. He couldn't remember being shot, either. It was probably better that way.

"The story was all over the news back when I was in college."

I was surprised I hadn't heard of it. Of course, back then I was immersed in my studies. When I wasn't studying, I was helping to take care of my mom who'd been diagnosed with cancer. I'd picked up extra jobs to help with the bills.

We reached my van and climbed inside. He picked up the papers from the files and glanced through them as I cranked the engine. "Sounds like a really interesting case, Gabby. I didn't put it together that Garrett was connected with those murders. I'm sure having some answers would mean a lot to him."

"You remember Garrett?" Again—how did he remember that detail, of all things?

"I remember you talking about your encounters with him when I was in the coma."

The coma.

My throat clenched at the memory. Those had been some hard, hard days. The uncertainty of not knowing whether Riley would wake up had wreaked havoc on me both physically and emotionally. Spiritually and mentally, too, if I were honest with myself.

I put the van in reverse, but Riley's hand covered mine.

"Wait a minute, Gabby. There's something I need to tell you."

Tension pinched my spine as I slid the van back into park. "Okay, what is it?"

He glanced down at his lap. "I've been thinking a lot lately, Gabby. I've been talking to my therapist about something, and I think I've finally made a decision."

"Made a decision about what?" Dread formed in my gut.

He licked his lips before his eyes met mine. "I'm going to go stay with my parents for a while, Gabby."

"Your parents? Why would you do that?" His parents lived up in D.C., about three and a half hours from here.

"Because my mom has offered to help with my recovery. She doesn't work, and my parents have the resources. They can transport me around without having to rearrange their schedules."

All the air left my lungs. "Please don't punish me because I have to work and I don't have resources."

He wiped a hair out of my eyes. "Punishing you is the last thing I want to do. I want to do the opposite."

"Then don't go," I hurried. All thoughts of exhaustion and being overwhelmed fled from my mind.

"It's the only way things are going to return to normal."

Tears rimmed my eyes. "You're breaking up with me?"

"No!" he rushed. "I'm just giving you some space. I'm giving *me* some space. I think this is going to be the best for both of us. At least I won't feel like a burden this way."

"A burden? I've never thought of you as a burden. If we were married—like we were supposed to be—this would just be one of those valleys, one of those 'for worse' moments—"

"But we're not married, Gabby." Riley's words caused

my heart to feel like a brick, like a solid lump that made it hard to breath.

"We should be married," I added. We were a week away from the big day when he was shot.

"Life isn't fair, Gabby. You and I both know that."

Circumstances continued to prove that to me again and again. Including this moment right now.

"I want you to stay," I finally stated.

He rubbed the top of my hands with his thumb. "This isn't forever, Gabby. It's just until I'm better. Until I don't have so many appointments. Until I can start working again. We'll still talk. Every day. I can come down to visit or you can come up to my parents' place."

A little bit of hope pooled in my heart. Still, I couldn't help but think this was the end for us. I couldn't help but envision him moving up to D.C. and staying. Or meeting someone else. A nice little nurse who helped nurture him back to health maybe. Or what if he felt like he'd always need his family's help and support? Or that D.C. was a much better place for his social justice law firm?

"My therapist agreed that I have too much pressure on myself here. I can't keep going on like nothing's changed. Everything's changed, and I have to accept that."

I pressed the corners of my eyes as tears threatened to overflow. "I can't change your mind, can I?"

"This is for the best, as hard as it may seem. It's not ideal, but it's the solution I've been praying for."

I stared ahead vacantly, trying to grasp another life change, another life disappointment. My throat squeezed out any words that wanted to escape. It was probably better that I didn't say anything else. I didn't want to stress Riley out, after all.

He squeezed my hand. "I love you, Gabby. Nothing will ever change that."

I nodded and stared back at the parking garage.

I wished I believed his words. But my past had taught me that love was hard to come by and even harder to make stick.

CHAPTER 3

Five days later, I sat in my apartment, staring into space. The soundtrack to *Les Miserables* played in the background. More precisely, the track "On My Own" played over and over again. I may or may not have set the CD player on repeat.

What could be more appropriate right now than a sad little melody about pretending your love was with you when he wasn't?

I mean, if I had a daisy I might pull off the petals and do a little "he loves me, he loves me not." But I was too afraid I'd end up with "he loves me not."

I'd almost watched "Message in a Bottle" or any of those other Nicholas Sparks' books-turned-movies that would leave me in tears. But I resisted.

Riley had moved out yesterday. By moved out, that just meant he wasn't physically at his apartment. He'd taken his clothes and toiletries, but his furniture and everything else remained.

That brought me a small measure of comfort.

Still, the whole apartment building was up for sale, which was just one more of many changes I faced in my life right now. Sure, the place was run down and old. And, there was the fact the residents of the old chopped up Victorian were as vastly different as my mood swings had been lately. But this place was home, and I had no desire to move.

Sierra, my best friend, plopped down on the couch beside me and squeezed my shoulder. Her little Asian face, usually determined and tense, looked so compassionate at the moment. "It's going to be okay, Gabby."

"Nothing feels okay. I don't want to whine. I want what's best for Riley, too. But I can't help but think this isn't it."

Chad—Sierra's husband and my business partner—sat on the other side of me. He still had that surfer-like air about him with hair that was too long and a face that needed to be shaved. He and Sierra were total opposites, but they seemed incredibly happy together.

My friends were attempting to have a "let's cheer up Gabby party," but it wasn't really working. They'd brought over a few of my favorite things, including pizza and cheese balls—something I only ate if I was really feeling down. We'd tried to play a game of Clue, but my heart wasn't into it.

"Tell me about this job offer you mentioned," Chad started, popping another cheese ball in his mouth. "This P.I. gig. It sounds right up your alley."

I shook my head. "It doesn't matter. I'm part owner of Trauma Care. I have other responsibilities." I had to stay focused and forget about any flights of fancy.

"I think you should take the job," Chad said.

I looked up at Chad, surprised. If I slacked off, he was the one who had to cover for me. That could mean some brutal hours. "It's too much work for you."

"Clarice is helping. I think we can manage, especially if you just give yourself a set time limit. I mean, we don't want you gone for months or anything. But a week or two? We'll be okay."

Part of me felt relieved; the other part of me wanted to think I was a little more indispensable than this.

"You said this investigation would take you to Cincinnati, right?" Chad asked.

I nodded.

"My cousin lives there. You could stay with her. She could show you around. Plus, she has some pull. She's a social worker, and her mom—my Aunt Lydia—is involved in more local causes than one person can count. I'd say between them, you'll have a wealth of resources at hand."

"Really? I didn't know you had connections with the area."

He nodded. "Yeah, I think you'd really like my cousin. Her name is Holly. Holly Anna, actually. We used to give her the hardest time about her name. *Holly Anna the Pollyanna*. She's a trip."

Maybe things were starting to fall in place.

"Gabby, I think it would be good for you to get away from here for a while. There are too many memories," Sierra started. "Some time away might help you clear your head, gain a new perspective. I know you don't want to admit it, but you've been through a lot."

"People have been through worse." I hardly believed the words myself.

"Seriously, Gabby," Sierra continued. "I was just reading up on the stress scale. I took the initiative to take it for you, and with everything that's happened in your life recently, you have a good chance of becoming physically ill or having a mental breakdown."

I stared at her a moment, unsure how to respond. Then I realized she was dead serious and truly worried about me.

Now that she mentioned it, getting away did seem like a good idea. Maybe Sierra was on to something. If Chad thought the business was covered, then perhaps there was nothing to keep me here. For a while, at least. It wasn't like I'd be moving permanently.

But there were other issues to consider. Issues I didn't want to own up to. But I knew I could trust Sierra and Chad. Besides, if I didn't open up to my friends, whom could I talk to? I had to start letting down the walls I'd so skillfully crafted . . . for my entire life.

I rubbed my throat, the memories threatening to take over. "There's also the issue of investigating a killer. I still have nightmares . . ."

Sierra squeezed my knee. I didn't have to finish. She knew exactly what I was talking about. "This is nothing. A little cold case. It's nothing like Milton Jones."

"It involves a killer who murdered an entire family."

"Ten years ago," Chad added. "I think you can handle this."

"It will be good for you," Sierra continued. "Of course I'll miss you like crazy, but then you'll come home and tell me all your wacky stories."

I thought about it another moment. She was right. I couldn't let what had happened stop me from doing what I loved. The only way to conquer my fears was to face them. And the only way to truly love someone was to let them go and pray that they came back.

Getting away actually sounded like a good idea. There were so many bad memories here right now.

I nodded. "You know what? I think you're both right. Getting away might just be the RX I need."

"That's the spirit," Chad said.

I stood up. "I'm going to call Garrett Mercer right now and tell him I'm accepting the job. For at least a week, I'm going to be an official P.I.—as official as you can be without the proper certifications, at least."

Finally, I had a challenge I was looking forward to.

And a reason for my mind to escape the dark prison

where "what ifs" chained me down.

***

On paper, the Mercer family had everything going for them, I mused as I cruised down the highway. They were wealthy, attractive, and well liked. Though they were British, they were living the American dream.

I was about to dig into that dream and try to find out what had turned it into a nightmare.

I'd left from Norfolk this morning at 7 a.m. to drive to Cincinnati. Garrett insisted on renting a car for me, and I accepted his offer as a job perk, along with a lifetime supply of GCI coffee. Garrett also gave me a wad of cash, more than enough to both cover my expenses and my overdraft bill.

Of course, Garrett hadn't actually done most of those things. His assistant Lyndsey had set everything up and been the consummate professional. Like any good employee, she'd even thrown in a handful of GCI pens.

As I cruised down the road, I turned up the radio as "Don't Stop Believing" by Journey came on. One of my full-time friends and part-time employees, Clarice, had made a point to change my playlist on my smartphone. I'd programmed songs like, "I Can't Make You Love Me" by Bonnie Raitt, "Nothing Compares to You" by Sinead O'Connor, and "You've Lost That Loving Feeling" by The Righteous Brothers. Clarice changed my songs to "I Will Survive" by Gloria Gaynor and "Firework" by Katy Perry.

Right now, it was nearly 6 p.m. The drive was supposed to take around twelve hours all together, plus I'd taken my time. I'd stopped for breakfast, lunch, and dinner. I'd gone inside for each of those meals—and saved the receipts for Garrett. He had told me to do that, so who was I to argue?

If my map was correct, I was about an hour away from my destination. I was on what was called the AA Highway, and all around me the rolling hills of Kentucky made my spirit feel a little more relaxed and at ease. It gave me that peaceful, easy feeling the Eagles sang about.

Until I glanced in my rearview mirror. The same silver sedan had been behind me since West Virginia. It was probably a coincidence, someone else simply traveling to the same destination as me. But something about the car put me on edge.

Sometimes the car was right behind me. Other times, a few vehicles were spaced between us. Even after stopping for dinner, that car had still reappeared about twenty minutes later.

I should be able to rule out the person following me as someone connected with this case. I mean, I hadn't even started investigating yet. Usually ominous, threatening things didn't start happening until I stuck my nose where it didn't belong. I hadn't done that yet.

The only hypothesis I could conjure was that Garrett had hired someone to tail me. The idea was kind of crazy, but maybe he wanted to make sure he was getting his money's worth. Maybe he wanted to make sure I was truly investigating.

I tried to ignore the driver and concentrate on the case.

I mentally reviewed what I'd learned from poring over those files. Edward Mercer worked his way up the corporate ladder, his final career move when he went from a consumer products company to the vice president of a drug company. His wife, Elizabeth Mercer, on the other hand, came from old money. People often said, especially in the early days of her marriage, that she'd married beneath her. In fact, she'd never worked, but was involved in some philanthropic endeavors. Garrett seemed a perfect mix of the two.

The daughter, Cassidy, had apparently gotten into some trouble for partying, once even driving her flashy sports car into a pole while under the influence of drugs. Even though she was only in high school, the party scene was a well-integrated part of her life.

I'd seen her picture and she had the sparkle in her eyes of someone who liked to try new things. But there'd also been an underlying loneliness. I didn't even know the girl, but I wondered if her wild ways were all efforts to get her parents' attention. For all I knew, they gave her plenty of attention. My gut told me they didn't, though. People that successful had to spend a lot of time on the job. And people who looked as nice as Elizabeth probably spent a lot of time at the spa, shopping, and at the plastic surgeon.

Again, these were all my assumptions, my gut reactions from what I'd read in the files.

According to the police report, at approximately 11:20 on Friday night, November 12, ten years ago, an unknown person entered the Mercer residence through an open bedroom window. Cassidy was shot first. Edward was downstairs watching TV and was shot next. The mother must have heard the commotion and come from the kitchen. She was shot last.

There were no signs of struggle, and the only evidence left behind was a footprint indicating a man's size 12 boot, which offered no leads.

Nothing was stolen, and the family had many things of value, including jewelry.

One witness saw a green Ford Ranger speed away, but police could never prove the vehicle was involved or connected to the crime. The nearest traffic light cameras were more than a mile away and turned up no evidence.

Phone records for the family revealed nothing out of the ordinary.

The local police had called in the FBI to help with the case. They'd profiled the killer to be meticulous, well planned, knowledgeable, and possibly someone who knew the family.

The contractor had been a suspect because of one rough encounter with Elizabeth. He'd been cleared, and he'd passed away from cancer a couple of years after the murders, so if he was guilty, we'd never know.

Edward apparently had some inappropriate relationships with several women. They were also cleared.

That left the police with the possibility, despite the FBI profile, that the crime had been committed by someone random, some crazy who just walked in off the street.

I didn't believe that. I'd bet the police didn't either. I was going to have my work cut out for me.

Another glance in the rearview mirror confirmed that the sedan was right behind me again. The tinted windows didn't give me any glimpses as to who was behind the wheel. I didn't have to see a face; I already didn't like this.

Spontaneously, I pulled off into a gas station. Just as I got to the pump, the driver continued past. I spotted the license plate. Virginia.

Hmm . . . coincidence?

Maybe. I had learned that sometimes there was such a thing. But it was too early to conclude whether that was the case or not right now.

Until I knew, I was going to have to keep my eyes open.

CHAPTER 4

An hour later, I pulled up to a moderately sized Tudor style home. With its neat flowerbeds, cheerful autumn flag, and welcoming wreath, the place was a diamond in an otherwise rough area of town.

Even in the darkness, I could make a few observations about the neighborhood. I based my conclusions on the number of people loitering on the street, the care of the buildings, and the types of cars along the curb. I'd been around bad areas of town before, and this classified as one. However, there was a stretch of homes that seemed to retain the glory of olden days. This was one of them.

Supposedly—if my directions were correct—this was where Chad's relatives lived. Garrett offered to pay for me to stay at a hotel, but I figured I'd be better off here. At least if I disappeared, someone would miss me this way.

I parked around the corner, on what appeared to be a quieter, less busy street. As I stepped out of my car and grabbed my suitcase, I noticed the change of temperature from Norfolk to Cincinnati. It was probably twenty degrees cooler here. I'd actually brought an old, black leather jacket with me. My friend Sierra was an animal rights activist, and I'd always felt guilty wearing the coat around her. I had no shame here, though. Based on the shiver that shimmied through me, I was going to need it.

I knocked on the door and, a moment later, a pretty girl with strawberry blonde hair answered. "You must be

Gabby! I'm Holly, Chad's cousin. I'm so glad you found the place okay."

She smiled a huge Julia Roberts type of smile—one that consumed her whole face, but in a nice, toothy way. Smooth curls cascaded halfway down her back and she wore a red dress that was fitted at the top and flared at the bottom.

"The one and only. Thanks for letting me stay."

"It's no problem. I'm glad we can help. Come on in." She extended her hand behind her.

I gripped my suitcase with one hand and my laptop with the other as I stepped inside, onto glossy, cherry wood floors. The place smelled like lemon and orange and vanilla. At first glance, the whole place could have been featured in *Better Homes and Gardens*.

I wasn't sure what I'd been expecting. Probably something a little more down to earth and homey. But this place was nice, showing an almost upper class kind of care.

She took my suitcase from me and led me inside. "I'm the only one home right now. My mom's planning one of those big fundraisers for a local nonprofit." She paused for long enough to lean closer, as if conspiring—even though no one else was around. "I can't keep track of which one, she's involved with so many. So you're stuck with me for the time being."

"I think it's the opposite. You're the one who's stuck with me."

"Oh, don't be silly. Any friend of Chad's is a friend of mine." She stopped in front of a staircase and put my suitcase down. "Can I get you some tea?"

I didn't really want anything except to be alone, but I didn't want to be impolite either. "I'd love some."

"I know you must be tired, so I'll fix you some and then I'll let you settle in for the night." We walked into the kitchen, and Holly nodded toward a little café-style table in the corner, a nook that was surrounded on two sides by an embankment of windows. "Why don't you have a seat?"

I set my purse and laptop down by the suitcase and did as she asked. My gaze wandered as far as my eyes could see. "Nice place."

Holly smiled as she put a kettle of water on the stove. "My mother is an interior designer and my dad was locksmith by trade, but he did carpentry in his spare time. They were a nice match and redid most of the house together."

"They did a great job." Everything looked clean and coordinated and cheerful. I decided right then and there that if I ever had my own house—and enough time and money—I wanted to hire her mom to decorate for me.

"Did you have a nice drive?" She turned and leaned against the stove, waiting for the water to boil.

I remembered the driver following me. I hadn't seen him again after I'd stopped at the gas station. Maybe all of it was just a coincidence, and I was reading too much into this. Maybe I was so used to danger that I saw it even when it wasn't there.

Ever since Milton Jones, I'd been jumping at the smallest sounds. I'd even bought a gun and taken shooting lessons. I hoped and prayed I never had to use it. But the 9mm Smith & Wesson was in my purse. I had a carry permit. And I would use it if my life was on the line. Or a friend's life for that matter.

I remembered Holly's question. "The drive wasn't too bad," I finally answered.

"I'm glad to hear that." The kettle whistled, and she poured me some tea, set it on a tray with some cream and sugar and cookies, and delivered all of it to the table.

For a moment, I felt like a queen.

Holly set a crisp, white porcelain cup on a dainty saucer in front of me before sliding into the seat across the table. "So, I understand you're here to investigate something?"

I added some sugar and milk to my tea. "I've been hired to look into a cold case."

"That sounds so exciting. Is that weird to say that?"

"No, not at all. But I have to say that this is my first time doing something like this." I tilted my head. "Speaking of which, have you lived in Cincinnati long?"

"My entire 27 years."

I grabbed one of the shortbread cookies, unable to resist them. "You ever hear about the murder of the Mercer family?"

Her eyes got even larger. "Everyone around here has. It's the kind of thing that gives you nightmares."

"What do you remember about the case?" I nibbled on the cookie and buttery goodness nearly had me closing my eyes with bliss.

"Well, you had this picture perfect family who had it all. A nice home, good looking kids, prestigious jobs. Then one day someone walks into their house, shoots all of them, and is never seen again. It's spooky really."

Spooky was one way to describe it. "Are there theories floating among the locals here?"

"Theories?" Her eyes drifted up in thought until she sighed, her bangs ruffling with the action. "I guess I've heard a few. I have to be honest, people still talk about the case and every once in a while some new lead seems to pop up and gets people all excited. It's almost like an urban legend at this point. The whole scenario has people playing their own real-life version of Clue . . . she said perhaps insensitively."

I smiled at her commentary on her statement. "So what were some of those theories . . . she asked curiously?"

"Oh, there were some crazy ones. Some people said it was like a Manson thing. Others said a cult had done it. A few thought the Mercers were spies from across the pond and that the government did it." Holly shrugged. "I don't know. To be honest, most people just think that a random crazy off the street—probably drugged up—walked in and let out his aggressions. Too many violent video games, too many drugs in his system, too little of a past for him to be on anyone's radar."

"Those are quite the theories."

She nodded. "I know, right?"

I took the last sip of my tea. "This was perfect. Thank you so much."

She grinned again. I had a feeling grinning was second nature to her. "Glad you enjoyed it. Let me show you to your room and I'll let you get some rest. If you have more questions tomorrow, just let me know."

She led me upstairs, I politely said goodnight, and then I fell back on the four-poster bed and stared at the ceiling for a moment.

As always, my thoughts went to Riley.

I hadn't told him yet that I was doing this. Somehow, I feared he'd think this news was justification for him moving and I didn't want him to think that.

I frowned as I thought about it. The doctor had said it was really important to keep his stress level low and not upset him. It would hinder his recovery or something.

I still couldn't believe he was gone. Coming to Cincinnati may have been the best thing for my psyche because staring at Riley's empty apartment and realizing he wasn't there would break my heart again and again.

Lord, give me Your wisdom. Shape my perspective. Remind me how to love and push away these insecurities.

Just then, my phone rang and my heart rate doubled. Was it Riley calling to tell me how he was doing? To say that moving was a mistake and that he was coming back? I yearned so much for just a touch of my old life that I was becoming delusional.

But I already knew that it wasn't Riley. The ringtone was all wrong. When I glanced at the screen and recognized Garrett's number, my heart fell.

I put the phone to my ear anyway. "Hey, what's going on?"

"You made it to Cincy yet?"

"Just got here an hour ago."

"Love that town. I think you will, too. You sure you don't want a hotel room? I could hook you up somewhere nice."

"No, I'm staying with a friend of a friend. I'm good."

"Excellent. I'm sure you're ready to dig in. Listen, I wanted you to know that I'm headed into town later this week."

I raised my eyebrows. "Really?"

"It's for a benefit gala. The speaker backed out at the last minute, and I've been asked to fill in. I'm their second choice, but I'm okay with that. I would have probably said no, but I figure the timing is providence, considering you're in town investigating."

"The timing is uncanny."

"Not to sound full of myself, but I do get these invitations quite often. And, like I said, I would have said no except for the fact that you're there . . . investigating. I'd like to connect with you while I'm in town."

"Sure thing, Boss." Who was I to argue? He was the one paying me.

"Looking forward to it. I'll call you closer to the time."

I hung up and stared at the phone a moment. Should I

call Riley? No, I decided. He was the one who wanted some space. I'd wait for his call.

I wished the waters were clear, but instead they were mucky.

I remembered the verse that I'd read last week. It had stayed with me since then.

Seek justice, love mercy, walk humbly with your God.

I had the seeking justice thing down pat.

But when it came to my relationship with Riley, I was going to need a lot of mercy and humility, it seemed.

***

In the bright morning light, I noticed that my room at the Paladins' could have doubled for a bed and breakfast—not that I'd ever stayed in one. But the space was decorated perfectly with everything coordinated.

After I showered and got dressed, I pulled out my notebook. I figured every good private detective should have one. I searched my memory, trying to recall if Magnum P.I. had ever carried one. I couldn't remember.

I checked my list of people to chat with. I was waiting for the lead detective to return my call. Garrett had also given me the name of one of his father's coworkers—Vic Newport—and the contact information for a fellow polo enthusiast named Sebastian Royce. I hoped to track them down while I was in town.

I leaned my back on the headboard. I honestly felt like I had no idea what I was doing, which was unusual for me. Usually, I started with a crime scene and moved from there. But I'd never worked a cold case.

When I heard movement downstairs, I decided to venture out. Some of the exhaustion of being on the road had left me, and the shower had helped wake me up. I stopped at the bottom of the stairs. No one heard me over the chatter in the room.

I cleared my throat, not used to being the guest in someone else's home and wishing my mom and dad had taught me a few more social graces. I smiled at the family sitting at the breakfast table. They were all talking, laughing, snatching food from each other, and sipping coffee. Holly sat in the middle of them, wearing another dress with a twirly skirt, her hair and makeup looking picture perfect.

My heart clenched. This was a family moment that I'd always longed for and dreamed about. My family had been dysfunctional growing up, to say the least. I'd dreamed about having a stable home life, but the reality was that it never happened.

I rubbed my hands on my jeans and cleared my throat again. Everyone went silent and stared at me.

Then the silence was broken with so many sentiments thrown out at once that I could hardly understand anyone.

"You must be Gabby!" A fifty-something woman with stylish, blond hair and smooth skin hurried toward me. "We're so glad you're here!"

She pulled me into a hug. I had to remind myself to unfreeze and return the gesture. I guess I wasn't a huggy kind of girl.

"I'm Lydia. Whatever you do, don't call me Mrs. Paladin. Even if you think I'm old enough for it, I don't feel old enough for it." She turned back to the table, pulling me with her. The scent of cinnamon and vanilla and coffee rose up to meet me.

I'd just stepped into a Norman Rockwell painting, I realized. Only a modern one. One that made an annoying longing well in me. Remembering Riley, the ache deepened. I'd been close.

Lydia motioned toward Holly. "Of course, you've met Holly Anna."

"Just Holly is fine," Holly said with a slight roll of the eyes.

"Then there's Alexandria the Great," Lydia continued.

A tall woman with dark hair and wearing a business suit fluttered her fingers in the air. "Just Alex works."

"And that's Ralphie over there." She pointed to a tall, exceptionally thin man wearing round glasses.

"Ralph, Mom. Ralph," he corrected.

Lydia didn't seem to hear any of them. "Would you like some coffeecake? It's Holly's specialty. How about some coffee? I ground it up fresh this morning."

Holly wasn't kidding when she said her mom was all about hospitality. I felt swept away in a whirlwind as I was whisked to my seat. In fact, I could only remember a couple times in my life where I was treated like such royalty. Before I could formulate an answer, Lydia had set a plate of yummy looking cake in front of me. The coffee appeared a second later.

My stomach grumbled in response. I hadn't eaten since dinner yesterday.

I realized that all that was missing from this scene were some blue jays swooping in to place a napkin in my lap. Add the birds and I just might feel like Cinderella for a moment. "This looks great."

"Holly Anna made it fresh this morning."

I glanced at Holly and she shrugged. "It's a recipe I found in an old cookbook from the fifties. The recipes from back then are actually much healthier and they use a considerably less amount of sugar."

I'd never heard of anyone reading old cookbooks, but it worked for me.

Lydia reappeared. "Cream? Sugar?"

"Yes and yes. Please. Thank you." I threw them all out, hoping one would work.

She laughed. "I love your manners. Your momma must have taught you right."

If she only knew. My dad had been an alcoholic, and to make ends meet my mom had worked two jobs, so I'd pretty much been left to fend for myself.

As if the moment could get any better, a dollop of whipped cream and some raspberries were sprinkled on top of my cake.

I met Holly's eyes and read an apology there. Her family had big personalities, and she seemed reserved compared to them. Was it because she was the youngest? I'd guess she was the youngest by quite a bit. I couldn't be sure.

I glanced around the table. "So . . . you all live here?"

They stared at me a moment before bursting into laughter.

"Not on your life," Ralphie said.

"I would never live it down at work if I still lived with my mom," Alex the Great added. "We meet the second Tuesday of every month for breakfast."

That made a little more sense.

"So, I heard you're a P.I.," Alex the Great started. "Interesting."

"I imagine, as a D.A., you probably don't have a high regard for the profession." I took a bite of the cake and it nearly melted in my mouth.

"I wouldn't say that. I've met some decent P.I.s in my time. As long as they stay out of my way, I'm fine."

"The person who hired me is hoping my background in forensics will help me. We'll see. I worked for the medical examiner for a while." A while being about a month until budget cuts did me in.

"It would be so wonderful if you solved the Mercer House murders." Lydia shook her head sadly. "That crime has haunted this town for years. Such a tragedy."

"How's it going so far?" Ralphie asked.

He was the one running for office, I remembered. With his thick blond hair, glasses, and sweater vest, he almost reminded me a bit of the boy from *A Christmas Story*, only thirty years older.

I shrugged. "So far, nothing. I'm hoping the lead investigator will eventually call me back. I'd love to start with him."

"You mean Detective Morrison?" Lydia asked. She nonchalantly took a sip of tea, her lipstick leaving a bright mark on the edge of the delicate cup.

My eyes widened. Maybe Cincinnati was a smaller town that I thought. "That's the one."

"I know Tommy. He's a wonderful man. Rough on the outside, but a teddy bear underneath."

"My mom knows everyone," Holly whispered.

I nodded, just trying to keep up with the fast paced conversation. "Small world." I wanted to beg on the spot for her to connect me.

She nodded again. "I'll call him and tell him you're a friend. If you don't mind me sticking my nose into your business, that is."

I shook my head. "No, stick all you want."

"You know, I should do that now before I forget. Excuse me a minute."

She disappeared into the other room, her cellphone already at her ear.

"So, you know Chad?" Alex asked. Her voice was deep, tough. I wouldn't want to go up against her in a courtroom.

I nodded. "We own a business together, so yes, I do."

"The crime scene cleaning thing, right?" Ralphie asked. "Fascinating."

"Some might say. It's definitely not a career for the faint of heart."

"I can imagine," he muttered. "Some would say the same about politics."

Lydia swept back into the room and handed the phone to me with a flourish. I hadn't known the woman long, but I'd bet she did everything with finesse. "Gabby, someone wants to talk to you."

Surprise ran through me. I quickly wiped my mouth, stood and took the phone from her. "This is Gabby."

"Gabby. It's Detective Morrison. I understand you want to speak with me," a gruff voice barked into the phone.

I paced away from the breakfast nook. "That's right. I'm investigating the death of the Mercer family."

"I've never gotten that case out of my mind. I have to tell you, though—we've had leading cold case investigators from around the world trying to solve this one. It's been the subject of TV specials and even a cable miniseries. I'm not sure how much luck you're going to have."

Based on my past track record, not much. Despite that, I still said, "I'd like to give it the old college try, as they say."

He paused. Hesitated was more like it. "Okay then. I'll give you an hour. Today at noon."

"Great. Just name the place."

He named a chili restaurant and said it was located down the street.

"I really appreciate this."

"Anything for Lydia. She's probably raised more money for the police auxiliary than anyone else in the city. We all owe her a debt of gratitude."

I hit END and handed the phone to Lydia.

Her eyes sparkled. "Well?"

"He said yes. Thank you so much for your help."

She waved a hand in the air nonchalantly. "I love connecting people. It's what I do."

"One of the many things she does," Holly quipped. "But you'll like the detective. He's a nice man. We were all sad to see him retire last year, especially with the stigma of not solving the Mercer family murders."

"What kind of stigma are you talking about?" I asked.

"People accused him of blundering the investigation," Alex interjected. "I never believed it. I think people just want a scapegoat. They said he focused too much of his attention on the tile guy. From there, the detective moved on to that killer in Missouri. Neither panned out, and no other new leads came to the surface."

"Failed investigation or not, he donated to my campaign, so he's on my good list," Ralphie added. He pulled back his crisp sleeve and glanced at his watch. "It's quarter till eight. I've got to get to work. Sorry to run out on you."

Alex downed her last bite of coffeecake. "Me too!"

Lydia pulled some lipstick from her purse and reapplied it. "Goodness gracious. Where did all the time go? I've got a board meeting across town." She stuffed her lipstick back away. "Gabby, if you need anything at all, you let us know. Make yourself at home."

And like three tornados joining together to create a super storm, they swept from the room and out the front door.

I let out a slow breath and glanced at Holly.

She smiled sympathetically. "They're a lot to take in, huh?"

I nodded. "You can say that again. And I don't mean

that in a bad way."

"Oh, I totally understand. They're great. If you want something done, they're the people you want to talk with. They're driven, type As, have detailed five step plans on how to organize anything, and succeed at everything they try."

"Sounds like I came to the right place. By the way, why don't you include yourself in that mix?"

She shrugged, a touch of sadness coming over her. "I was more like my dad. Laidback. A dreamer. Idealistic. I like to take life at a slower pace and smell the roses. I always say I was born in the wrong era. I think my dad was the only one who understood that."

I'd wondered where her dad was. The past tense Holly spoke with made it clear. "I'm sorry. I lost my mom. It's hard."

"Yes, it is hard." She frowned before pulling in a quick breath. "The good news is that, since I have to take the next few days off or lose the time, and since I have always been fascinated with mysteries, I'm at your service."

"Really? You wouldn't mind doing that?"

"Not at all. In a way, you'd be letting me live a long buried fantasy of being Nancy Drew."

I smiled. "I'd hate to hold you back from doing that."

"I actually have an idea for you, if I'm not being too forward."

My curiosity was pricked. "No, please."

She grinned. "Okay, here goes. Fasten your seat belt, though."

CHAPTER 5

Holly shifted and tapped a cotton candy pink fingernail against her snow-white coffee mug. "It's like this: My friend is a part of this group of armchair detectives who like to try solving cold case files online. It's kind of crazy sounding, but they've actually solved twenty some crimes. Not my friend specifically, mind you, but the hundreds of members in the group . . . she said to clarify."

"Sounds fascinating."

"I was hoping you might think that." She glanced at her watch. "In fact, I thought I'd introduce you to her."

"That sounds great. You're all going above and beyond. I can't help but feel like . . ."

"Like maybe God ordained all of this?" She smiled. "Me too. I'm a big believer that there are no coincidences in life."

The doorbell rang.

Holly grinned and pointed toward the front of the house. "And right on time, here she is. She's so punctual that you can set your clock by her."

They were making my job too easy. At least all the excitement was taking my mind off the fact that Riley hadn't called.

Except, that thought had reminded me that Riley hadn't called.

Poo.

Holly answered the door and ushered in a black

woman with super curly hair springing from her head like rays from the sun. "I'm Jamie. You must be Gabby."

I extended my hand. "So nice to meet you."

She had a laptop tucked under her arm and a curiously mischievous expression on her face. "I love cold cases. But as soon as I heard you were investigating, I wanted to help. I hope you don't mind."

"Help is always good. Can you tell me a little bit about what you do?"

"We're an organization—unofficial—and we like to stick our nose where it doesn't belong."

"I like you already."

She snapped her fingers. "I know, girl. I always say, blessed are the nosy ones for they find things out. Important things."

I couldn't help but laugh.

"I haven't solved a crime yet, but I will." She pulled open her laptop on the breakfast table. She typed in a few things and a moment later a website popped up. "So, this is what we do. My friends and I post information on cold cases—mostly missing persons or unsolved murders. We have thousands of visitors to our site every day."

"Thousands?"

She nodded. "Our total reach so far is four million."

"Enough said."

"You know it. Everyone wants to be an armchair detective, you know? People scour the Internet, and it's amazing how word spreads, especially now thanks to social media. We post one thing online, people share and then friends of those people share it. The message gets passed along at an amazing pace. The few cases we've helped solve have been because someone has recognized a picture. They would have never seen that picture without our help."

"Sounds both practical and amazing."

"Girl, we're totally on the same wavelength." She gave me a fist bump.

"Right on." I tapped into my inner soul sister.

She began pattering away. "Okay, I'm going to start simple. I put together the basic information on this case, and I'm going to post it later today on our website—if that's okay with you. It's all been posted before, but I'm going to start recirculating it."

I nodded. "Sounds good to me."

"I'll ask people to post it around and see if we can discover any other information. We get a lot of false leads, but sometimes there are major payoffs."

"Payoffs are good."

"If you need me to do any kind of online research for you, just let me know. I'm available. Don't tell anyone, but I'm also pretty decent at hacking into systems, if you know what I mean."

"I may have to take you up on that online research."

Jamie pointed from Holly, to me, and back to herself. "I'm thinking we could be like the MOD Squad. One black, one white, and one blonde. What do you think?"

I laughed out loud. "It's a definite possibility."

"I can scour the thrift store for some old bell bottoms," Holly offered.

"I've already got the afro." Jamie pointed to her hair.

I laughed again. "You could be on to something, but . . ." I glanced at my watch. "We'll have to talk more later. Right now, I've got to get to my meeting."

"I've got to run, too. Gotta do an interview for an article I'm writing." Jamie waved goodbye and scurried out the door.

Holly gave me directions to the chili joint, and then I grabbed my purse and stepped outside. I rounded the corner where I'd parked and I stopped in my tracks.

The tires of my rental car were slashed.

I walked closer and bent down to examine each one. What in the world? Was that impending feeling that someone was following me *not* my imagination? I'd briefly thought that maybe Garrett had hired someone to tail me, but it wouldn't make any sense for Garrett to pay someone to do this.

With a sigh, I stood and went back inside the house. Holly looked up in surprise. "That was fast," Holly said.

"My tires were slashed."

Holly's mouth gaped open. "No way. I mean, this isn't the best area of town, but stuff like that doesn't happen that often. I mean, never before to us. Unless getting egged once counts."

"I'm going to need to call the police, I guess. But I've got to meet the detective. He only had a short window of time."

Holly stood. "I'll take you. We'll call the police when we get back."

***

I settled down in an ordinary looking restaurant in a not so great part of town for some Cincinnati style chili—a sweet tasting meat sauce served over spaghetti noodles and topped with handfuls of shredded cheddar cheese. Though I hesitated at the idea at first, when I tried it, I actually liked it.

But I liked the fact that I was able to meet with the detective even more.

Detective Morrison was a trim man in his sixties. He still had a head full of gray hair. His face was squarish and slightly wrinkled and his eyes contained a certain world-weariness that I'd seen before on too many law enforcement personnel who'd been worn down by the cruel reality of how heartless people could really be.

He ordered what was called a four-way chili because it also had beans, a large diet soda, and a side of garlic bread. Holly opted for a salad.

"Thank you for meeting with me," I started when we all had our food.

"An hour," he reminded me. He cast me a tired glance while still bent down toward his food.

I got the message: He was doing this as a favor. Certainly, a lot of people had knocked on his door over the years, trying to track down information on the case. I was sure he had better things to do.

"Understood." I pulled out my pad of questions, so I could take notes.

"Got your notepad, huh?" He looked amused and maybe even skeptical.

I offered a half shrug. "I left my trench coat and magnifying glass in the car."

He stared at me for a moment then a chuckle emerged, growing until it became a full out laugh. "I like that." He rubbed his cheek. "That's a good one."

A moment of relief filled me. Maybe I'd gained his trust. For once, my smart mouth had worked in my favor.

His smile dipped, and he reached into his wallet and opened it. He slid something across the table to me.

A picture of the Mercer family.

"This case haunts me every day. I try to let it go, but it's hard."

"I can't imagine," I offered.

"It's like this. Everyone thinks they can find something I missed, ride in like a knight on a white horse and save the day by solving the case." He shook his head and leaned back in his chair. "Look, I welcome someone else to solve this case. I do. It's not that I'm being prideful. I couldn't sleep for years when I thought about what had happened to that family. I even had a new alarm system put into my own house because I couldn't stop thinking about what it would be like to have something like that happen to my own family."

I had a feeling he felt like a failure when it came to this case. The community had been counting on him to put a killer behind bars and it hadn't happened. Law enforcement could be like that, taking on the burden of unnecessary guilt. I could spot that disease a mile away, mostly because I struggled with it myself.

"I'm not going to pretend to be a genius. I'm not. Nor am I going to pretend like I think I can solve this," I started. "Garrett Mercer hired me, so I'm going to give it my best shot. The fact is that we're all in this together, whether we want to be or not." Great, I'd taken to quoting musicals without even trying. I hoped the detective didn't notice the *High School Musical* reference, and think of me as young and immature. The singsong inflection I'd added wouldn't help my case.

The former detective drew in a long, deep breath before meeting my eyes again. "The person who did this needs to be found. They need to pay for the damage of their actions. The crime was horrific. No one should get away with an offense like that."

"I agree. You were the original detective on the case?"

He nodded. "I was. Of course, I had other detectives help out. The FBI got involved. Even when they took over, I couldn't stop looking for answers."

"What was your gut reaction to the case?"

He sighed and ran a hand down his face. "Whoever did the crime was someone with a mission. They knew what had to be done. There was planning involved. The whole family was home—minus Garrett. But it was unusual for the family to all be in the same place. All of their lives went in different directions, kind of like bystanders fleeing from ground zero. They may have been a family, but it was in blood only."

"What do you mean?"

"Elizabeth and Edward looked like a picture perfect couple in photos. But their marriage was a turbulent one."

"Sad." Garrett had mentioned something about his dad being unfaithful.

"Too often a reality." He shook his head. "Anyway, even the daughter seemed to be something of a lone ranger. She was involved with clubs at school and hung out with her friends. My impression was, after interrogating people close to the family, that her parents didn't parent very much. They were too caught up in themselves."

"I suppose even when you look at the crime scene, you saw a little of that, right? The dad was watching TV, the mom was in the kitchen, the daughter was in her room upstairs."

The detective nodded. "Exactly. I doubt the daughter even heard anything happen downstairs. Her radio was blaring."

"Is there anyone you'd wished you'd investigated, but that you didn't have a chance or means to pursue?"

He shook his head. "If I had even an inkling that someone might have been involved, I questioned them. If I had even a hint that someone wasn't telling the truth, I re-questioned them. As far as I'm concerned, I left no stone unturned."

"I see. What about Arnold James, the man who committed an eerily similar crime out in Missouri?"

"He didn't do it. The thing about most killers—killers

like Arnold, who's a true psychopath in my opinion—is that they want people to know who they are, to discover them. They're twisted like that. They want the fame that being a murderer brings. If Arnold had done it, he would have owned up to it. Besides that, there's the logistics. He was seen in Missouri on the morning the Mercer family was killed. There's little chance he could have made it here in time, especially when you consider the planning that went into this crime." He shook his head. "There's just no way."

"What about the man who did the tile work inside their house? I know he passed away, but do you really think he was innocent?" I finished the last bite of my chili, my stomach full and satisfied.

Detective Morrison sucked in a long breath. "He was my best lead. I really thought he could have done it. He even had a criminal history of abuse, but we could never prove anything. His wife claimed that he was at home that night. We tested his hands for gunpowder, his clothes for blood. There was nothing."

"Just one more question. About Edward Mercer. I've heard rumors of his liaisons. Did you talk to the women he was involved with?"

He nodded. "All of the ones we could round up. More and more kept coming out of the woodwork. Believe me—we thoroughly questioned each of them. We came up with nothing." He wiped his mouth. "The truth is that all of the people you just mentioned were our best guesses. The problem is that the whole case felt like a guessing game, and that's the shame in it all. No one should get away with murder."

"I agree."

He finished his food and glanced at his watch. "Hour's up. I don't feel like I helped."

I wasn't sure if he had either. But at least I had a feel for the case from his perspective. "Thank you for your time. I've got the check."

He waved goodbye to Holly and then left.

This was going to be a harder case than I thought, and I wondered if I should call Garrett right now and tell him I was going back home and forget about it. I had to give it a little more time, though. Just a little more time.

CHAPTER 6

As I was paying my bill, a shrill yell sounded from my purse. "Help! Get me out of here! It's so dark. Someone, save me . . . !" The voice was tinny and almost cartoon-like.

Holly looked at me, her eyes wide with alarm. "What is that?"

I smiled sheepishly as I reached into my purse and pulled out my cell. I held it up. "My friend Clarice not only put together my playlist for me, but she also programmed the ringtones on my phone before I left. She thought it would make me laugh, and I haven't figured out how to change it yet."

"Funny. I think I like this Clarice."

I glanced at the screen, knowing it wasn't Riley. Clarice had programmed his ringtone as "That's Amore."

I didn't recognize the number, but I answered anyway. "Hello?"

Silence stretched on the other line, first irritating me then raising my suspicions.

"Hello?" I repeated.

I was about to hang up when—

"Stay away from this one," a gravely voice rumbled through the phone line.

I froze, wishing with all of my might that the man was talking about the restaurant. I knew better. "What?"

"Drop your investigation."

Tension pulled at my muscles. I finished paying, excused myself, and stepped onto the sidewalk, wanting both privacy and a chance to see what was going on around me. "Why would I do that?"

"Some things are best left buried."

My eyes scanned my surroundings. Old buildings with graffiti and chipped bricks and sprinkles of litter surrounded me. Storefronts, many abandoned based on the outdated, crooked signs, were on the lower level of the three or four story buildings. Apartments were over many of them, several with AC units in the windows and sheets covering the glass.

Nothing stood out to me, though. No *one*, I should say.

"I think justice is always best when it's alive and well," I ventured.

"Some skeletons weren't meant to come out of the closet."

A shiver crawled up my spine. "Who is this? The same person who slashed my tires?"

"Most people call me the Watcher."

My throat tightened at the ominous name. "Who assigned you as guardian over this case?"

"That's not important."

"I'd say it is."

"Stop looking for me. You won't find me."

The air froze in my lungs. Despite that, I continued to scan the buildings around me, looking for a sign of someone. But everyone seemed engaged, moving. Not watching, waiting.

"Maybe we could meet sometime and talk about this." Riley would have told me that was the dumbest idea ever. Sadness pressed down on my heart at the thought. The emotion quickly dispersed though as my adrenaline took over all of my senses.

"That won't be necessary. But consider this a warning."

I didn't like the sound of that. "And if I keep investigating?"

"You don't want to find out. That is all." The line went dead.

My gaze swept the area one more time. Still nothing. I hurried toward the corner.

A movement in the rundown apartments there caught my eye. I moved closer, the third story window of a grungy yellow building never leaving my sight. Had the curtain moved? I couldn't be sure.

I stepped nearer.

A car horn blared. I nearly jumped out of my skin. My gaze skittered to a black sedan. The woman behind the wheel had her hands raised in the air, as if asking me what I was doing.

If only she knew.

I waved an apology and started back toward the restaurant. It looked like things were getting interesting. Very interesting.

***

I stepped back into the chili joint, convinced that if I died in the near future, it would be death by a car. I'd had two too many close calls lately.

Holly stuck a chocolate mint in her mouth and waved me over. "Everything okay? You look like you saw a ghost."

"Something like that." I grabbed my coat and told her about the call as we walked out to the car.

She gasped. "That's terrible. And strange. I mean, who would do that?"

"Someone involved in the crime, I suppose. But what I can't come to terms with is how they know I'm investigating. It's not like I'm closing in on someone. Whoever made that phone call has no reason to scare me. Yet he's trying to."

"I suppose the question is 'why' then? They must see you as a risk somehow."

I shook my head. "I guess."

She pulled her cute little purse up higher on her shoulder. "Listen, I'm free for the afternoon. Anywhere you want to go? I know the area pretty well. I'd be happy to take you."

"I would actually love that. Norfolk is tiny compared to this place." I looked down at my paper. "I need to go to 123 Birmingham St. Know where that is?"

"I can find out fast." She tapped something into her phone, studied the screen for a moment, and then nodded. "I know exactly how to get there. Want to go now?"

"Why not?" I might as well jump in.

A moment later, we were in Holly's baby blue, vintage Mustang. In my rush this morning, I hadn't really taken it in. I'd been too preoccupied with my slashed tires and trying to formulate what I was going to ask the detective. I definitely hadn't commented on it. "Nice ride."

"I know, right? I love all things old." She backed out of the parking lot, and we started down the streets of Cincinnati.

"Old cars, dresses that could have been popular in the fifties, recipes from a bygone era. I'm seeing a pattern here." I assumed the dresses were probably designer pieces.

She touched the hem of the pale yellow dress she wore. "This old thing? I do love my dresses. I find them at thrift stores."

My opinion of her went up a few more notches.

We cruised down the city streets for a moment, and I absorbed the urban life around me. I loved the character of Cincinnati. The buildings and streets all seemed to tell stories of the past, of the history of the area.

I really needed to get out more, I decided then and there. There was so much of the world—of the United States—that I hadn't seen. My circumstances had always limited my travel. I hadn't even realized that I wanted to travel until this moment. Growing up, I'd gone to North Carolina to see some relatives a couple of times. In college, my friends and I had gone down to Florida for spring break. That was it.

"I can't believe Chad is married now." Holly's voice cut into my thoughts. "He seemed really happy last time I talked to him. I can't wait to meet his wife."

I smiled when I thought about Chad and Sierra. "They both seem really happy. An odd match, but they work together." I glanced her way. "Are you two close?"

"I feel like he's my brother, even though we never see each other anymore. I really admire him. Not many people give up an established career and a steady paycheck to follow their dreams. His mother nearly flipped when she heard his plans. My mother did flip."

I liked Holly already. Despite her overly girly appearance, she seemed down to earth and friendly, not stuck up like I first thought she might be. Plus, she was a social worker. The job wasn't exactly prestigious. Most people did it because they were concerned about the well being of others. I could admire that.

"It does take some courage. He paved the way for me. My family thought I was crazy to become a social worker. Said I couldn't support myself or make a comfortable life on that salary. But it's what I wanted to do."

"Life is too short to live for someone else's dreams,

isn't it?" I was pretty sure there was a country song about that.

Holly frowned. "You're absolutely right. We have to make the most of the time we've been given. And it wasn't that my family doesn't think social work is noble; they were okay with me helping people in need. They just wanted me to be able to take care of myself in the process."

We drove for about thirty minutes, Holly giving me a quick tour by pointing out buildings, stadiums, bridges and colleges. We finally pulled away from the busy interstate and the crowded streets. Trees became more prevalent. To my right was a glorious view of the Ohio River. We climbed through the hills and finally Holly slowed and pulled down a long drive marked DEAD END.

Appropriate, I couldn't help but think.

The car climbed up the winding lane until the woods ended and a huge mansion appeared.

Holly braked. "Whoa. What a place."

"You're right about that." I knew Garrett had come from privilege, but wow. This was a one-percenter kind of home. Gray bricks comprised the exterior. Huge columns surrounded the front door in a circular colonnade. A black, iron fence could be seen in the backyard and maybe even a tennis court.

As Holly put the car in park, I stepped out. The day was brisk already, but on this hill, the wind was particularly biting. I pulled my leather jacket closer and stepped toward the house. There were no cars in the driveway, but the place looked well kept.

I glanced at Holly as she joined me. "What are the chances the current homeowners would let us take a tour?" I asked.

"As someone who knocks on people's doors for a

living, I'm going to have to say they're not great. Not great at all."

I frowned. "Yeah, my thoughts, too. I wonder who lives here now." The place was still well cared for. The grass—even though it was cool outside as winter approached—was neat. The bushes were clipped. The trim looked freshly painted.

Suddenly, a woman came running from the woods.

I sucked in a breath before I spotted her fuchsia sweat suit and ear buds. A jogger, I realized. Just a jogger. She stopped in her tracks when she spotted us.

Her hand went over her heart before she plucked out her earphones. Based on her fine wrinkles, the woman was probably in her early fifties, but her slim build added a hint of youthfulness. "I had no idea someone was here. I nearly wet myself."

And I nearly snorted. But I didn't. Score one for me.

"We weren't trying to trespass," Holly started. "A friend of Gabby's used to own this house."

Her gaze fell on me. "Is that right? It's been a long time since anyone's lived here."

"How long?" I asked.

"Well, the Mercer family still owns this place. The son refuses to sell. Wants to hang onto it, for some reason."

"But it looks so taken care of. And Garrett doesn't live around here." Not that I could see him doing the maintenance work himself.

"A caretaker comes out a few times a week to keep everything up. That's about it. Occasionally, a news crew will come to film an update—which is weird, considering there really aren't any updates." She shook her head. "Honestly, it's probably better that this house doesn't go on the market. Who would want to live where such a tragedy occurred?"

I remembered the case I'd last worked. I remembered the people I'd come across who were fascinated with murder. They'd even sold mementos from crime scenes and serial killers. Any one of them would *love* to live at a place with a past like this. It was disturbing.

"Did you know the family?" I asked.

She nodded. "Not well. They hadn't lived here long and they primarily kept to themselves. But when something like this happens, you just feel close to people, you know? Even though I didn't know them, I mourned for their deaths. No one deserves to die that way." The woman seemed to think twice about everything she was saying. "You said you were friends with . . . who?"

I raised my chin. "Garrett. Sort of. He's hired me to look into the deaths of his family."

The woman drew in a deep breath. "I'd like some answers. That's for sure. I couldn't sleep at night for what felt like years. I upgraded my alarm system. I got a guard dog. It's only been in recent years that I've let down my guard some. I was afraid at first that it was some kind of psycho serial killer on the loose."

"What do you think now?" I asked.

She let out her earlier breath, long and slow. "I've spent many a night trying to figure that one out. And I have no idea. No clue even." Her eyes focused on me a moment. "I see Garrett on TV. I'm so glad he's done well for himself. This tragedy could have easily ruined his life, and no one would have blamed him for going downhill. But he really rose out of the ashes and pulled his life together."

"He's doing good things and seems happy," I offered. As much as the man got under my skin, I couldn't deny that he was making a difference in the world.

"Good to hear. It's hard to know if it's all an act." The

neighbor nodded toward the distance. "I gotta keep running. Good chatting with you both!"

After she left, I turned to Holly.

"I want to peek into the windows." If Holly weren't with me, I would have marched right up to the house without thinking twice about it. But I barely knew the woman, and it was too early to offend or shock her.

Holly looked at me a moment before shrugging. "I always say that life is too short to be afraid of taking risks. Don't you think?"

I nodded. "I think."

"Then let's go for it."

CHAPTER 7

"Are you always this adventurous?" I couldn't help but ask as we approached the house.

Holly shook her head. "No, I usually play it pretty safe. But sometimes things happen in life that change your perspective."

I didn't know her well enough to ask any questions about her statement. But her eyes misted over for a minute, and I wondered what emotions were hidden beneath her smiles and social graces.

"I know all about life changing moments," I offered. "If I were a drinking woman, I'd toast you over that statement later."

Holly laughed. "Yeah, I know what you mean."

Just out of curiosity, I tugged at the front door. It was locked. Of course.

Instead, I moved to the window and peered inside.

From what I'd read, the intruder had come in through the window in Cassidy's room. She'd been shot first.

Garrett's father had been in the living room. The TV was on when the police arrived, so most assumed that he'd been watching football. He was shot next, right beside his chair. Elizabeth Mercer was found in the kitchen.

As I peered inside now, I could see a chair and a TV beyond that.

Had Garrett left the house just as it was? Was this

place some kind of shrine for the family now? I didn't know.

I wondered what I'd do if I were in Garrett's shoes. I had no idea. It was easy to jump to conclusions. Maybe this house was all he felt like he had left of his family.

"Do you see anything?" Holly asked.

"I'd bet that everything has been left just the way it used to be." Except the crime scene had been cleaned up. Someone had done a most excellent job. At least, they had from my vantage point at the window.

Holly shivered. "I just can't imagine."

I had to remember that not everyone had been surrounded by the things I had. I wasn't immune to death's sting or the mourning that came with the loss of life. But I didn't blanch at death the way others did. Death had become part of my job, both as a medical legal death investigator for the Commonwealth and as a crime scene cleaner.

We walked around the back of the house. Sure enough, there was a tennis court, as well as a large garden with a fountain in the middle. There had been a swimming pool at one time, but the area had been filled in. Probably for insurance purposes, if I had to guess.

I stood there a moment, trying to figure out my next move. "I don't know what else we can do here. I just wanted to see the place, you know?"

She nodded. "I guess we should get back and report those slashed tires, huh?"

"Yeah, I guess so."

We climbed into her car, and she cranked the engine. Well, she tried to crank the engine. The Stang whined and moaned. I was sensing some kind of theme here involving animosity between cars and me.

"I can't believe this," she muttered. She climbed out

and popped open the hood.

I joined her, though I had no idea what I was looking for. Fixing cars wasn't my thing. I was more of an expert when it came to picking skull fragments from walls.

She wiggled some wires or hoses or something before shaking her head and muttering, "Why does this always happen at the worst times?"

"This has happened before?"

She frowned. "Every few months, I think."

"Should we call a tow truck?"

Her frown deepened. "No, there's someone else I can call."

She dialed a number and stepped away from me. I let her have her privacy, wondering if she was calling an ex-boyfriend or something. That's what I would guess based on that frown.

I crossed my arms as I waited. My gaze scanned the woods surrounding the property. Suddenly, I shivered.

There were two different kinds of shivers: the kind you got because you were chilly and the kind you got because your gut told you something was off.

Something was off.

I continued to scan the woods, but I saw nothing. Not even the jogging neighbor from next door.

I scooted closer to the car, remembering the phone call from earlier. What had that man called himself? The Watcher? Not the most original threatening name, but threatening enough that a touch of fear spread through me. Was the Watcher here now? Had he followed us?

Holly came back over and rolled her eyes. "I have someone coming to help me out."

"You sound thrilled."

"I . . ." She ran a hand through her hair. "I just don't want to lead him on. That's all."

"I figured there was a story there." Unrequited love. I was usually on the other side of that equation.

She leaned against the car. "He's the guy that everyone thinks I should date."

"Everyone but you?"

She nodded. "Yeah, everyone but me. The thing is, there's nothing not to like about him. He's a great guy. I should want to date him. I just don't feel that spark, you know?"

I nodded. "Yeah, I know about the spark."

"Have I let Hollywood movies infiltrate my thinking too much? Maybe I'm holding out for something that doesn't exist."

Not that I was one to give advice on relationships, but . . . "Look, romance isn't always like it is in the novels or in the movies. But love and romance can be great. You should have chemistry, have a spark. There's nothing wrong with holding out for that." My voice cracked.

That's what Riley and I had.

Had. I'd thought in past tense. Was our relationship really over? Or was its impending demise just in my mind? Was I preparing myself now as a way of protecting my heart when things definitively went south?

The only comfort from this conversation was that for a moment I'd forgotten about that feeling of being watched.

"I get what you're saying, but . . ." Holly's voice drifted off, until she finally shook her head. "Never mind. It's a long story. I guess it boils down to the fact that I've always wanted one of those great loves. You know, I want to find someone and be one of those couples who just seem like they belong together."

I nodded.

"My mom and dad had that. They were always just so happy together. My mom told me once that you don't find great love, though. You create it. You cultivate it. You decide on it."

"Makes sense. A lot of sense actually."

My skin crawled again, and I reached into my purse. My fingers wrapped around my gun.

I prayed every day that I would never have to use this. But sometimes God didn't answer prayers in the way you wanted. He had other plans. Better plans. Even if it didn't feel like it at the moment.

"What's wrong?" Holly asked.

I scanned the woods. "Does anything around here look strange to you?"

"Besides the fact that this house is like a shrine to a deceased family?" She surveyed the landscape. "Not really. Why?"

"I keep feeling like something is off. Like someone is watching."

"Like, the phone call off?"

I nodded. "Yeah, like the phone call off."

Just then, a car rumbled down the road. A black Mercedes appeared a moment later.

"Here he is," Holly announced. "His name is Brian."

A shorter man climbed from the car. He wore a tailored business suit, had a neat haircut and a head full of hair. He was stocky but fit, but his thick jawline made him appear heavier than he was.

His eyes lit up when he saw Holly. He reached forward, gripped her shoulders, and kissed her cheek. Holly smiled and thanked him for coming.

He extended his hand as he approached me. "You must be Gabby."

"Word gets around."

He laughed, deep and hearty. "Anything with the Mercer family sparks interest with people around here."

"I can imagine."

"Let me check this out." He pulled off his jacket and asked Holly to hold it, then he approached the car. "So, more car problems? You sure you don't want to trade this baby in for something a little more reliable?"

"But with much less personality and character," Holly quipped. "I like to think about where this car has been, what it's done. It's like a piece of history."

"An unreliable piece of history." He stuck his head under the hood.

I tuned them out and scanned the woods again. This time I saw the fading sunlight reflect on something in the distance.

Something shiny.

Like binoculars.

I hadn't been imagining things after all.

CHAPTER 8

"Gabby?" Holly asked.

I snapped back to my immediate surroundings. "Maybe we should leave your car here and have someone pick it up later."

My mind began replaying my encounter with Milton Jones. He was a serial killer, and I'd been his captive for a few days. It had felt like a lifetime. I still remembered the darkness, the fear. I still couldn't look at a bucket of water without wanting to throw up. And, as a crime scene cleaner, I saw a lot of buckets.

"Gabby?"

My gaze found Holly. "Yes?"

"You're as pale as a ghost."

I searched for the source of that reflection again, but it was gone. That's when I pulled my gun out. "We really need to go."

Holly's eyes widened. "Wowzers."

At that moment, the hood slammed down. Thankfully, my finger wasn't on the trigger. I was jumpier than a flea on a trampoline.

"All fixed," Brian announced. "One of the cables leading to your battery came unplugged. Kind of weird but fixable. You should probably bring this over for a tune up sometimes, though."

"Like you don't have enough on your plate."

"I always have time for you." He shrugged. "At least

take it into the shop."

I'd much rather pay attention to their little soap opera, but there was a potential crazy person out there. I had to keep the bulk of my attention focused on the distance.

"Whoa," Brian suddenly said. "That's a . . . gun."

"A girl can never be too careful," I mumbled, sounding tougher than I felt.

"You want to be careful somewhere else?" Brian asked. "I've got a campaign to run. Ralph doesn't stand a chance without me."

"That's not true." Holly scowled.

"You know it is. I'm the man behind the man."

"Your conversation is cute and all, but there's someone watching us." I nodded in the distance. "He's over there."

A wrinkle formed between Brian's eyebrows. "Someone watching us? For real?"

I nodded. "Unfortunately."

Brian raised his hands in the air. "Look, I'm not going to pretend to be a hero here. I'm only a superstar in the social media world. I think we all need to get in our cars and get out of here."

Holly nodded. "Sounds like a good idea to me."

I gave the woods one last glance before climbing in the Mustang. No way was I trying to chase someone down myself, especially since I didn't know whom I was up against.

But this case was starting to leave a bad, bad feeling in my gut.

***

Holly drove down the streets closest to Garrett's property, and I looked for a suspicious vehicle parked on the side of the road, some kind of clue as to who had been in the woods. I saw nothing and no one. But I was sure someone had been there. He must have left when he'd realized we'd spotted him.

When we got back to the house, I'd had dinner with Lydia and Holly, and then I'd excused myself for the night. I needed time to let my thoughts percolate.

Right now, I sat on my bed and stared at my notes. Which led me nowhere.

After I stared at my notes, I stared at my cellphone. Which led me nowhere.

Riley still hadn't called. Was my memory faulty or had he said he'd call every day? I was fairly certain that's what he'd said.

The fact that he hadn't made an effort seemed like a prophecy of our doomed relationship. How could things have been so great just a few months ago? I would have never envisioned then that I'd be at this place now.

But I knew, deep in my heart, what had happened. Milton Jones had happened. He'd rocked my world and Riley's world. To think that we'd ever be the same would be ludicrous. But I could hope to move on, to be a better person.

If I didn't, then Milton Jones would win, even from his grave. I couldn't let him do that.

As I stared at the phone, it rang. My heart raced for a moment. I knew it wasn't Riley calling, but was it the Watcher? I put the phone to my ear and answered.

"Gabby, it's Vic Newport. You left me a message."

I straightened. "That's right. Thanks for calling me back."

"I have time to meet with you tomorrow at ten. Are you available then?"

"Ten? Ten works. Yes."

He gave me directions, and we hung up. At least I had

that lined up. Maybe Edward Mercer's best friend would have some answers for me.

I stared at the phone another moment before deciding to swallow my pride. There was no room for pride in relationships. That's what my pastor had told me once.

My hands were shaky on the buttons as I dialed Riley's number.

The phone rang. And rang. And rang.

But Riley didn't answer.

My heart fell. Had he seen my number and avoided my call? Could it truly just be a case of him not hearing his phone ring or being involved with something else? The thing was, it was seven at night. He should be getting ready for bed. He'd been turning in early ever since he came home from the hospital. Simple, everyday routines left him exhausted.

I shook my head. I had to get control of my thoughts. I'd been down this whole feel-sorry-for-myself road before, and I didn't want to go there again.

Where did broken hearts go? I silently asked Whitney Houston. She hadn't figured it out in her lifetime. But I was determined my story wouldn't end the same way as hers.

As the phone beeped, I found my voice. "Hey, Riley. Just calling to check on you. Call me back when you get the message. I'll be awake."

I hung up, tucked the phone beside my pillow, and waited, convinced I'd done the right thing. Now I just had to wait for him to call back.

In the meantime, I decided to call Sierra and check on things back in Virginia. Unlike Riley, she answered on the first ring. Make that, Chad answered on the first ring.

"Hey, Gab. What do you think of the family?"

"I think they're a hoot. They could have their own reality show, for that matter."

"For real. Hey, listen. Did you already bill the Batemans again? My records are showing it's been a month since the first bill went out . . ."

We caught up on business for a few minutes. A moment of guilt panged through me. I should be there, helping to earn money. Chad seemed to read my thoughts.

"I've got everything under control. There's nothing for you to worry about."

"You sure?"

"Absolutely. Violent crime in the area seems to be down this week, so your timing in leaving was impeccable."

"Good to know."

"Alright, I know you didn't call to talk to me. Here's Sierra."

"Hey, you," Sierra started. "Get this. Some company came out today and put a new 'For Sale' sign up. I guess the other realtor wasn't aggressive enough."

My heart thudded in my chest. "That's too bad. I kind of liked the nonaggressive one."

"Yeah, me too. I keep wondering where we'll move, if it comes down to that."

That apartment building was all I had tying me to Riley right now. If we were all displaced, I might never see Riley again.

But that was doomsday thinking. I tried to push it aside. "Let me know what happens."

Sierra paused a moment. "You talked to Riley?"

"Not yet," I answered softly. "I left him a message. Hopefully, I'll hear back from him tonight."

"Okay. I just wanted to ask. I'm sure he'll call."

I wished I felt that certain.

***

Riley had never called last night. I'd checked my phone several times to make sure I hadn't missed something. But there was no denying the truth. He hadn't tried to contact me, even after I left the message.

I pushed away the fear and anxiety that tried to grip me, that tried to occupy my thoughts. I was going to turn over a new leaf. I was going to trust that everything that happened was for my good, even when my feelings didn't match. My pastor always said that emotions could be used for good or evil. I was going to choose "for good."

Holly had some kind of appointment in the morning, so she couldn't hang with me. But she did drop me off to get a new rental car. Thankfully, the police had come and taken a report. Then the rental company had told me— after nearly an hour on the phone—to have the car towed in.

Despite my misgivings about trying to navigate this city on my own, I had no choice. Vic Newport was available to talk. He and Edward had apparently been BFFs.

I pulled off the Interstate. Straight ahead, I spotted a six-story building with Wimbledon Pharmaceuticals stretched across the top in bold, blue letters. I'd heard of them before. They not only made general medications like pain relievers and acid reflux aids, but they also had created some groundbreaking cancer and MS drugs.

I'd done a little research on the company before leaving and had discovered that they generously gave to many charities, that they'd nearly gone under eight years ago when another company beat them at distributing a new chemotherapy medication, and today they were on the Fortune 500 list. The company was started by Reginald Wimbledon and taken over by Reginald Wimbledon, Jr. He ran the company until last year when he passed away.

Since then, his son Smith Wimbledon had taken over.

I found a parking space, then hurried inside. A receptionist ushered me upstairs, walking at such a fast clip that I was still trying to catch my breath when I reached a conference room.

The woman forced a smile and pushed the door open. "He'll be here in a moment."

I paced around the room, trying to cool my nerves. There was nothing to be nervous about. I'd done this a million times before. Just ask questions. Be nosy. Do what you do best.

Still, this felt different. I'd never been paid to ask these questions before, which seemed to raise the stakes.

I paced over to a marble topped coffee bar and ran my finger across it, staring at a stain there, just as the door opened.

"Ms. St. Claire?"

I straightened myself, a little too quickly. So much for appearing professional. "Mr. Newport. Thanks for letting me come out. I know you're a busy man."

Mr. Newport wasn't tall and wasn't short. He had a severely receding hairline and an expensive suit. He must like jewelry too because he had a thick gold watch, a couple of bracelets, and even a necklace.

"Anything I can do to help Edward and his family."

Maybe I could earn points with this man, just like I'd earned points with Detective Morrison. "In exchange for your time, I can give you a great trick for cleaning that marble top with just some baking soda and crushed chalk."

He stared at me a moment and said nothing.

So much for earning points.

He pointed to a stiff looking chair at the table. "Have a seat."

I obediently sat down at a long, glossy, conference

table, rationalizing that I wasn't the corporate type. Not with the sour faces, the stiff suits, and the office politics. Two other men filed into the room.

I froze. I hadn't expected anyone else to be joining us.

Mr. Newport must have noticed my confusion because he paused. "I also have Smith Wimbledon here. Mr. Wimbledon's grandfather founded the company and today Smith serves as the CEO. He knew Edward and thought he might add something."

Smith nodded. He was younger than I expected. Probably in his mid-thirties, but he had a head full of hair, an easy smile, and kind eyes.

"My father was the CEO when Edward Mercer worked here," he explained. "Unfortunately, he had a heart attack last year and here I am now, trying to fill big shoes."

I nodded, trying to calm my anxiety. "Thanks for being here."

"And this is Gil Portman from our PR department," Vic continued.

Portman, a forty something man who looked like he tried to be young and hip with his snug business suit and gelled hair, stood. "I'm just here to make sure the company doesn't get any bad press. We're not anticipating it, but we've had some experiences in the past where words were taken out of context, mostly with reporters. We don't take any chances. Any interview taking place at Wimbledon is attended by a member from our department."

"Understood."

I bit back disappointment. I was counting on a nice private conversation where I could get this man to open up about the real Edward Mercer. Instead, this would be more like a board meeting where everything I asked was analyzed. Wonderful.

All three of them sat with their fingers laced in front of them—had they planned it that way?—and stared at me.

"Now, what can we do for you, Ms. St. Claire?" Mr. Newport asked.

"I'm investigating the deaths of the Mercer family, and I understand that you were close friends with Edward."

He nodded curtly. "That's correct. Our families often got together for dinners and other social events."

"Did Edward have any enemies?" The question sounded lame and expected, but I had to ask.

His face twitched ever so slightly. "We all have enemies, Ms. St. Claire. Some people because they're too ruthless and others because they're too kind. There will always be people who don't like us for one reason or another."

"Why didn't people like Edward?"

Portman from publicity spoke up. "I'd like to add that people here at Wimbledon respected Edward. We believe in nurturing people and creating a safe, healthy work environment."

I supposed they didn't want to be known as a workplace full of bullying. I nodded. "Excellent."

I turned back to Vic Newport and waited for his answer.

He adjusted one of his gold bracelets before coming out of his trance-like scowl. "Some people disliked Edward because he worked his way up at the company so easily. Others didn't like him because his wife came from wealth. Like any good businessman, he was focused and some people saw that trait in him as an almost shark-like quality."

I wondered if that meant Edward saw people as a commodity? I didn't ask.

I needed to redirect my question. "Was there anyone

in particular who had especially hard feelings toward him?"

"No one that the police haven't already questioned." The answer came from Wimbledon, who had a compassionate smile on his face.

Perhaps he'd noticed that Mr. Newport was a little too businesslike and not warm enough. Had he intervened for the sake of the company's good name? Or was it because he was truly kind?

"Edward wasn't a perfect man, but he was a great asset to us here," Newport continued, glaring at Smith Wimbledon. "While he was successful at business, I fear he thought of himself as a failure when it came to his family."

"I'm sure working a high-stress, demanding job like this will do that to a person." Since my stain removal tip didn't work, I tried a new tactic. I tried sounding like I was on their side, like I was sympathetic. I thought many things in life were more important than money, though.

Mr. Newport nodded. "Something's got to give. You know the saying, 'You can have it all'? Well, you truly can't."

"For the record, we do encourage our employees to utilize their vacation time in order to strengthen family relationships. However, we also feel like a person's personal life isn't ours to interfere in," Portman added. "We believe in personal responsibility."

I glanced around the room. At least I agreed with that sentiment, even if Portman did sound like he was talking out of both sides of his mouth. "Could you tell me a little more about the company?"

"We're a pharmaceutical company," Wimbledon interjected. "In a nutshell, we manufacture and develop drugs that save people's lives."

"Sounds noble."

"We like to think we're in the business of bringing hope to the hopeless. That's what this is all about. We help to extend lives, as well as ensure a better quality of life for those faced with unfortunate medical conditions," Portman added with the spin of anyone worth his weight in the PR field. "We take our jobs here very seriously. In the past, we've lost millions we put into drug research because we discovered deadly side effects. That's what sets us apart from other drug companies: Money isn't our bottom line. People's wellbeing is."

"Admirable."

Portman nodded. "And, if you're interested, I have a sheet I can give you before you leave with a list of our philanthropic endeavors."

"Did Edward ever have any problems here at work?" *Backstabbing, whistleblowing, stomping on people below him?*

"None whatsoever. Edward was a hard worker, and we were so sorry to lose him," Wimbledon jumped in. "He brought a lot of experience in management to the company and really helped to tighten up the way the company is run."

"You have any theories as to what happened to him?"

Mr. Newport grimaced. "A random crazy. It's a reality I'd rather not think about, but it's the only thing that makes sense to me."

"Would someone that random really leave no evidence behind?" I threw the question out just to see the reaction.

Tension crackled in the room. "I suppose that's for the police to figure out," Mr. Newport said, his lips puckered. "I don't consider myself a detective. I leave that to the authorities."

The man had agreed to meet with me, but he certainly didn't seem too fond of having me here. Was this his personality? Was he like this with everyone? Or was the man acting like this because he had something to hide? I wasn't sure. Best I could tell, the man didn't have any motive to kill his best friend.

Wimbledon stood. "I hate to cut this short, but we do have a board meeting. Have all of your questions been answered?"

I nodded with a touch of hesitation. "I suppose."

"We wish the best of luck in finding this killer, Ms. St. Claire. No one deserves to get away with murder. I'd love to see justice for this family." Wimbledon shook my hand. "You let us know if you have any more questions."

I told everyone thanks and then a thirty-something short woman with brittle, over-processed blonde hair escorted me toward the elevators.

"Is Mr. Newport always that terse?" I asked. I probably shouldn't have. I shouldn't have pulled her into this. But asking questions never hurt . . . until they almost got me killed, at least.

The woman waited until the doors closed before answering. "Work is his life."

"I gathered that."

"That's why I like my job. I've been offered promotions—based on merit, not on connections—but I just stick to being a midlevel manager. Sure, I may not make the most money, but I go home every day at 5 p.m., and I don't take any work with me. No weekends, very little overtime. My husband's job is the same way. We may not be rich, but we're happy. I have time for friends, for books, and for a good movie on occasion."

I smiled, noticing we were almost to the first floor. "I guess Mr. Newport isn't married."

"Not anymore. I doubt he'll marry again. Not after that scandal involving his wife."

I perked. "Scandal?"

"I shouldn't really say anything." She looked around, even though there were only the two of us on the elevator. "But it was bad. What woman wants to feel like second place, though? His wife was neglected. Not that that excuses anything."

"You said scandal." I wasn't dropping that point. "Was their conflict public?"

"Everyone knows about it. No one speaks of it, though. Maybe it's better that way."

I had more questions. Like, what kind of scandal was it? Certainly Portman from publicity wouldn't approve of this conversation.

The elevator dinged, and the secretary snapped back into professional mode so quickly it was almost comical. Her head jerked up, her eyes took on a cool appearance, and she strode forward like the two of us hadn't spoken a word on the trip down.

"Please sign out before you leave. We like to keep track of all of our visitors."

I nodded, knowing this conversation was over. No way did this woman want to risk her job by talking to me about things of this nature. And as stringent as the company seemed about their PR, she very well could lose her job over the comments she made.

I chewed on her words as I signed out. The Mercer family and the Newport family had been friends, and I knew that Edward wasn't always faithful to his wife. Had he been unfaithful with his best friend's wife? Would that give Mr. Cold and Calculated Newport a reason to kill? The man certainly seemed meticulous enough to pull off a murder spree without leaving evidence behind.

I shook my head as I stepped outside. Certainly I was reading too much into this. Certainly the police had looked into him, checked his alibi.

But right now, Mr. Newport was all I had to go on.

Mr. Newport and a mysterious man who was watching my every move.

CHAPTER 9

I had just enough time to grab lunch, so I decided to eat some more Cincinnati chili. It might be my new favorite food. I decided to branch out and try a chili-cheese sandwich, which was actually like a coney without the hot dog. I gobbled up every bite.

After washing my food down with some soda, I called Jamie. Since she'd offered to help with research, I decided to accept. I asked her to see what she could find out about both Vic Newport and Sebastian Royce, who was next on my list. She quickly accepted.

Sebastian was one of Edward's friends and apparently they liked to play polo together at a local country club.

I pushed aside any judgments that formed in my mind at the idea of polo and put my car into drive. I was beginning to get a better feel for navigating the city, and that was a good thing. I'd learned through life that the fewer people I had to depend on, the better. It was an unfortunate but true fact.

My cellphone rang and, thanks to the handy-dandy Bluetooth feature, I was able to talk hands free. It was Jamie.

"Where ya headed?" she asked.

"I'm off to meet Ralph Lauren."

She let out a deep belly laugh. "You think that's what this man will look like?"

"Doubtful. Very doubtful. But it's my first foray into the

world of polo—beyond the shirt, that is. Did you dig up anything on him?"

"I'm still looking."

"Not hacking, right?" I had to admit that the idea was intriguing. Too bad it was also illegal.

"Give a sister some credit. I'm not hacking. Not yet at least. I'll let you know if I find out anything, though."

"You're the best. Thanks."

Twenty minutes later, I reached the east side of town and pulled into the drive of Rolling Hills Country and Golf Club. Well-manicured greens were on either side of the lane, adorned with preppy golfers who braved the cold weather with their caddies all for the sake of the game. Sacrifices. That was what life was all about.

Memories filled me of the last time I'd felt like a fish out of water. I'd attended a law school reunion with Riley at a resort called Allendale Acres. Most people who frequented the place made more money in one month than I made in a year, and I wasn't exaggerating.

At least I'd worn my Sunday best today—casual black pants with a soft royal blue top and an infinity scarf. My dressy would never compare to Holly's girly-girl dressy, but I was okay with that.

Though I spotted a valet at the front doors of a massive white building in the distance, I tucked my car into a parking space. I wasn't too cheap to pay a valet—I'd be reimbursed anyway. I just didn't like the hassle. I was perfectly capable of parking my own car.

I hurried up to the steps, nodding to the valets like I knew what I was doing and that I belonged here. I paused by the front desk. "I'm here to see Sebastian Royce."

The woman nodded. "Name?"

"Gabby St. Claire."

"He's expecting you. Go straight ahead and you'll reach

the White House Restaurant. The maître d' will help from there."

The woman's reverent tone alerted me that, even among the wealthy, Sebastian Royce was like club royalty. Garrett's note had said the man owned a line of successful sporting goods stores with attached athletic complexes that included batting cages and driving ranges.

I tried to look like I belonged as I stepped into the restaurant. Before the maître d' could say anything, I simply said, "Sebastian Royce." The man nodded and led me to a window table.

A man with what I'd guess to be premature white hair and oversized glasses sat at a table there. His face was nearly wrinkleless, he had a mustache that curled up on the ends, and an air of importance seemed to surround him. He was more King Triton than a Jamaican crab who randomly burst into songs like "Under the Sea" and "Kiss the Girl." While I was making mental references to *The Little Mermaid*, I supposed I might cast myself as Ariel.

King Sebastian didn't even look my way as I approached.

The maître d' seemed hesitant to disturb, but I wasn't. I slid into the seat across from Sebastian Royce and waited until he looked at me. Finally, he slowly turned away from his phone and stared at me without so much as a hint of warmth.

I smiled—a little too brightly, just for effect—and said, "Thanks for meeting with me."

"I'm sure this will be a waste of my time," he started. He put his phone down and clasped his hands together on the table. "This case gets reopened every couple of years. People clamor to talk to me since I was a friend of Edward Mercer. There's nothing new I have to offer."

It wasn't exactly a warm and fuzzy greeting, but I'd

heard worse.

"I don't expect you to have the answers. I'm just trying to gain insight into the family. I was hoping you could help."

"The only reason I agreed to meet was because of Garrett. I know he needs answers. Anyone in his shoes would. I'd hate to seem unsupportive."

I had a feeling that if I weren't a woman, Sebastian Royce would have suggested we meet in the sauna to discuss this. With cigars. He just seemed like a guy's guy who was stuck in a mindset prevalent many decades ago.

"Can you tell me about your friendship with Edward Mercer?"

The man stared out the window. "We met through a mutual love of polo. It was a stress reliever for both of us. We met here at the club a few times a week to shoot the breeze."

"Had anything been troubling Mr. Mercer in the weeks leading up to his death?"

"Nothing other than the usual."

"And what was the usual?"

"Being a successful CEO or Vice President of a company comes with a cost. There are long hours, hard decisions, people who like you just for your money, charities that stick to you like a tick to a hunting dog. You trade one set of problems for another. When you can find people who are in similar places in life and whom you can relate with, it's a welcome respite."

"I see."

"That was ten years ago. Ten years ago, I was just getting started and making my way up. We had a lot in common."

"Had Edward ever mentioned moving?"

He raised his bushy eyebrows. "Moving?"

"There was something that Edward Mercer wanted to talk to his family about. It must have been big if he wanted the whole family there." Maybe Edward was going to own up to his own scandal. Doubtful, but maybe. "Perhaps it was about his job."

"No, he loved his job. Talked about it all the time. Believed he could be making a difference. They were talking about him making the head honcho one day." He leaned closer, amusement sparkling in his eyes. "Head honcho. Sounds like a big deal, huh?"

I nodded, not wanting to offend the man, whose personality was an odd mix of self-absorption and peculiar humor. "I suppose. So he wasn't going anywhere?"

"Not that I was aware of. And he would have told me."

"Do you think he was getting divorced?"

"I doubt it. They didn't have a perfect marriage, but Edward and Elizabeth seemed in it for the long haul. They'd adjusted."

I didn't like the sound of that. "By adjusted, do you mean that Elizabeth had come to terms with Edward's unfaithfulness?"

He shrugged, as if I'd asked him about the weather. "I suppose."

"So, in your opinion, their relationship wasn't caustic?"

"It may have been years ago when things first began to crumble. But they'd both gotten to the point where they accepted things for what they were. They were married in name only."

"Excuse me. Mr. Royce?" a new voice said.

I looked up and saw a man, probably in his mid-thirties. He wore a button up shirt and khakis, and as he stood there tapping his foot and cradling an electronic tablet, he was the living, breathing definition of high strung.

"Yes, Kevin?"

"One of the board of directors is on the phone. He wants to speak with you."

Sebastian shrugged. "Tell him I'll call him later."

"Sir, he says it's important."

Sebastian scowled this time. "I said, tell him I'll call him later."

Kevin stared at his boss for a moment and then scurried away. Sebastian scoffed when Kevin was out of sight. "He's a faithful employee. Not necessarily a good one, though."

"He's your assistant?"

Sebastian nodded. "Has been for the past twelve years. Started as an intern. Surprisingly, he's stuck with me."

"You always bring him with you here to the country club?"

"I started coming here as a stress reliever from work. Now I bring my work here with me as a stress reliever. I handle my calls and correspondence here as often as possible. In between polo and golf, of course. So, yes, I do."

I nodded and decided to ask the question pressing on my mind. I wasn't sure if it had to do with the case or my curiosity. "Are you married, Mr. Royce?"

"I tried four times. Now I'm thinking that maybe Edward and Elizabeth were on to something."

His words made my heart feel heavy. Most of the time I still felt hope for my future. I wanted a marriage built on love and respect. I wanted to spend forever with someone.

What I didn't want was to treat marriage like buying a car, enjoying it for a while, and then trading it in for something better or more exciting. I wanted to grow old with someone. I was even okay with the fact that one day the butterflies might wear off. That I'd see the other person at their worst. That there would be bad days and hard times and moments of angst. Even knowing that, I still wanted to be committed.

Mr. Royce wasn't done. "Are you married, young lady?"

I fingered my engagement ring. "No, I'm not."

"Smart girl. You'll be even smarter if you stay single."

"No offense, but that's a horrible thing to say." If I said "no offense" before an offensive statement, that made it okay, right?

"Not horrible. It's the truth. People ask me my advice on success, and that's always what I want to say. Of course, I never do. But what I really want to tell people is that in order to achieve big things, you've got to be focused. All my ex-wives did was take my money and make my life miserable. Whatever temporary happiness we had . . . it wasn't worth it."

Was that Riley's thought process, also? He had to be focused in order to achieve his healing? Maybe this was everyone's secret to success, and I was just now hearing about it.

I'd never considered myself idealistic—at least, not to the extreme—but that's how I was feeling now. I wanted to believe that you could be focused *and* relationship minded.

Then I thought about my own life. Was the reason I wasn't successful because I'd let people hold me back? I'd dropped out of college to help my dad. I hadn't explored other job options with my degree because I wanted to stay local and be closer to Riley.

Both of those things had gotten me nowhere. They'd left me with a crime scene cleaning business and a flash in the pan P.I. assignment.

"I made you think, didn't I? There are people who'd pay big bucks to get advice from me, young lady. I gave you that one for free." He snapped his fingers and pointed at me.

I couldn't bring myself to say, "Thank you." No, make that I *refused* to thank him. People always trumped other things in life. As a Christian, that should be obvious to me.

I shook my head, feeling sorry for the man. I decided not even to acknowledge his statement. "What were your thoughts on who committed the crime?"

"As a businessman, I don't make assumptions." He raised his hand and a waiter refilled his wine glass.

"As a businessman, certainly you make projections—on how much you'll make for the year, amongst other things. You just assumed if you raised your hand, the waiter would refill your glass. We all make assumptions. Certainly you've given the murder of your friend some thought."

Apparently, that entertained him because he chuckled. "I suppose it is all a matter of word choice. Of course I thought about it. Who didn't?"

"And?" I prodded.

"Edward did tell me—and I passed this on to the police—that his wife had felt uncomfortable with the way the tile man looked at her. I guess there was one occasion where she caught him in her bedroom."

I perked. I hadn't heard that yet. "What did he say? I'm assuming she confronted him."

He nodded. "She did. He said he wanted to check out the tile work he'd done in the master bath to make sure the patterns matched."

"Was he going through her things or simply in the room?"

"I seem to remember that he was looking at the pictures on her dresser. Despite that, she fired him. He wasn't happy about that. Said he was depending on this job in order to pay his bills, that he'd turned down other jobs in order to complete the one at their home."

"Didn't they have a contract?"

"People like the Mercers knew how to write a contract, how to get out of them, how to make complicated clauses work in their favor. This worker knew that. He knew he wouldn't stand a chance and that a lawsuit would be too expensive."

"Sounds like they were sharks."

He raised one of his bushy eyebrows again. "I call it survival of the fittest."

By fittest, I figured he meant richest. I didn't dislike rich people, nor did I feel entirely comfortable around them. But rich, arrogant people who took advantage of the poor did bother me.

Despite my thoughts on the social classes, one thing became clear. Perhaps the most promising suspect in my investigation was the same as the police's: the tile guy. But since he was dead, no one might ever know the truth as to his guilt.

One other thought remained. I'd heard of this man's sporting goods stores before. And I knew they sold guns.

Which meant that Sebastian Royce most likely owned some.

CHAPTER 10

As soon as I got back into the car, my phone rang. It was Jamie again.

"Perfect timing, girl. What's going on?"

"Get this. Before Sebastian Royce was a business mogul, he had several failed businesses. I'm not sure there's any tie in to those businesses at all, but I figured it was worth mentioning."

"You never know when those facts can come in handy."

"I also discovered that the man used to be a sharpshooter several years ago. Won some contests even before abruptly dropping from the scene. He definitely had the know-how when it came to pulling the trigger with precision."

"What would his motive be, though?"

"Okay, so you know he owns this chain of stores called Winners. He originally started the company fifteen years ago with a man named Warner Crush. Twelve years ago, the company had some problems and nearly split over differences and financial problems. Two years after that, Edward Mercer and his family died. Coincidence?"

"Probably. But something about that timeline bothers me. Whatever happened to Warner Crush?"

"I was hoping you might ask. He actually started a new company, specializing in just batting cages. His small chain of stores isn't nearly as successful as Sebastian's market-dominating enterprise. But he's local. In fact, his headquarters is off of 21st St."

"I know where I'm headed next."

I pulled off into a gas station, typed the address into my phone, and ten minutes later, I pulled up at Swingers, an interesting name for a batting cage chain. The place wasn't especially polished, but maybe batting cages weren't supposed to be. I knew little about baseball.

I walked toward the building, which apparently operated as not just the company headquarters, but also one of their flagship locations. Everything was white, accented in a hideous shade of orange.

Inside, I ignored the smell of leather and sweat, I went straight for the desk. I pulled out my wallet and flashed my driver's license, hoping the guy wasn't paying attention. "I need to see Warner Crush about an investigation."

The man raised his eyebrows and nodded behind him. "Go through the door in the back. You can talk to Mr. Crush's secretary."

I'd gotten past one gatekeeper. Would I make it past two?

I bypassed the sporting equipment, entered a hallway lined with painted cement blocks, and searched the names on the doors until I saw Warner Crush's. I pushed inside and flashed my driver's license again at the fresh-out-of-high-school girl sitting behind the desk, staring at her phone.

"My name's Gabby. I'm a P.I., and I need to talk to Mr. Crush."

She stared at me, never moving her head, and her phone still raised. "I'm sorry. He's busy."

"This is important." I stared at the door behind her, wondering if that's where Warner was now.

She blinked, her head still not moving. "You'll need an

appointment."

"You do understand I'm in the middle of an active investigation, right? This is a little more serious than a game of Candy Crush."

Her bottom lip dropped down. I'd hit the nail on the head. But her moment of awe was short lived.

"He has a very busy schedule."

"It's about Sebastian Royce."

Suddenly, the door behind her opened. Warner Crush stepped out. Bingo! "You're investigating Sebastian?"

"In relation to the death of the Mercer family."

He looked at me a moment, and I could see something simmering in his gaze. Finally, he nodded. I was pretty sure that was satisfaction I saw in the depths of his eyes. He was trying to disguise it as duty and responsibility, though. "I can give you a few minutes. I need to go test out one of the machines. You mind if we talk out there?"

I smiled. "If that's what it takes."

***

"So, how did you and Sebastian know each other?" I asked Warner Crush, who in the few minutes since I'd met him had already become "The Crusher" in my mind.

Through the course of our initial chitchat, I'd learned that The Crusher was a former minor league baseball player who'd done a number of jobs throughout the years, including being a high school baseball coach. Later, he managed some travel baseball teams. Then he'd started the business with Sebastian, and now he ran these batting cages.

He was well over six foot tall, had the build of a wrestler, and closely cropped blond hair.

He took a swing at the ball.

If I knew anything about baseball, I might try to impress him now. But I didn't, so I didn't. I just tugged my helmet in place as I watched him swing and grunt and avoid eye contact.

"Sebastian Royce and I met because we were both on the board for a local sports association. We started talking. I had managing experience and a history in playing the minors. He had business sense and some cash."

"How'd he get that thus stated cash? From what I understand, he lost money on his past businesses before hitting it big with Winners."

That earned me a glance and a snort. "He has a way of schmoozing with the right people. He can find investors faster than Everth Cabrera can steal a base."

I had no idea who Everth was, but I assumed the man was a baseball player and that he was fast. "I guess it didn't work out that well. At least not in the early years."

The Crusher hit a ball even harder. Was he really testing the machine or was he getting out some pent up anger? I didn't know the man well enough to say.

"Sebastian may have been able to raise capital, but he didn't have a lot of sense. At least, not back then."

"What happened between the two of you?"

He missed a ball and let an expletive escape. He quickly recovered and got himself in position to hit again. "He thought I was ruining the store. I thought he was ruining the store. I guess he was right. We split ways and the store succeeded."

"Why would you think he was ruining the store?"

"I thought he wanted to grow too fast. All the capital we had disappeared in the first year. We weren't turning a profit. He, in the meantime, thought the solution was to borrow more, to open more stores, to expand rapidly. He thought I'd done a poor job at managing employees, that we'd hired too many, that we were paying too much."

"What happened after you guys split?"

The Crusher shrugged. "I only heard rumors. I sold my share of the company to him, so officially, I was out of the loop."

"Unofficially?"

"I heard a few things. Nothing confirmed. But you said you're investigating the murder of the Mercers, right?"

I nodded. "That's correct."

"I always thought it was strange. I have a hunch that Sebastian took a loan from Edward Mercer. We had a couple of social events over at their house, and I saw them in some heated discussions."

I tried to remain expressionless. "Is that right?"

He hit a button and the machine must have stopped. He set his bat against the wall and turned toward me. This was really what this meeting was all about, wasn't it? The Crusher couldn't stand the fact that Sebastian had created a successful business for himself while his had floundered. With that knowledge, I had to try and ascertain the truth from anything he told me.

"I know Sebastian and Edward had a huge fallout about a week before the murders. I wonder sometimes if Edward's death was the only reason the company was successful. Since Sebastian didn't have the money to pay Edward back, it was practically free cash."

"What kind of loan are we talking about here? How big?"

"To keep the stores open, he needed around ten million."

My eyes widened. "That's a nice chunk of change. Did Edward Mercer have ten million to loan?"

"I couldn't tell you that. I know his wife was loaded, but she kept a tight rein on her money. I heard rumors that it was off the books, thanks to some foreign bank account."

I leaned against the metal cage behind me. I wondered exactly what Elizabeth Mercer would have thought about a risky loan like that. "Do you think your friend—former friend—is capable of murder?"

"Something always seemed a little off about him. Some people called him eccentric. But maybe the line between eccentric and crazy is thin."

"Did you ever tell the police about your theory? About this rumor?"

"No, I didn't. I had no proof. Without proof, you have nothing."

He should have gone to the police because maybe they could have found proof. I didn't voice my thoughts aloud. "What about the person who told you that information? Did they have proof? I'm assuming the information came from someone who still worked for Sebastian Enterprises."

"Sebastian's assistant spilled the news."

Kevin? "How do you know his assistant?"

A smirk formed across his face. "He uses the batting cages here."

"What?"

"I know. It's odd. But he said he has to get away from the toxic environment where he works. He comes in every day after he's put in his hours. I guess this is his way of rebelling. He has to be a 'yes man' all day. Depending on how stressful his day was, he might say too much sometimes."

"Why doesn't he quit then?"

"Sebastian pays too well. This guy knows too much. Besides, I told him to go to the police, but he refused. He was afraid he might end up dead if he did."

99

CHAPTER 11

I had a lot to think about as I drove to the Paladins'. I was at the tail end of rush hour traffic and, I had to admit, Cincinnati's rush hour made Norfolk's look like a drive through the country.

By the time I reached my temporary home, my head was spinning and my stomach was grumbling.

I stepped inside and found Holly sitting at the kitchen table, her head cradled in her hands. She smiled when she saw me, but still looked exhausted. "Hey, Gabby."

"You feeling okay?" I asked.

She nodded. "Just tired."

I hadn't planned on doing this, but I needed someone to talk to right now, and Holly seemed like a good candidate. Between the investigation, my thoughts on Riley, and my lingering doubts on my future, my head was ready to burst.

"I need a drink. Coffee, that is. Maybe some food, too. Something fattening that I'll feel guilty about later, but that will comfort me immensely for the time being."

Holly's eyes lit. "Funny you should say that. I've had one of those days, too. Want to go to a coffeehouse and chill? I know a great place for homemade soups. They've got good coffee and pies. Lots of pies."

"Sounds great."

A few minutes later, we were out the door. She wove through Cincinnati until we reached a place that Holly told me was part of the University of Cincinnati. She parked in a crowded lot and then we hurried across a people-laden street to a shop located in the basement level of an apartment building.

"I frequented this place all the time in college," Holly told me. "It remains one of my favorites to this day. Life was so different back then."

I knew all about life being different. Even small things—like being here at the coffee shop—made me think of life back home. It made me think of The Grounds, my favorite hangout. Riley and I used to go there all the time. Since his accident, he didn't like coffee anymore. He couldn't even stand the smell of it. That had meant that whenever I'd been over at his place to help him out— sluggishly tired, most of the time—I'd had to leave my coffee at my place. It was a sacrifice I'd been willing to make, but changes like that in life were so strange.

We were seated. I ordered a mushroom and brie soup, and Holly got chicken tortilla. While we sipped away, I filled her in on my day. I told her all about Vic Newport, Sebastian Royce, and Warner Crush.

I was hoping talking about it might make the answers—I'd even take a decent theory—magically fall into place, but it didn't. Maybe that was because what I really wanted to talk about was personal. Maybe that part of my life needed the most sorting now. I finished my soup and ordered a piece of banana caramel pie.

When a moment of silence fell, I found myself blurting, "So, in case you're wondering why I carry a gun with me, I thought you should know that my fiancé was almost killed by a serial killer who wanted to exact his revenge," I started. My words sounded too ordinary, too mundane. I took a sip of my coffee, trying to wash away the bitter taste in my mouth. "It turned my life upside down, to say the least."

Holly's eyes widened. "That's horrible. I can't even imagine."

"I still have nightmares."

"Is that why I hear you crying out in your sleep at night?"

My cheeks flushed. "Sorry about that."

"Don't apologize."

"Yeah. I have night terrors. All of the time." I shook my head. "Anyway, my fiancé came out of the coma, but he hasn't been the same. As the ultimate slap in the face, he decided to move back home with his mom and dad last week." The words still made me balk. "He thought they could take care of him better than me."

"Ouch."

"Yeah, ouch. That's when I decided to come here. I decided some time away might be the perfect medicine."

Holly frowned, a certain somberness coming over her. "Life has a funny way of slapping you in the face sometimes, doesn't it?"

"You can say that again," I muttered. I drew in a deep breath and listened to the muted strands of acoustic music crooning through the overhead. For a moment—and just a moment—I pretended like the past couple of months hadn't happened. I tried to pretend like my heart didn't hurt, that the future looked bright, and that life didn't feel so uncertain.

"Sometimes getting away can allow our vision to clear. I'm going to pray for you, that you can see things more clearly. I hate clichés—I really do—but there's one that says God never closes a door without opening a window. I don't know what God has in store for you, but keep trusting Him. He has a plan and He's got the timing down pat."

I thought about Sebastian's words today, about how you should focus on your career and how relationships could mess you up. I didn't really believe that, but now that the thought had settled in my mind, I could see a glimmer of truth in the statement. Of course it was easier to get ahead when your only priority was yourself.

Though I constantly felt like I was out of my comfort zone, maybe God wanted me totally in a place of uneasiness in order that I might rely on Him. Truly, His power could be made perfect in my weakness.

Or, maybe the fact that I always had a crisis in my life was more a reflection of me than it was anyone else. Maybe I brought these things upon myself.

"Have you ever heard the saying YOLO?" Holly played with her coffee stirrer.

I nodded. "You only live once? Yeah, I've heard it. Why?"

She nibbled on her lip for a moment. "Here's something weird. I know it sounds crazy that I'm telling you this, but I was diagnosed with subcutaneous panniculitis-like T-cell lymphoma."

I sucked in a quick breath, uncertain if I'd heard her correctly. "Lymphoma?"

Would that explain the glimpses of sadness I caught in her eyes? The moments of exhaustion?

"The exact name is a real mouthful, isn't it? This type is a rare but terminal illness that my doctor said is fast acting and essentially untreatable. Basically, my life has an expiration date."

"I'm so sorry, Holly. I would have never guessed." Her news made my problems seem small. For a moment, I felt guilty for whining. I decided if I were to assign people songs that fit their lives, I would give Holly either "Put on a Happy Face" or "I've Got Sunshine." And it wasn't because

I thought she saw life through rose-colored glasses. It was because she looked for the good in the hardest circumstances. Her attitude despite that news was amazing and admirable.

"It strikes at the strangest times, you could say. Most of the time, I'm okay. But every once in a while, I can feel the disease that's ravaging my body. Dying gives you a new perspective on living."

"I bet." I didn't know what else to say.

She traced the rim of her coffee mug. "I know I need to make some changes. I've got to break away from the expectations that everyone else has for me and listen to my heart. Listen to what God's been impressing upon my heart. I've made a so called bucket list."

I could only imagine the expectations that her family had for her. Being extroverted with dominant personalities could easily turn into being overbearing and pushy. "It sounds like our families might be on opposite ends of the spectrum. They had no expectations for me. My mom might have had some, before the cancer got to her."

Something about the conversation seemed to create an instant bond between Holly and me, one that I didn't often feel. I was grateful for it, though. Through our pain, somehow we were able to relate.

"My mom died when I was in college. I had to drop out and take on some extra jobs to help with the bills. I wanted to study forensics and go into law enforcement. I thought crime scene cleaning would be the next best thing. It would keep me close to the evidence, you know?"

"Makes sense to me. Some of the nicest things people did for us when my dad died was to come over and clean up and bring food. They were such simple acts of kindness, but they went such a long way. Cleaning is an admirable profession, so saith I, at least."

I half smiled. "So saith you."

She waved a hand in the air and rolled her eyes. "I have this thing about King James English. People always make fun of me for it. Every once in a while it slips out, henceforth creating some strange looks from people."

"I think it's charming," I offered, raising my mug. "You really do like eras gone by, don't you?"

"I dream about days when life was slower, more thoughtful, more relationship oriented." She cleared her throat.

"When did your dad die?" I asked.

"My dad died two years ago. He was the only one in the family who understood me. Who could understand why I'd want a job that paid so terribly but that brought all the satisfaction in the world."

"We all need someone like that in our lives." I certainly longed for it. And I did have people like that. Sierra and Chad, for example. We didn't always see eye to eye, but they supported me. Unless I was doing something stupid like almost getting killed. I cleared my throat. "So, tell me about this bucket list."

She smiled. "At first I wanted to do all of these crazy things for myself. I wanted to go to Europe. Go wild for once in my life. Do things that were death defying. Have crazy flings with handsome, Italian men and explore haunted castles and eat as much chocolate as possible." Her smile slipped. "Then I realized the most fulfilling way to spend my final days was to make other people's lives a little easier, a little better."

"What do you mean?"

She shrugged. "You know, random acts of kindness. Helping those who can't help themselves. Giving to the poor. Standing up for the voiceless. Those kind of things. I upped my volunteer hours at a local youth shelter. I surprised my brother and cleaned his house when he wasn't home—and never took credit for it. Things like that."

"I think that sounds really great, Holly. The happiest times in life are when we're giving to others. You're right. Focusing on yourself—" myself being a case in point "— can just make you miserable."

I wondered if I was one of those random acts of kindness. Holly had bent over backward to help me out since I'd been in town.

"Absolutely."

I gripped my coffee. "What's your family say about your diagnosis? They certainly seem optimistic still." They were all so close knit, despite their differences. They were like the family I'd always wanted but never had.

She grimaced. "They don't know, actually, she said with confusion and some regret."

I stared at her a moment, again uncertain if I'd understood. "What do you mean they don't know?"

Holly let out a long breath, any earlier hint of lightheartedness disappearing. "It's like this: When my dad found out he was dying, his life—his final days—became all about his death. I don't want that. I don't want people to look at me all the time and just feel sorry for me. So I haven't told my family. Not yet, at least."

"You've got to tell them."

She shrugged. "My sister is planning her wedding. My brother is running for office. There's so much going on right now. I want them to have their moments."

"Time is ticking away, though. I mean, I'm no expert. But if someone I was close to was diagnosed, I'd want to know. When I found out my mom had cancer, I just wanted to be around her as much as possible. Nothing else was as important anymore. My priorities changed. Looking back, I wish I could have spent even more time with her."

She stared off into the distance a moment before her gaze met mine. "This is going to sound strange, but I've only told two people: Jamie and you."

I blinked in surprise. "You're serious?"

She nodded. "Totally. I guess you feel like a safe person because you're only here temporarily, you know? I know you won't tell anyone . . . will you?"

I shook my head. "Of course not. It's not my news to tell."

"It's been really nice getting to know you, Gabby."

I smiled. "You, too, Holly."

I only wished I didn't feel like already mourning for her.

She was a new friend, but sadness still pressed in on me.

Her words remained with me, the reminder about living as if you didn't have much time. Maybe that was a lesson I needed to remember, as well.

Especially in the P.I. line of work.

***

I downed the last sip of my coffee, my mind gravitating toward my own bucket list. What would be on it? Finding a career that I'd dreamed about? Finding happiness outside of men? Maybe even seeing more of the world. I didn't know. I was usually concentrating on surviving the moment.

Holly stared at me from across the table. "How about you, Gabby? No jobs with the medical examiner?"

I shook my head. "None even close. Maybe I'm holding myself back."

"You could just be a P.I. instead."

"I've never even thought about it. I don't know. I want

to be proactive, not just go wherever life takes me. But I just feel like I need resolution. I need to know where Riley and I stand. I need to know Chad would be okay in business by himself. That my dad will be taken care of. I don't feel like I can leave until I have that peace." The words left my heart feeling heavy.

"Sounds like you're looking out for everyone but yourself. I'm not saying that's a bad thing either. Or a good thing. It's just an observation."

The words rang true. Guilt had captured me, making me a slave to the emotion so many times.

"Maybe that resolution will keep you in Norfolk. Maybe God wants you to be a crime scene cleaner. Maybe He wants you to wait because He has an even better job for you. Or maybe you need to get away from the chains of your past. Maybe moving would be the best thing for you. That's something you have to pray about. God will answer you. He said that His sheep will know His voice. It's just going to take some time. But you'll know."

"You're pretty wise, you know?"

"I wish I had this kind of clarity before I was given a year to live. Now I realize that all of that worrying, all of those fears . . . they didn't add a single benefit to my life."

I had a lot to think about. One thing was for sure: I could honestly say that God brought me here to Cincinnati for a reason. Maybe it was just to meet Holly and get a new perspective. She was right: Life did have a funny way of working out. I just had to learn to trust God in the meantime.

Just then, our waitress put a piece of paper on the table. "Some guy asked me to give this to you."

I wagged my eyebrows at Holly. "A guy? Maybe this is something that should be on your bucket list."

"Life is too short to worry about men," Holly

announced with the roll of her eyes.

"Isn't that the truth," I agreed. Yet I didn't. I wanted to agree, I wanted to be independent, and to feel like I could do anything on my own. In theory, I could. In reality, I missed having Riley by my side.

Holly's eyes narrowed as she unfolded the paper. "I think this is for you."

She slid the note across the table to me.

As I read the words, my blood went cold. *Don't say I didn't warn you.*

There was no signature, but I knew who had sent it. The Watcher.

He'd been here.

CHAPTER 12

I rushed outside and looked for the man—not that I had any idea what he looked like. I searched for someone suspicious, someone hurrying away, someone looking at me.

Unfortunately, I'd made a scene when I ran toward the door so quite a few people were looking at me. This had to be against some kind of unspoken code that trained P.I.s knew about. *When searching for someone, don't draw attention to yourself.*

Whoever had left the note was long gone.

I sighed and shuffled back inside. I went straight toward the waitress, who was collecting a tray full of food behind the counter. "What did the man look like who left this?" I held up the note.

She shrugged and popped a bubble with her gum. "I wasn't paying attention. He wore a hat down low over his eyes. He was a white guy. Not tall, not short. Not fat, not extremely thin. No accent. Lousy tipper. I don't know. He could have been anyone, huh?" She grabbed two bowls from the window behind her. "I see so many people in here. They all get mixed up in my mind."

"Do you have cameras here?"

She snorted and started hurrying through the restaurant to deliver the food. "No. We're a simple establishment here. Nothing fancy. Sorry."

I found Holly and gave her the update. At that point, I

was so rattled that there was no need to finish my pie, no matter how delicious it might be. We went back to her car. I checked the tires, the backseat and the underside, just to make sure no one had done any damage—not to mention to make sure no one was lurking there.

I saw nothing.

I half expected the engine not to start again.

But it did.

Still, the threat was ominous. The Watcher was planning something, and I had no idea what.

My thoughts swirled as we drove, volleying back and forth between the case, the threats, and my personal life.

No immediate answers or solutions came in regards to the case.

Which left me with thoughts of Riley.

I made up my mind. I was going to call Riley this evening. I was going to swallow my pride and try to find out what was going on.

***

I sat in bed that evening. Even though I wasn't cold, I had the covers pulled up over my legs, more as a security blanket, really.

My phone trembled in my hands, which was ridiculous. I should not feel this nervous about calling Riley. But I knew it wasn't calling him that had me nervous. It was the possible outcomes of our conversation that put me on edge.

What if he hadn't missed me? What if he'd decided to stay up in D.C. permanently? What if the doctors changed their opinions and now concluded that Riley would never fully recover? There were so many scary possibilities.

But sometimes it was better to face those possibilities

than to flounder in "what if" land.

I dialed Riley's number, but my call went straight to voicemail.

My heart dropped. Why wasn't he answering? He still hadn't called me back after my last voicemail. That meant that the last time I'd spoken with him was Sunday night.

He'd moved Saturday, and he'd called the next day. We'd spoken, but only briefly. He'd told me he'd gotten to his parents' house and was getting settled in. He thanked me for being understanding and told me that he'd call again soon.

That was three days ago.

Were my expectations too high? Maybe calling once a week was more appropriate. I didn't know anything anymore. I just knew that I missed him.

Which was why I decided to take a big leap and call his parents' house.

Things had been shaky between his parents and me ever since we'd disagreed on Riley's care while he was in a coma. All of us had since apologized, but I couldn't help but feel like our conflict was still hanging over our heads.

The immature side of me tried to avoid talking to them all I could, simply because I wanted to avoid potential conflict. And I had to face the fact that sometimes I spoke without thinking—which inevitably made things worse.

His mom, Evelyn, answered on the first ring with a whispered, "Hello?"

"Mrs. Thomas. It's Gabby." My chest tightened.

"Gabby, how are you?" Her words didn't convey an overly thrilled tone, but she also didn't sound annoyed.

"I'm doing okay. How are you?"

"We're managing up here."

What did that mean? Probably nothing, I reminded myself. I had to stop reading into things. "I'm trying to get up with Riley. Is he there?"

"He just laid down for the evening. He had a day of intense therapy, and he was utterly exhausted when he got home. So it was dinner and bed for him."

Disappointment pressed on me. "I see."

"I'll let him know you called."

"That would be great."

"You're taking care of yourself, aren't you?"

"Absolutely."

"I'm so glad to hear that. I'll let Riley know you called after he wakes up in the morning. I know we have another full day, but hopefully he'll be able to grab a moment to talk. I'll insist that he does."

Maybe she was trying to be helpful, but what I heard was: I'll make him call you, even if he doesn't want to.

I thanked her, said goodbye, and dropped the phone on the bed. I pulled a pillow over my chest and hugged it for a moment.

It was going to take a whole lot of trust in God to keep myself from dissolving into worry and fear on this one.

But Holly was right. God did do everything for a purpose. Maybe He was just trying to refine me now. And if I was going to live a life of transformation, I was going to have to start living out my faith.

***

By 10 a.m. the next morning, my cellphone was all-abuzz. My first call was Jamie. I filled her in on the case, and she told me that she hadn't gotten any creditable leads from the website.

My next call was from Sierra.

"Someone toured the building," she told me.

I frowned. "Really?"

Why would anyone want to buy the old rundown place? That's what I wanted to think. But I knew the truth. Other people would be able to see it as I did: as a treasure, as a lovely historical house that could be restored to its glory.

"I tried to eavesdrop, but all I know is that it was a man and woman in their fifties. They looked kind of uppity. I heard something about tearing down a wall and support beams."

I swallowed a little too hard. "That's too bad."

"Nothing's for sure. I told you I'd give you an update, though."

I heard Chad talking in the background.

"And, of course, my husband wants to talk to you again. Here he is."

"Hey, Gab. You know how we talked about expanding?"

"I remember you *mentioning* expanding more than I remember us actually *talking* about it."

"I can't stop thinking about it. I was going to wait until you got back to talk again, but now I'm thinking that offering a full range of contract services might just be the solution we're looking for."

"You mean, permanently?" Sure we'd taken on a few other jobs, but . . . . "We're crime scene cleaners. That's what we do."

"We'll still be crime scene cleaners. That's going to be our focus. But instead of having to hire subs to do some of the work, I want you and me to be able to do it ourselves. That way we'll make more of a profit and it will streamline our work load."

"What I'm hearing is that you want me to learn to put down carpet."

He paused. "In a manner of speaking, yes. I do. There

are a lot of things we can do ourselves. If we expand, we can also hire some more employees to help carry the workload."

"Which then eats into our profit."

"Not if we pick up more jobs. We've both done mold remediation and we know how to handle water damage. There are possibilities out there."

"The idea is . . . intriguing, to say the least."

"So, you'll think about it?" His voice lifted with each word. "I have some friends who are contractors who could teach us both what we need to know to get the jobs done on our own. I could really see this becoming a profitable business, Gabby."

Part of me wanted to scream "no!" I wanted to scream that things should stay the same. That I'd had too much change lately. That I just needed for life to feel normal again. But I didn't do that. Life went on, whether I wanted it to or not.

Finally, I nodded. "You know what? We should consider your idea."

I expected him to sound excited, relieved. Instead, he said, "There's one more thing."

"What's that?"

"I think we should change the name," he blurted.

I blinked, trying to buy myself some time as I processed his idea. "From Trauma Care?"

"We need something more generic. Trauma Care sounds very . . . traumatic."

I'd named the business when I'd started it. I'd been on my own for a while, until Chad and I decided to join forces. Trauma Care had been my brainchild. I'd had all of the forms printed up to start the business. I'd even spent way too much time trying to develop jingles and ensure that people left positive online reviews.

Trauma Care was mine. Was I just being territorial and stupid? Probably.

But I could hear the hope in Chad's voice. He was married now, ready to make a living and settle down. He had no reason to think small.

Then there was me. I hadn't been able to carry my weight lately, not the way I usually did. There just seemed to be so many changes happening at once, and I was having trouble handling them.

In honesty, I had bigger wars to battle at the moment. "Let's do it. I think it's a good idea, Chad."

"Really?" His voice came out high pitched.

"Yes, really. Everything you said. I think it's a good idea."

"Wow. That's great. I wasn't expecting the conversation to be so easy. I thought I would be safer with an audience. Otherwise, I would have brought it up sooner."

"That's me. I'm easy." I heard what I said and shook my head. "But not like that. Anyway, did you have an idea for what the name change might be?"

"I was thinking, 'The Cleaning Crew.'"

I scrunched my nose up. "I don't love it. Why don't we think about it some more?"

"Got it. Thanks, Gabby. Stay safe."

We hung up, then Garrett called. I needed some sorbet or other palate cleanser, only for my brain, which was spinning from all my conversations I'd already had.

"Hey there, Love. It's Garrett."

I wanted to sigh every time he called me "Love." However, I knew the pet name wasn't reserved just for me, so I let it go. In a move ripe for a lawsuit, I'd heard the man call his assistant the same thing. "Hi, Garrett."

"I just got into town. Would you mind meeting me at

my place to catch up?"

"A professional meeting at your place sounds great." I had to add the professional part. I knew the man was a player, but I needed to keep my boundaries clear.

"Can you be here in an hour? That enough time?"

"Yup." Yup? Speaking of being professional, certainly I could do better than "yup."

I quickly freshened up. I didn't want to appear too dressy or like I'd primped for Garrett, nor did I want to look sloppy and inappropriate. I settled with a pair of nice jeans, a striped top, and my black leather jacket.

"You look nice." Holly caught me as soon as I stepped out into the hallway.

I tugged at my shirt. "I'm meeting with the boss himself."

"Garrett, you mean?"

"He's the one." I paused. "Listen, I just wanted to let you know that it was really great chatting last night. Thanks for your insight."

"God gives us experiences for a reason. Sometimes, it's just so we can share what we've learned with others."

"You're absolutely right." I glanced at my watch. "I'd love to chat more, but I've got to get to that meeting. What are you up to today?"

"I'm feeling a little tired. I think I'm going to take it easy."

"Sounds wise."

I climbed in my car and set off down the road. I kept an eye on my rearview mirror, watching to see if anyone else would follow me. Because if there was one thing I'd learned it was to keep my eyes wide open.

CHAPTER 13

Twenty minutes later, I pulled up to an apartment building in an area of town called Mt. Airy. The neighborhood reminded me a bit of where I lived in Norfolk. It seemed kind of quirky and eccentric and artsy. I already liked it.

I stepped into the lobby of what must have been a fifteen or sixteen story building and called Garrett. He met me downstairs a moment later.

"Let's talk up at my place." He hit a button on the elevator. "We'll let your head clear a moment."

"Your place, huh?"

"A friend of mine actually owns it. He lets me use it when I'm in town. I run some of my operations out of the city."

"You never fail to surprise me."

"There's a lot I could surprise you with, Gabby."

I didn't know what that meant. I wasn't going to ask. The elevator dinged, and we stepped inside. Garrett pressed the "16" button.

"Penthouse?" I asked, not surprised.

"Sounds quite presumptuous to say it that way, doesn't it? The 'really big one at the top' sounds a little less intimidating."

The elevator stopped, and we stepped out. Garrett ushered me to a black leather couch. I sank there, and Garrett sat a respectable distance away.

"Any updates?"

I told him what I knew. Wrinkles formed at his eyes, deepening with each new detail.

"You have no idea who this person is who's calling?"

I shook my head. "No idea. I don't even know how they know me or how they got my number. Nothing makes sense."

"Perhaps the police can trace the call."

"I've thought of that but, with cellphones, it's complicated. Let me wait and see if he calls again."

Garrett assessed me with his gaze. I felt my cheeks flushing—against my will—and I looked away. Thankfully, at that moment, his cellphone rang. "It's my assistant. Excuse me one second."

He slipped away, and I immediately relaxed. I was in love with Riley but, for some reason, this man was making my body react in ways I didn't want.

I knew I wouldn't act on any of the things I felt, so I was safe in that regard. Still, I didn't like feeling a touch of attraction to anyone else. I was regaining control of my emotions when Garrett reappeared.

Garrett sat down beside me. "I'm so sorry, Love."

He squeezed my shoulder, briefly massaging the tight muscles there. I told myself it didn't feel good, but man did it ever.

"This case has been dormant for a while," Garrett started. "I'm unsure why someone is being stirred and upset by it now. The person behind the crimes has been hidden away for a long time. Coming out and threatening you is only risking his own freedom."

I nodded. His words made sense. "You're right. Why would someone take that risk?"

He sighed and leaned back. "Maybe I should take you off this case."

I shook my head. "I don't like being bullied, Garrett, and that's exactly what this person is trying to do."

He plucked a hair from my cheek. "And I don't like putting people I've hired into danger."

I scooted back slightly. He had to stop touching me. "Really. I'll be fine."

I stood and stretched, hoping the action looked natural and not like I was tenser than a cat on a tightrope. Everything still felt surreal. I felt like this couldn't possibly be my life, that maybe I'd stepped into someone else's. For a short time, at least.

My gaze scanned my surroundings. The place was modern and trendy and masculine. Quite a change from my apartment complex, which was old and creaky, but it had lots of personality. Maybe Holly and I had more in common than I thought.

"Nice place," I muttered, desperate for a change of subject.

"Isn't it?"

"You think your friend would let me stay here if my apartment building sells?"

Garrett gave me a questioning look. I shook my head and waved him off. "Ignore me. The building I've lived in for the past five years is on the market. We're all watching and waiting to see who will buy it."

"Sounds like the place means a lot to you."

I nodded. "It does. People have come and gone, but that building has remained steady."

"Well, hopefully the new owner will let all of you stay."

He reached down and picked up a glass. He raised it to me. I had a feeling it wasn't full of coffee this time. It looked like something stronger. More likely liquor. "Can I get you something to drink? Something to take off the edge?"

"I'm good. Thank you."

He set down his glass, crossed his arms, and leaned against the window. "You have beautiful hair. Has anyone ever told you that?"

I touched one of my curly locks. My red hair had defined me almost all of my life. It was only recently I'd learned to control it so it didn't frizz out all the time. Now it only frizzed out *half* of the time. "Thank you. I've been called many things in my life because of it. Little Orphan Annie being the most prominent."

He tugged on a curl and then released it. It *boinged* back into place. "No, not Orphan Annie. That wasn't exactly what I was thinking. About that girl from *Brave*?"

"The cartoon character? Interesting."

He grinned. "Cartoon or not, she was spunky and valiant."

And sometimes stupid. I didn't add that part.

He leaned back, his full attention on me. "I was actually surprised you took this case, you know. I figured you'd have other plans. Wedding planning and such."

I reached for my engagement ring. "Yeah, well, a girl's gotta do what a girl's gotta do." My voice quivered, a telltale sign making me want to scream.

He tilted his head, his look inquisitive. "I have a feeling there's a story there."

"A story I don't want to talk about." I frowned.
He raised his hands. "Understood. How about we go grab a bite to eat and talk some more? There's a place just down the road. We can walk there. Sound good?"

"I wouldn't have it any other way."

***

"I have some questions for you," I started, stabbing my

French fry into a glop of ketchup on my plate. I had to keep this conversation focused.

Garrett nodded. I sensed a new heaviness about him. His normal glib disappeared as he stared at me from across the lunch table. "Of course. Anything you need to know. I'll do whatever it takes to find out who murdered my family, Gabby. I don't think I'll have peace in my life until the person who's behind their deaths sees justice."

We'd walked down the street to a pub-like restaurant. The place had dark walls, matching wood trim, low ceilings, and pictures of dogs playing poker. I ordered a burger and fries, and Garrett got fish and chips. Billboard's top hits blared overhead and a pool table looked lonely in the corner, beckoning someone to play.

I tapped my finger on the glossy wooden tabletop, feeling the need for full disclosure. "You should know I've never worked a cold case before."

"I have confidence in you."

At least someone did. Riley certainly hadn't. My heart panged at the remembrance, and I immediately scolded myself. I was supposed to be turning over a new leaf.

He pulled something out of the canvas bag he'd brought with him. "I brought some more notes I found. I gave you the basics before you left, but I thought these notes could be helpful, as well. They're from the last P.I. I hired."

"The last P.I.?" This didn't sound good.

"His name was Bradley Perkins, and he wasn't as determined as you. Not by a long shot."

"Maybe you shouldn't get your hopes up."

His eyes sparkled. "In case you didn't hear me the first time, I have confidence in you."

"I appreciate that. But . . ."

"I think some fresh eyes on the case will do wonders,

Gabby."

I sucked in a deep breath and pushed my thoughts aside. "Okay then. Let's take a look."

He pulled open the first folder. The picture of a smiling family was on top. I picked it up and studied the faces there. Smiling faces oblivious to what the future would hold. This really could be anyone, any family. No one ever thought they'd meet a violent end until the crime happened to them, and it was better that way. People shouldn't have to live in that kind of fear.

"Beautiful family." I had a feeling I already knew a lot of what he was going to say. I had the sense that Garrett needed to talk about it, though.

A sad smile feathered across his face. "Thank you."

I pointed to the teenage boy in the photo. "This you?"

"How'd you guess?"

"Same grin." He was handsome even back then. He was already tall and lean. He'd filled out as he'd gotten older, but part of that filling had been muscles. With time, the stupid arrogance in his eyes had turned into real confidence that came with being proven and successful.

Beside him was a blonde, teenage girl who looked picture perfect. She had bright, shining eyes and glossy hair. The girl took after the mom, who looked exactly like her except twenty years older with a more sophisticated hairstyle and a few more wrinkles. The dad looked like Garrett.

"Cassidy would have been twenty-five this month."

The familiar pang of loss resonated inside me. I knew the feeling all too well. "I'm sorry."

He put the picture down. "If I'd only come home earlier that weekend as I'd told my family I would, maybe none of this would have happened."

"Or you could have died, too."

123

He sighed. "I used to think that was a better option than living with loss."

"What convinced you otherwise?"

"I don't know. Soul searching. Looking outside of myself. Faith."

"Faith? Are you a Christian?" I was curious now.

"I believe in God," he answered easily. "I'm not sure which one. But I like to pray to him."

His statement didn't settle well with me. "You're not sure which one?"

He shrugged. "I think all religions have good and bad qualities. I want to embrace the good things and have nothing to do with the bad things. The hatred religion causes. The moral absolutism. The holier-than-thou attitudes."

"Interesting," I mumbled, when in reality I thought his statement was quite ludicrous. Maybe I should say something and argue the merits of a relationship with God. But my reasoning wasn't my most dominant quality at the moment. Besides, the man had hired me. I'd always heard it was a bad idea to mix work with religion. "Maybe we could talk about it more another time."

"What I'm hearing is that you're looking for excuses to spend more time with me?"

I waved my finger in the air. "No, what I'm saying is that I really would like to hear more of your thoughts on God, in exchange for listening to my story about how Jesus has changed my life."

He stared at me a moment. I couldn't read his expression, but finally he nodded. "It's a deal."

I smiled. "Great. Now, in the meantime, I'd like to ask you a few questions about this case. I want to hear the answers in your own words."

He leaned back. "I think I can handle that."

CHAPTER 14

Garrett ordered another beer for himself, mumbling something about taking the edge off. "You sure I can't get you something?"

"I don't drink."

His eyebrow quirked. "Really? Just one more fascinating quality you have."

"Nothing fascinating about it. My dad is an alcoholic. I've seen the effects of alcohol on not only the person drinking, but also on the people around the person who drinks. I don't want anything to do with it."

He stared at me a moment and then set his drink back on the table. "What were those questions you had? I'm an open book."

I settled back in the booth. "Tell me more about your family. How did they adjust to being here? Was it really just a better job offer that brought you across the pond?"

He didn't flinch. "My mum and dad were having some marital problems. They needed a fresh start."

"Define marital problems."

His gaze darkened. "My dad had taken on some lovers."

I tried not to visibly cringe at the word "lover." How I hated that word. It made me squirm every time I heard it.

Garrett continued. "I don't think his indiscretions meant anything to my dad, but they meant the world to my mum. Broke her heart. But she didn't want to give up on the marriage. My dad agreed to move, if that's what it took to keep the marriage together."

"Were your father's . . ." I squirmed again. " . . . lovers investigated?"

He grinned. "Why are you blushing?"

"I'm not."

"You're uncomfortable. Does the idea of a lover flummox you?"

I scoffed. "I'm just collecting data here. You're the one reading into things."

He leaned back, a satisfied look on his face. "You're funny. Perplexing sometimes. But funny."

"I just want to keep you guessing." Had I just said that? The last thing I wanted was to flirt, to lead him on. On the other hand, the attention felt good. I knew I was headed to treacherous waters if I didn't remain cautious. "Besides, why do I have a feeling that you fall back on being charming and flirtatious so people won't see the real you sometimes."

He twitched his head to the side. "You could be right."

"I've been through some stuff, too, you know. Not like you have. But I've been through enough. Don't feel like you have to cover up your pain around me."

"You're certainly plainspoken. I appreciate it."

I cleared my throat, realizing I'd just gotten personal—something I had no intentions of doing. "Any other indiscretions I should know about?"

"You mean professionally? No. My father was at the top of his game. He was a fair, honest man . . . except when it came to marriage."

"Did your mom ever retaliate and have any affairs of her own?"

He shook his head. "Not that I know of. I can't imagine my mum doing that. She was dedicated to the family."

"But probably lonely." I shook my head. "I could unearth some skeletons best left alone." The Watcher had indicated that much.

"I've thought about that, and I'm prepared to face the facts, no matter how unpleasant they might be."

I nodded. "Okay then."

One thing was for sure: Focusing on someone else's tragedy sure beat focusing on my own.

"Garrett, could I see the inside of the house?"

He wiped his mouth. "Of course. I would have given you a key if I'd known you were interested. There's not much to see there."

"I'd still like to get a feel for your family, for the crime."

"How about if I take you then?"

I nodded. "That sounds great."

He put his napkin on the table. "Let's go."

***

I stood in the living room, trying to show my due reverence and respect. I'd been in plenty of scenes like this before. I'd been in scenes like this before with grieving family members.

But the fact that an entire family had died here—minus Garrett—just made this even more somber than usual. I couldn't even begin to imagine the hole this had left in his life. I thought my life had been hard, but my grief didn't even begin to compare.

Garrett's shoulders slumped as we stood there. His hands were stuffed casually into his pockets, but I could sense his heaviness.

Against my better instincts—or perhaps because of them—I squeezed his forearm. "I'm sorry."

"I thought the pain would go away. But it's always

lingering there, you know?"

I nodded and pulled my hand away, tucking it safely into my pocket. "Yeah, I know. Death is like that."

"Investigators say that my father was shot right there." He pointed toward a recliner in the distance. "That's not the original chair, but I bought one just like it to replace it. Strange, huh? Probably makes me seem a little off my rocker."

"Not so much. Sometimes people do things that seem unusual in their grieving process. Everyone grieves in different ways, though." I tried to push the memories away, but they came anyway. "I talked to my mom for a long time after she died, as if she was still with me. Sometimes I'd forget and think she would be coming home."

"I remember those days."

"My mom used to leave Tootsie Rolls on my pillow. She called me Tootsie sometimes. After she died, I would buy them. Sometimes I'd drop a couple on my pillow and pretend she'd left them there." I shook my head. "I haven't thought about that in a long time."

I'd pushed away a lot of those painful memories. Memories of feeling alone and incapable of fixing my family. My mom had been the only one holding us together.

He nodded at a picture of his dad. Garrett appeared to be a younger version of him. Both were handsome with sparkling eyes. "I'd still love to call him for advice sometime."

"Were you close?"

"As close as you could be with a man who worked all the time. All the time. Never made baseball games or school plays or award ceremonies. My nanny was there."

"I take it nanny isn't a name for your grandmother?"

He shook his head. "No, my actual nanny. My dad was a good man. He was smart. But he wasn't a family man."

"I'm sorry."

"If there's one thing I learned from him it was that life had to be about more than business. That's why I make an effort to treat my employees well. To know their names. To really listen when they talk."

I remembered his giggling assistant and wondered if I'd read too much into their interactions. Maybe he was just being personal and caring.

"Your father would be proud of you, you know."

He shrugged. "I think he would be. I still feel guilty that I wasn't here. Especially when I think about my sister. I'd always thought of myself as her guardian."

"Even if you were here, it probably wouldn't have changed anything, Garrett. There would just be one more casualty to the whole situation. You."

He raked a hand through his hair. "I know. Maybe that would have been easier, though." He drew in a deep breath, snapping out of his melancholy mood. He turned toward the kitchen. "My mum was in the kitchen. That's where her body was found."

"And you saw the aftermath of all of this?" That would be completely awful.

He nodded. "First one on the scene. After I found my mum and dad, my first thought was my sister. I prayed that she was okay, that maybe she'd gone out with friends. I prayed I wouldn't find her."

There were no words. I simply nodded, knowing already what the outcome was.

"I went upstairs and found her in her bedroom. Her music was still blaring."

"Can we go up to her room?"

He nodded. Silently, we climbed a grand staircase,

walked down the hall, and stopped in front of a bedroom. Garrett pushed the door open but didn't step inside. "This is Cassidy's room."

The room still looked like a teenage girl. Posters of her favorite rock bands, a sash with "Homecoming Queen" across it. A couple of tiaras, some old stuffed animals. Various pictures were shoved in the corners of her mirror.

"Can I go inside?"

Garrett nodded.

I entered with reverence. The first things I examined were the pictures along her dresser. I'd yet to consider that maybe the killer was somehow connected with Cassidy. Could she have had an upset boyfriend? She was into the party scene. Could one of her friends been drugged out and committed the deed?

"She always liked it cold in here."

Garrett's voice broke me away from my thoughts. He walked over to the window and tugged at the latch.

At the mention of the word "cold," I shivered. It was cold in here now. The heat was probably on just enough that the pipes wouldn't freeze.

"I'd come in here to check on her and, in the middle of winter, she'd have her window up and would be wearing a hat and gloves. I never did understand that. Nor did my dad. He was the opposite. As soon as it was cool enough to start a fire downstairs, he would. When he was home, that's where he was. In front of the fire, watching football—he'd become quite fond of the American version of the sport—and drinking a cup of coffee."

"That's how the shooter got inside, right? Through her window?"

Garrett nodded. "That's what investigators said."

I walked across the room. "She had her own balcony, though?"

Garrett nodded. "Perk of living in a house like this."

"I'd say." I'd been happy to have my own 8 x 12 room, furnished by things we'd purchased at a thrift store.

"I always wonder what she would have grown up to be like."

I stared at the pictures of Cassidy on her dresser. There was one of her with some friends on the beach. Another of her with a boy. One of her in front of an elegant Christmas tree.

I pointed to the guy in the photo. "Who's he?"

"Marty Alvin. Cassidy dated him for . . . I don't know. Eight months?"

"Nice guy?" I asked.

Garrett shrugged. "He was okay, I guess. Cassidy liked him."

I made a mental note to see if I could talk to him while I was in town—if he even lived in the area still.

I pointed to the Christmas picture. "Are holidays hard for you?"

He shrugged. "I always get away. Go on vacation."

"Alone?" I couldn't resist the question.

I could tell by the look in his eyes that the man didn't go alone. I'm sure he had a pretty woman at his side, basking in the luxury of going to a fancy resort with a handsome man and living the good life.

The good life for me meant paying my bills.

He shrugged again. "Not always."

"Uh-huh." I said the comment with a little too much satisfaction.

"What was that for?" He pivoted, soaking me in with a tilt of his head.

"What?" I asked innocently.

"That little 'uh-huh'."

I skirted away from him, uncomfortable with his

closeness. As I walked toward the closet, I decided to play it straight with him. "I don't imagine you to have a lack of companionship."

"Perhaps I'm a little pickier than you think I am."

"Oh, I'm sure you're picky." Tall, leggy blondes probably. Women like his "assistant" back at GCI.

He stepped behind me, tugged at my arm until I turned, and looked down his nose at me. "You think you have me figured out, but you don't. For the record, I don't see myself having a permanent relationship—even a meaningful one, for that matter—until this killer is caught. I don't want to risk a future wife or child's life, knowing this killer could still be out there, might still be waiting to do something else."

I swallowed, my throat suddenly achy. "I see."

"To be honest, one day, I want to settle down and raise a family. Here. In this house. With the woman of my dreams. Someone who's strong, but gentle. Someone who can be tough when she needs to be tough."

The way he looked at me caused my heart to beat double time. I swiped a hair behind my ear and looked away. "I hope you get that resolution."

"I hope I do, too."

Something in his gaze hinted at more. I could read the insinuations there.

"I'm engaged," I reminded him.

"But there's trouble in paradise. Am I right?" His eyes didn't leave my face. I could tell he was watching for the truth.

The truth was something I didn't want to admit. I huffed and turned away. "I don't have to discuss this with you."

"No, you don't. But if you want to, I'm a pretty good listener."

I pulled back my emotion. Of all the people I'd talk to about Riley, Garrett Mercer was the last on the list. Well, at least he was down there with my ex-boyfriend Chip Parker and my dad. That was pretty low.

"We should just stick to the task at hand," I insisted. "Finding a killer."

"Very well then."

"Any friends who were suspects?"

"Not that I know of."

"This case really is perplexing. There are just no good leads."

"I've heard that before."

I didn't know what else could help me up here. "Can we go back downstairs again? Would that be okay?"

He nodded.

A moment later, I paced the kitchen. I pictured everything that happened. The images caused me to blanch. The crime was clear; the motives, however, were not. Garrett stood against the wall, watching.

I stopped pacing, hoping the pieces would magically fall into place. They didn't. A new question did pop into my mind.

"Is it a coincidence that you hired me right before the ten year anniversary of their deaths?"

He shook his head. "The gods smiled down on me. I'd been thinking about it, and then I met you. It was providence."

"The gods, huh?"

"Why do I think you're judging me again?"

My neck twitched. "I'm not judging."

"It was just an expression. Why does it matter to you?"

Why did it matter? It was a good question. I shoved my hands into the pockets of my jeans and let out a long breath. "I think I've met people who go to church, but it makes no difference in their lives. They live unchanged lives; there's no transformation. Then there are other people who go to church and they live sold out lives for Christ."

"So the only people who are really Christians are the ones who carry their Bibles everywhere and preach on the street corners?"

"I didn't say that."

"What are you saying?"

"I just don't want to be complacent."

"And by me saying there could be more than one god . . ."

"It insults everything I stand for, which probably doesn't sound very hip." I shook my head. "I think this boils down more to me than it does you. I apologize if I seem harsh. The truth is that, when my faith was tested recently, I feel like I failed. I chose to have faith in everything except God. I realized that to truly be a Christian means to be transformed. To truly live it out." The fact just then became clear to me.

"Look, Gabby, I may not be a theologian, but I've heard that the Christian God is supposed to be a God of grace. Maybe you should have more grace for yourself."

I swallowed hard. "Maybe I should."

I hated to admit it, but maybe Garrett Mercer was pretty wise.

Just then, something crashed upstairs.

This nice little talk about believing was going to have to wait.

CHAPTER 15

I reached into my purse and pulled out my gun.

"A gun?" Garrett's eyes widened.

Impressed or scared? Scared, I decided.

Why were so many people uncomfortable with guns? More likely, they were uncomfortable with *me* having a gun. Knowing Garrett, he was probably anti-gun. Of course, I had to stop being so judgmental.

"Stay here," I ordered, sounding braver than I felt.

"You were hired to be a P.I., not my bodyguard."

"I've got this." My insides felt like gelatin, though. I kept thinking of Milton Jones. If I was ever going to conquer my fears, I had to face them.

That meant I had to confront the boogieman.

"That's ridiculous. I'm coming with you." Garrett quickened his pace until he was beside me.

I hesitated at the stairs. What would I find up there? Did I really want to know? Would a smart girl turn and run the opposite way right now?

Probably. But playing it safe rarely got me anywhere.

I held the gun in front of me, trying not to tremble, trying not to show my weakness.

Garrett started to talk again, but I shushed him. We needed to listen, especially if there was someone in the house.

We reached the top of the stairs. I didn't know where the sound came from. But I had a feeling it was Cassidy's room. I went there first.

I stared at the door with trepidation.

Lord, I don't want to be stupid. Guide me. Stuff like this has gotten me in trouble before.

The door was half open. I saw no signs of movement inside.

Slowly, I nudged the door the rest of the way open.

After lifting up another prayer, I peered around the door.

I held my breath, expecting the worst.

Instead, everything appeared just like we'd left it.

Except that the French door leading to the balcony was wide open, a November wind whipping inside. We definitely hadn't left it like that. Was that the sound we'd heard? The wind smashing the door into the wall?

I turned quickly and searched behind the door. There was no one.

I inspected the perimeter of the room, leaving no space unchecked.

It was clear.

A movement outside caught my eye. I hurried to the balcony just in time to see a man wearing all black running through the yard toward the woods.

"What is it?" Garrett asked.

I nodded outside. "Your intruder."

I raised my gun. Should I shoot? Not to kill, but to slow him down, to find out his identity? The moral dilemma caused me to pause.

I couldn't bring myself to do it, not when I wasn't in immediate danger. Besides, I was a lousy shot.

Garrett rushed beside me, his gaze following the man outside.

"Someone *was* up here," he muttered.

Just then the intruder turned. Raised his gun.

Without thinking, I pushed Garrett down, just as a bullet hit the wall behind us.

***

Time froze as I waited for whatever would happen next.

I prepared myself for more bullets, for more of an attack.

Instead, there was silence.

That's when I realized that I was lying on Garrett's chest. I scrambled off of him and pulled myself to my feet, shaking off any dust, as well as feelings of discomfort.

I tried to snap back into professional mode as I reached for Garrett's hand. "Are you okay?"

"Thanks to you I am."

I peered over the balcony. The gunman was gone. There was no hope of catching him now.

Garrett stood and brushed the dirt from his elbows and pants. He stared at me, a look in his gaze that I hadn't seen before. "You just saved my life."

"That could be an exaggeration."

He touched the bullet hole behind him. It was at chest level and had hit right where Garrett had been standing. "Seriously, that could have killed me. I owe you a debt of gratitude."

A raise would be nice. I kept that thought silent, though. I wasn't that desperate for money. Not yet, at least.

"You're not hurt, are you?" He stepped closer.

I ran through a mental checklist of symptoms. "I think I'm okay."

He touched my forehead. "You've got a little cut. We should get you cleaned up."

I willed him to stop touching me.

I craved love and affection so much. I had for my entire life. But I should be able to fill myself up with God's love for me. I didn't want to fall back into old habits.

I loved Riley. I hoped he still loved me too, despite what my emotions were telling me right now.

I quickly took a step away and started toward the stairs. "This place still have water?"

"As a matter of fact, yes, it does."

"Great." I hurried down to the kitchen, grabbed a paper towel, wet it in the sink, and dabbed my forehead.

Garrett—who'd been at my heels—took the towel from me and held it at my hairline. "There. All better," he insisted.

I scooted back, not liking how close we were. "We should call the police. They need to know what happened."

Finally, he nodded. "Okay then. I can't very well say no to the woman who saved my life."

***

Three hours later, Garrett pulled his gas efficient hybrid to a stop in front of my car. "Here you go."

I opened my door. "Thanks, Garrett."

"No, thank you. I really mean that, Gabby. You continue to impress me."

I felt my cheeks heating, which was a sign that I should immediately change the subject. I stepped onto the sidewalk. "I've got to run."

Garrett rolled down his window. "You know, you looked pretty sexy with that gun."

I ignored him and unlocked my door.

"Gabby?"

I paused, bracing myself for what he might say next. "Yes?"

"I have an event coming up where I'm the keynote speaker. One of my friends will be there. She owns a company that makes the products crime scene investigators use. Everything from evidence bags to more advanced stuff like blood testing kits and UV lighting. It might be a long shot, but perhaps you'd like to meet her? It would be a great connection for you."

I stared at Garrett, trying to measure his sincerity. "You'd do that for me?"

"Of course I would. It would be nothing really. Besides, it's the least I can do after you saved my life. Sometimes finding the right job is all about networking."

Garrett seemed like the networking type. I, on the other hand, wasn't. Not by any stretch of the imagination. In fact, sometimes I thought I did the opposite by being too in people's faces and isolating.

"I'd love to meet her." I could brush up on my social skills and maybe make a good impression. Maybe I could end this hideous bad luck streak I was going through.

Garrett's grin widened. "Great. The event is tomorrow evening. Dress is semi-formal. That a problem?"

I'd guess that Holly would let me borrow something. "That will be fine."

"Great. I'll pick you up at your place at six."

***

No one was home when I walked in the Paladins' house, which was fine with me. I could use a moment to sort out everything that had happened today. I hurried up to my room and called Jamie. I wondered if she'd discovered anything about Mr. Newport.

"Hey, girl. Do I have some news for you."

"Let's hear it."

"Vic Newport's ex-wife was Rebecca Newport," Jamie started. "She wasn't embroiled in a scandal with Edward Mercer. At least, if she was, that news didn't make the front page of any publications. No, Rebecca caused trouble when it was discovered she abused prescription drugs manufactured by Wimbledon Pharmaceuticals. The police never figured out how she got her hands on those drugs, though."

"That's interesting."

"The woman was given two years probation, plus community service," Jamie said. "That burns me up."

"Why does it burn you up?"

"I think rich people can get off easy. They have connections and political reach."

I wondered if Mr. Newport did have influence in the justice system or if this was simply a matter of a first-time offender not being given jail time because of overcrowded prison conditions.

"Anyway, I know that's not what you wanted to talk about," Jamie continued. "I checked the timeline. All of that scandal with Rebecca Newport happened four months before the Mercer family was murdered."

"I wonder if she's somehow connected," I muttered. It was a possibility, I supposed.

"Well, I found her phone number and called her."

"What did she say?"

"It went straight to voicemail. I left her a message, though, and asked her to call me back."

"Good work." I was seriously impressed.

"Remember, I've got some mad hacking skills, too. I meant it when I said to let me know if you ever want me to utilize them."

"Seriously?"

"Seriously."

We hung up, my mind still spinning with all the new information.

In the meantime, I found the phone number for Bradley Perkins, as well as some other pertinent information on the man.

He was still a P.I.—a professional one, at that. He was based out of Pittsburgh, had expensive rates, and had endorsements from a couple of police officers.

On a whim, I called him.

He answered on the first ring. "Brad here."

His voice sounded clipped, and nasal. I instantly pictured the man as short, small, and fast paced.

He probably had a dimly lit office in a shady part of town and liked to smoke cigarettes. That's what stereotypes would tell me, at least.

"Hi, Brad. My name is Gabby St. Claire. I was hoping to ask you a question about your investigation into the murder of the Mercer family."

He grunted. "I've got pressing matters at hand—matters that actually involve getting paid. You ever heard the saying that time is money? That's my life."

"I promise to be short. Please. I've been hired to investigate. As a P.I." The words still didn't sound quite right.

"Really? You know every reporter around has been calling me lately, wanting some kind of scoop with the anniversary to their deaths approaching."

"I'm not a reporter. I'm just like you." Only totally green and not official. "Just trying to find answers."

"Good luck with it." His voice had a touch of northeastern briskness, and I wondered if he was from New York or New Jersey originally.

"Why would you say that?"

"I certainly didn't get very far on the case."

"Why was that? The case was too complex?"

He snorted. "Because I valued my life."

A chill brushed my skin. "What do you mean by that?"

"Look, it's been a while. Three years maybe? But Garrett Mercer hired me. I worked the case for about two weeks before quitting."

"Why did you quit?"

"The threats started. I was married at the time. I didn't want anything happening to my wife. Couldn't care less now that she left me for someone else. Looking back, maybe I should have kept going. But, at the time, I was head over heels. I backed off the case. My life was worth more than finding a killer."

Surprise washed through me. This was not where I'd expected this conversation to go. "Wow. Did Garrett know about this?"

"Yeah, I told him."

Interesting that Garrett hadn't mentioned those details to me, especially after everything that happened. "What did he say?"

"I don't think he believed me. I think he thought I just wanted off the case, assumed I had a better opportunity."

I'd have to mull over that theory longer. "How'd the two of you connect?"

"Look, lady, I don't have time for all of these questions. I'm in the middle of a stakeout. I've got to wrap this up because I actually have a paid gig. Earning a living is a beautiful thing. I highly recommend it. I also highly recommend that you be careful."

"Any idea who was behind the threats?" I rushed, not ready to finish this conversation.

"Didn't know. Didn't care."

The man sounded like a real winner. Where had Garrett found him? Why had Garrett chosen him out of all of the other P.I.s out there? He certainly didn't seem especially astute or determined.

"Just one more question. Please." I expected him to refuse.

"Yeah, yeah. You're on overtime hours now. I'm only saying yes because I'm a gentleman."

I pressed onward. "Did you discover anything of interest? Anything that's not in the files?"

"Besides the fact that the family was shadier than they let on? If I were you, I'd check out Edward's past."

"I talked to his coworker and polo partner. What other part of his past are you talking about?"

"Probe deeper. There's more there. I didn't have time to dig in like I wanted. I had other priorities, like keeping my family alive."

Then there was me. I didn't have anything to lose, did I? I didn't really have anyone to live for. Who depended on me. Who needed me at home.

Was that really true?

That was something I was going to have to decide.

CHAPTER 16

As soon as I hung up with the P.I., my cellphone rang again. My heart raced when I heard "That's Amore." Riley. Riley was finally calling me. Both anxiety and excitement spread through me.

I took a deep breath before answering.

"Hey there." I tried to keep my voice light.

"Hey, Gabby. How's my favorite girl?" His voice rolled over the line. Man, did I ever miss that sound.

My nerves calmed but only slightly. Riley had called me his favorite girl. That was a good sign, right?

"I'm hanging in," I responded.

No need to go into all the details with him of everything that had happened. I had to try and keep his stress level low, so he could heal quicker. I had to keep reminding myself of that. I was so used to sharing my life with him.

"I'm glad to hear that. You won't believe this, but I lost my cellphone. I thought I'd turned if off before therapy and left it at the office. Turns out it was in my suitcase the whole time."

"Glad you finally found it." I leaned back into the bed, trying to relax—something I wasn't very good at doing. I had to focus this conversation on Riley. "The bigger question is: How are you?"

"I have to say that I'm doing better. I feel calmer and more single-minded. I think being up here has been good for me. I can just focus on my recovery."

My heart squeezed. I was so glad he was doing better, but at the same time sad that he wasn't doing better with me.

"That's great." I forced the words out. I meant them, but my emotions still rebelled.

He paused. I gave him time to formulate his thoughts. Tried not to rush him.

"I was talking to my therapist today, Gabby. You know, more about the emotional stuff that guys never want to talk about."

My heart squeezed even more. I desperately wished I was the one he was talking to about all of this. "Okay."

"She thinks we should indefinitely postpone the wedding."

I nearly choked on nothing but air. I lurched forward, a physical ache in my chest. "What?" Certainly I didn't hear him correctly.

"I know it's not what you want to hear. But she thinks the wedding is putting too much pressure on me. She said I needed to focus solely on my recovery."

"I thought the wedding would give you something to work toward." If I were in his shoes, getting married would motivate me. At least, in theory it would. But I hated that my voice took on the injured tone it did. I tried to tamp the emotion down.

"I feel too much like I'm letting you down," Riley said. "I feel like my recovery is hindering your life. It's hindering you from moving forward."

"You're not letting me down," I insisted. "I want you to get better."

"Then you understand why we need to call off our engagement for a while?"

I bent over again, the pain that spread through me

nearly too great for me to contain. I forced down a few deep gulps of air. "You're serious?"

"I'm sorry, Gabby. This isn't what I wanted, either. But my therapist says that oftentimes people with brain injuries change. She said if we stay together, we'll need to start over with dating again and see where it ends up. If we decide to do that, we should wait a while. Wait until I finish therapy."

"You're not serious." Even the professionals were against me. That's how it felt, at least. This only made me hate Riley being in D.C. even more.

"I don't know anything anymore, Gabby. She did say my injuries weren't as serious as the other cases she'd seen. But she warned me that I can't expect things to go back like they were. At least not for a while."

I couldn't find the right words, either, so I decided to own up to that fact. It seemed the safest bet at the time. "I don't know what to say."

"Don't read too much into this, Gabby. I love you."

If you loved me, you would marry me. You would believe in our future and think it was worth fighting for. I voiced none of those thoughts, though.

It seemed that keeping his stress level low meant mine ricocheted to dangerous levels.

"I know this is difficult," Riley continued. "The doctors are still expecting me to make a full recovery. I just need some time."

"Does this mean we've broken up?" I didn't even want to ask the question. But I did. I had to know, I had to have some clarity.

"It means we've taken some steps back."

"I see." It was all I could manage to get out.

"Please don't be upset."

I was upset, but I couldn't let him know that. "I just

really want what's best for you, Riley. If this is what your therapist says you need to do, then I support you. Your health is more important than anything else right now."

I meant it. I did. But I couldn't help but think that there had to be another way. A better way. A way that didn't involve my heart hurting so much. But I supposed that was asking too much.

"You don't know how relieved I am to hear that." Riley's voice took on a softer, more relaxed tone. "I've been dreading this phone call, putting it off. I just don't want to hurt you."

Too late! I twisted the engagement ring on my finger and then pulled it off. I stared at the diamond solitaire, a picture of what could have been.

And so the story of my life continued.

"I know, Riley," I whispered. "You just get better."

As soon as we hung up, I fell back on the bed. I didn't cry. No, crying would be too much of a relief. I just stared at the ceiling as an achy heaviness spread through every part of my body. Then I resigned myself to a life where everything I wanted was dangled in front of me, only to be snatched away before I obtained it.

***

"You okay?" Holly asked. "You seem a little distracted today."

I'd texted her last night and told her I was turning in early. Then I'd stayed in my room with the lights out, trying to make sense of life. It didn't do any good because this morning I felt just as confused as ever.

Right now, we cruised down the road, on our way to meet with one of Cassidy's old boyfriends. I'd given him a call this morning, and he'd agreed to meet. Holly had offered to come with me, and I didn't refuse. I could use some company since being alone with my thoughts felt like torture.

I reached for the empty spot on my finger where my engagement ring used to be. "My fiancé called off the wedding last night." My voice sounded as dull as my soul felt.

"Oh, Gabby. I'm so sorry. I had no idea."

I nodded. "Yeah, I had no idea either."

"Did he say why?"

I stared out the window at the urban buildings we passed, at life as it continued on as usual. "It was his therapist's idea. She said he needed to focus on getting better and to eliminate any sources of stress in his life." My voice took on an unfortunate mimicking tone, one of my not so fine qualities and defense mechanisms.

"Ouch. Was the therapist implying that you were a source of stress?"

I shrugged. "The wedding was. Apparently, he felt pressure and that pressure was hindering his recovery."

"Did he say anything else?"

"He claimed he still loves me, and that he hates doing this." I shook my head, dumbfounded. "I don't know what to think anymore."

"I don't know him, Gabby. And I'm only getting to know you. But give him some time. Men like to be strong for their women. They don't want to be seen as weak. Maybe he just needs some space to get his masculinity back."

Her words made sense. Guys did have their pride. Maybe I was reading too much into this. Maybe the stress of everything had worn my spirit down to the breaking point.

I said nothing.

"I know this is hard for you in the meantime, though," Holly continued. "The uncertainty has to make you feel insecure. If I could go back to two years ago and talk to myself, I'd remind myself that emotions aren't bad, but that I need to take things in stride."

I glanced at her, curious now. "What happened two years ago?"

She glanced over at me and frowned. "I was engaged, actually."

"Were you?"

She nodded. "But it was right when my dad had been diagnosed with cancer. I didn't want anything to hinder my time with him, so I put off the wedding."

"What happened?" She obviously wasn't engaged now. Nor was she married.

"My fiancé got tired of waiting, got tired of being second place. He broke things off with me—a month before my dad died."

"Wow. That had to be hard."

She nodded. "It was. But looking back now, I see it was for the best. Boy, did I wish I could see it back then. But I was blinded by too many emotions. I was pulled in too many directions. I couldn't see anything clearly—except for my dad. Our emotions can be a wonderful thing, or they can lead us astray."

"Yes, they can." I'd been thinking a lot about that lately.

"I know it sounds cliché and that I'm repeating myself, but with every closed door, there is an open window. We just have to look for it. We have to know that everything that happens in this life is for our best. It's all about trusting God."

"It sounds like you've got that down pat." My words were sincere; I only hoped that sincerity came through in my voice. "She said genuinely," I added at the end, just to clarify.

Holly threw me a quick smile before continuing. "I had some very frank talks with God when I was diagnosed. There was a lot of pity. A lot of whys. But I'm trying to focus on the eternal and not on the temporary things of this earth."

"I wish I had your faith, Holly." I was no better than those people I'd accused of going to church but showing no evidence of transformation in their lives. Garrett Mercer and I were more alike than maybe I wanted to admit.

And that was a fact that I hated.

"Faith is a choice I make every day. I'm not perfect. I'm nowhere near perfect, for that matter. Just ask my family. They'll tell you that I'm idealistic and impulsive and too much of a dreamer. But, I've said this before and I'll say it again: Dying can put living into perspective."

For a moment, I pictured myself being given an expiration date. If I knew I only had a month to live, would I be wallowing in self-pity? Definitely not. I'd be trying to live to the fullest.

And the truth was that none of us knew how long we had left here on this earth. Maybe it was time to stop bemoaning all that had gone wrong and start looking for the things that were going right. I had to get rid of this negativity in my life.

Her words caused a new determination to settle over me. I was going to start trusting that everything did happen for a purpose—even this stalled engagement. I didn't know where that path would take me, but I was going to have faith that all things did work for the good of those who were called in Christ Jesus.

Holly pulled to a stop in front of a surprisingly humble

home—at least for the likes of the Mercer family. "We're here," she announced. "Marty Alvin, AKA Cassidy's boyfriend's house. You ready for this, Sherlock?"

I nodded, ready to focus on something other than my troubles. "Let's go, Watson."

**

Marty Alvin had probably been handsome in his younger days. Today, he was 27 and he looked like he'd lived a rough life. Probably, if I had to guess, he'd been mixed up in too many drugs and too much alcohol. Those addictions could age a person more quickly than they'd ever want to admit.

Based on the glazed look in his eyes, those rough days weren't behind him.

His hair was too long, his whiskers too unshaven, and his clothes too unlaundered.

Some people could get away with that look, but only if they did it on purpose. On a positive note, he bore a faint resemblance to Marky Mark, from Marky Mark and the Funky Bunch back in the 90s. The comparison was both because of his physical features and his hip hop culture attitude.

As soon as he appeared, I could smell body odor, something frying in the kitchen, and the stale scent of a house that didn't get enough air circulation.

"Marty?" I asked.

"That's me."

"I'm Gabby, and this is my friend, Holly. Thanks for agreeing to meet with us."

He grunted and shoved the door open. He offered no smile—just a vacant kind of stare—and waved us inside. The interior of his home looked like a dump, and one glance at the man and woman in the background seemed to indicate that he was still living with his parents.

No, this was not the kind of man I pictured Cassidy Mercer with.

Had he changed in the years since she died? Or had he always looked and lived like this? I wanted to find out.

I was thankful that Holly was with me right now. She had experience with stuff like this. Visiting people. Assessing their situations. Making determinations.

I had experience with assessing crime scenes and bloodstain patterns. I was getting better with the people part. But I constantly had to watch what I said so I wouldn't offend anyone. Holly seemed to have more of a gift with words and social graces.

Marty Mart gestured toward the couch.

"Have a seat." His words slurred together.

Holly and I shoved some magazines out of the way—and a couple of fast food wrappers, as well as beer bottles—and then sat down. Marty lowered himself onto a torn barstool across from us. He grabbed a brown bottle and took a long swig.

He sat the bottle on the table with a loud *clank*. "I'm not sure how much help I'm going to be."

"You never know when something someone says might reveal a clue that investigators haven't picked up on yet," I started. *Of course, if you weren't drunk, you might think more clearly.* On the other hand, sometimes people revealed more under the influence of alcohol, so maybe I shouldn't complain. "So, how long did you and Cassidy date?"

He shrugged. "About six months."

I pulled out my handy-dandy notebook—like any good detective would—and began jotting some notes. "Where did you meet?"

"At school. I went there on a scholarship, much to the disappointment of Cassidy's parents. They sent her to a private school to get her away from kids like me."

"So, there was animosity between all of you?" I asked. It made sense to me.

"To say the least." He let out a long belch before tapping his chest with his fist. "We kept our relationship quiet after the first blow out with her mom."

"What was that blow out like?" I prodded.

"Her mom was hot under the collar when she found out the two of us were dating. Thought Cassidy could do better. She was right. She could have done better. A lot better. She thought I was going to bring her daughter down."

I could see why, but I kept that thought silent, and instead asked, "What did Cassidy say to that?"

"Cassidy wouldn't let me break up with her. She insisted she loved me, and that we just had to keep our relationship on the down low."

"Do you think she really cared for you?" I kept my voice soft, trying not to sound judgmental. But it sounded like Cassidy Mercer was the type who might do things like date a bad boy just to get her parents' attention.

He shrugged. "Yeah, I like to think so. She stuck by me, even when I acted like a jerk."

"Did her parents ever find out that you stayed together?" I continued.

He nodded. "Yeah, about a week before they died. They ordered her to stop dating me. Said they'd send her to boarding school if she didn't."

"How did she take that news?"

"Not well. Cassidy liked to do her own thing."

"Did you ever wonder if you were just one way Cassidy was trying to get her parents to notice her?" Asking the question was a risk, but I wanted to take it.

"Of course. A girl like her? A guy like me? We were an unlikely match, to say the least."

"But you both liked to party?" I projected. "Is that what you had in common?"

"I didn't. Not at first. After Cassidy and I started dating, she introduced me to some party drugs. I tried to stay away from that scene, but I'd tag along with her, trying to keep an eye on her. Eventually, I tried a few things to take the edge off."

Cassidy got him hooked on drugs? That was an interesting and unexpected development.

"It sounds like you really cared about her," Holly started. "That you were trying to watch out for her."

He frowned. "I loved her. I wanted to marry her after she graduated. She said she had to go to college, but that I was cute. I felt like she was being condescending at the time. But there were areas of her life where she rebelled and others where she felt like she needed to be compliant. College was one of those compliant areas."

"Can you tell me anything about the night she died?" I continued.

"Yeah, we were supposed to go out. My friend was having a killer party. Mr. Mercer insisted that Cassidy had to stay home. Said that her brother was coming into town, and that they needed to have a family meeting. Cassidy talked about sneaking out. I told her not to." His face looked pinched. "For once I was trying to be responsible, and look where it got me."

"You couldn't have known," Holly said, her voice soft with compassion.

"The one time she wasn't rebellious, and she ended up dead. Isn't that just like life? The ones who eat healthy get cancer, the ones who drive carefully are hit by drunk drivers, the ones who are faithful in marriage are cheated on."

I glanced at Holly, hoping what he'd said about cancer didn't upset her. She didn't even flinch.

"Did she have any idea what the meeting was about?" I asked.

He shrugged. "Not really sure. She thought the family might be moving again. Apparently, the Mercers liked to move every three or four years. She said she wasn't going to go with them, that she was going to stay with me, finish high school, and then go to college."

"And you said?"

"I reminded her that her trust fund didn't become available until she was 21 and that she'd have a hard time making a way on her own. I loved Cassidy, but the girl had no idea what real life was like. She didn't know what it was like to want anything or to have to work for things, to earn them."

"Did she mention the family having any problems?" I asked.

He shrugged and took another chug of his beer. "Just the normal stuff. Her dad was never home. Her mom just wanted to look pretty. I mean, I guess they cared about her, in their own way. I've never understood rich people."

I stared at my paper, contemplating what else I needed to ask. I came up blank. "Anything else you want to add?"

He straightened on the stool. "There is one thing. I was sneaking to see her once, and I overheard something that's stuck with me to this day."

I leaned closer. "What's that?"

"Mr. Mercer was outside, pacing on the patio. I'd snuck to their house. I'd parked on the road and cut through the woods. I came up around the side of the house, and he didn't see me. I didn't see him. I heard him first. He was on the phone and he was yelling at someone. He said something about an agreement that he had with someone. He shouted about money. He sounded steamed."

Finally, something that could lead somewhere! "Did you have any idea what the conversation was about?"

"To be honest, I assumed he was probably trying to pay off some woman so that she'd stay quiet about an inappropriate relationship." He used air quotes as his words slurred. "Cassidy said he had a history of that."

I nodded, noting the common thread. Apparently, everyone knew about Edward Mercer's reputation with women. I felt sorry for his wife, and even amazed that she'd stuck with him through all of that. "I've heard that from more than one person."

Marty Mart scowled. "Listen, I want justice for my girl. I haven't been the same since she died. So there was one other thing I remember hearing from that conversation."

I leaned closer. "Okay."

"I heard a name. Sebastian."

CHAPTER 17

I sucked in a quick breath. "Did you tell the police that?"

Marty Mart shook his head. "I was going to. But then someone left a note on my door. Said if I said too much that the same thing that happened to the Mercers would happen to my family."

"So you stayed silent?"

He shrugged. "Can you blame me?"

In all truthfulness, I guess I couldn't.

"Besides, I was the primary focus of their investigation for a while. It was awful. I couldn't keep up with my studies and dropped out of the private school. It was fine by me. Too many bad memories there anyway."

"Why would they think you were guilty?" I had a few theories, but I wanted to hear what he had to say.

He counted it out with his fingers. "Turbulent relationship with her parents. Them forbidding us to see each other. Me coming from the wrong side of the tracks. I'm sure you can fill in the blanks."

"But you wouldn't have murdered Cassidy if that was the case," I reasoned.

His eyes lit, and he slapped one hand into the other. "Exactly. That's what I kept saying. Her death tore me up. There's no way I would hurt her."

"I mean, maybe if she'd broken up with you—" I stopped mid-sentence. "She didn't break up with you, did she?"

He scowled. "No, she didn't break up with me. Ask her BFF and she'll tell you the same."

I studied his face a moment. Could I trust what he was telling me?

"What was the police's reason for suspecting you then?"

"They said I was drugged out and that I hadn't realized the extent of my actions. Drugs can make you do crazy things. I won't argue that. But I didn't kill anyone. Especially not Cassidy."

"Why'd they finally let you go?"

"They couldn't find any evidence to hold me. Everything was circumstantial." He snickered. "Yeah, even I learned a few things from that ordeal."

"But let me guess. Your DNA was at the house probably. You own a gun—or had access to one. You were doing drugs. And you probably left tire tracks on the road outside their home from your visits."

His gaze darkened. "I know that looks bad. But here's the other thing I forgot to mention. I had an alibi that evening. I got into a car accident coming from a party about twenty minutes before the crime occurred."

***

As we were walking to the car—and before I even had a chance to rehash the conversation with Holly—my cellphone screamed for help from inside my purse. I really had to change that ringtone.

The number had the same area code as the Pittsburgh P.I. Could he be calling me from a different phone, maybe to give me an update? A girl could only hope.

I answered. "This is Gabby."

"This is Detective Larson with the Pittsburgh Police Department. I'm calling about Bradley Perkins."

I slowed my steps. "Okay."

"Would you mind giving me your name, ma'am?"

I had my hesitations about giving out my name. But if this man really was a detective, there was a good chance he already knew my name. "My name is Gabby St. Claire."

"Ms. St. Claire, did you know Mr. Perkins?"

"No, sir. I'd only spoken with him yesterday." Where was this going? If my gut was right, it wasn't any place good.

"May I ask about the nature of the call?" the detective asked.

"Certainly. Mr. Perkins was a P.I. He worked a case that I've currently been hired to work. I called to pick his brain on information he may have discovered in his investigation." I swallowed the lump in my throat and climbed into the Mustang.

"So, you're a private investigator?"

"I'm new to the scene, but yes, I am."

"Where are you now, ma'am?"

"I'm in Cincinnati. If you don't mind me asking, what's with all of these questions? I didn't exploit any confidentiality issues when I spoke with Mr. Perkins. I simply asked a few questions."

"Mr. Perkins was found murdered this morning. We're looking into everyone who was in contact with him in the days before he died. Yours was the last number on his cellphone."

"Murdered? Are you sure?"

"A bullet through the head doesn't lie."

I closed my eyes and froze. "That's terrible."

And it was the same way the Mercer family had died. Coincidence? I couldn't be sure.

159

But my gut told me no.

"Did he mention anything suspect to you?"

I replayed our conversation. "He said he was meeting with someone later that day. A reporter was my impression. He was apparently being paid to talk about the murder of the Mercer family."

Puzzle pieces began fitting together. What if that meeting was just a ploy to kill him? But why? Why would someone kill Bradley Perkins?

After I hung up, I turned to Holly. "The plot thickens."

***

"What are we doing?" Holly asked as we pulled up to Rolling Hills Country Club.

I stared at the building in front of me. "It's like this. Sebastian borrowed a substantial amount of money from Edward Mercer before he died. Apparently, the two of them had a misunderstanding as far as the terms of the so-called loan."

"How much are you talking?"

"Ten million."

"That's a lot of moolah."

"Maybe enough moolah to kill over. Maybe enough moolah that the killer is desperate not to be discovered, which might happen if investigators started following the moolah."

"So, why are we here, though?"

I tapped my fingers on the armrest. "I'm contemplating confronting Sebastian."

"That sounds like a terrible idea. If your theory is right, he's a dangerous man."

"I'm out of ideas. At this point, Sebastian is my best lead."

"We shouldn't get ahead of ourselves. I don't think confrontation is the best idea at this point. Is there any other way you can find out information on this Sebastian guy?"

Just then, I spotted a familiar face emerging from the doors of the country club. It looked like I'd just hit the jackpot. "That's his assistant."

"And . . ."

"Let's follow him."

Casually, we pulled out behind his truck. I remained a couple of car lengths behind him until he pulled to a stop at The Crusher's office and batting cages. "Stay low," I whispered to Holly as we got out of the car.

Kevin scurried inside. We stayed a safe distance behind him and watched as he disappeared into a locker room.

"Look like we belong here!" I urged.

Holly nodded and picked up the first thing she saw on the shelf. She crossed her eyes as she examined it. "What is this? Some kind of protective breathing equipment?"

She put it over her face and took a deep breath. "Luke, I am your fath—"

I swatted her hand down.

"What?" she asked.

"Holly, do you know what this is?"

"Obviously it's not a mask fit for Darth Vader."

"It's an athletic cup."

She still looked puzzled.

I leaned closer. "A jock strap."

Her cheeks reddened and she calmly placed it back on the shelf.

Just then, Kevin emerged wearing exercise clothes. I knew where he was headed.

I turned toward Holly. "You up for hitting some baseballs?"

She raised her eyebrows. "I can't say I'm much of an athlete unless you count Zumba."

"Works for me."

***

We walked to the desk against the far wall and inquired about using the cages. Though the man eyed us suspiciously—could it have anything to do with Holly's dress?—he instructed us on how to buy tokens and how they would pay for a certain number of balls.

I couldn't help but smile. Yes, we'd be a sight to see out there. But sometimes a girl had to do what a girl had to do.

I ignored the strange looks a few people gave us as we wandered outside. Act like you knew what you were doing. That's what I always said.

We found our assigned stall, slipped inside, and I handed Holly a bat. Apparently, you were supposed to bring your own, but there were a couple of extras on hand for situations like this.

"Why am I doing this instead of you?" she asked, readjusting her helmet.

"I need to be free to chase down this Kevin guy and ask questions if I need to. You don't mind, do you?"

"I'm the one who just put a jock strap on my face. If I can survive that humiliation, I suppose I can survive this."

"Thanks for being such a good . . . sport."

Anyone else would have scowled. Holly laughed.

"Life is too short to care what people think of you." She raised her bat. "So let's get this party started."

I dropped some tokens into the machine beside me and then heard a motor start up. A moment later, the first ball flew toward us, and Holly screamed when it almost hit her shoulder.

I had to cover my mouth to keep from smiling. She'd just gotten in place to hit again when another ball came flying toward her. She ducked, sending the ball flying into the net behind the stall.

The people on either side of us stopped to stare.

That's when I saw Sebastian's assistant turn toward us. He was still behind the cages, swinging the bat, and warming up.

His gaze lingered on Holly, and I waved him over, seizing the opportunity while I could. The man strode over. "Anything I can help you with, ladies?"

"Is this thing working correctly?" I asked. "The balls are coming awfully fast."

"You can slow down the speed."

Holly screamed again as a ball flew her way. The man grinned, looking amused and perplexed at the same time.

"How about if I give you a hand?" he offered.

"That would be wonderful." I nodded back toward Holly and lowered my voice. "She has delusional dreams of going pro."

"Really?" he asked.

I shook my head. "No, she actually has to play . . . for a work assignment." Work being my investigation. "You know how those things go sometimes? Team exercise building and such." If Holly and I counted as a team, that was.

He nodded, seeming to buy my story. His gaze latched on to me for a moment. "Do I know you?"

I shook my head. "I don't think so. I just have one of those faces."

He nodded, apparently satisfied. "You mind if I come inside?"

"Please do."

He looked Holly up and down. Approval tinged his gaze. "First of all, next time you come, you've got to dress to play baseball."

"But this dress is so cute." Holly's eyes twinkled.

She was playing an airhead. I had to somehow thank her for this in the near future. Maybe with pie and coffee.

"Cute will get you nowhere in baseball. Hitting the ball will. Now, you've got to swing it like this." Kevin, in a textbook flirtatious move, put his arms around Holly and helped her move the bat in a smooth motion.

I had to cover my smile.

"Swing just like that. Keep your movements controlled, purposeful. And don't scream. The ball won't hurt you."

Just then, the ball hit her shoulder. "Ouch! It *does* hurt."

"You've got to keep your eye on the ball. Take out any pent up aggression on it. But always remain in charge of your actions. That discipline will make you stronger."

I leaned against the fence. "You must come here a lot."

"Every day."

"Does that mean you have a lot of pent up anger you need to get out?" I ventured.

He helped Holly hit the ball, and she squealed in delight.

"I might have some frustrations. Who doesn't? Coming here helps on a multitude of levels."

I crossed my arms casually, hoping not to appear too anxious. "What do you do for a living anyway? And I never did catch your name."

"Kevin, and I'm the executive assistant to the CEO of a company."

"Sounds cushy," Holly said, swinging again but missing.

"Not so much. I feel like a glorified servant most of the time."

"Why not quit?" I asked.

"Long history, I suppose. I started working for this guy right out of college. I was an intern, actually. He was a practical nobody back then. He kept me on, and I was grateful for the job. Every time I want to quit, he seems to sense it and gets all nice. He'll give me a raise, a bonus, a comp vacation."

"Comp vacation? Maybe I'll apply to work for him. Is he hiring? Cleaning just doesn't pay what it used to."

"Beats me. I know he hires people to do everything for him. Wouldn't surprise me if he hired someone to wipe his mouth after he finished eating." He chuckled, low and dopey, at his own joke. "You'd have to ask him."

I wondered if that included hiring someone to assassinate people for him.

"So, why are you so frustrated then?"

He swung the bat with Holly, more forcefully this time. "You'd have to meet the man to understand."

Oh, I could understand perfectly.

The machine ran out of balls, and Holly straightened. I could see the relief on her face. "That went by quickly."

Kevin winked. "I've got this one for you."

He ran a card through the machine and balls started flying again.

"Between the three of us, I actually work for the competition. This store's competition, I mean. I get a strange satisfaction out of coming here."

"Oh, aren't you sneaky?" Holly said. She'd drawn the short straw and gotten the role of dingbat. But she had the acting thing down pat.

"I'm sneaky, and I'm free for the next three days." He raised his hands in victory. "Speaking of which, here's my number. Maybe we can get together."

Holly raised her eyebrows and slipped the business

card into her sweater. "Thanks."

"Why are you free for the next three days?" I asked.

"My boss just left yesterday to take a tour of some of his stores in Pennsylvania."

My heart nearly stopped. Now that was a curveball I hadn't been expecting. "Pennsylvania. I've got some relatives there. What part?"

He shrugged. "Beats me. I think he's stopping in Pittsburgh then Philly."

Pittsburgh? That couldn't be a coincidence . . . could it?

Despite what Holly might think, we'd just batted a thousand.

But we still had more bases to cover in this next inning.

Holly hit the ball, squealing in delight.

"There you go!" Kevin cheered.

She hit another ball.

"Looks like a lucky streak."

A lucky streak? I wished I could say the same for my life.

CHAPTER 18

I straightened up the knee length black dress that Holly had let me borrow. A sheer, sparkly layer of black flared overtop the sheath underneath. I sucked in my stomach and stared in the mirror.

Not bad. In fact, I kind of felt like a million bucks at the moment.

Holly let out a wolf whistle. "You look fabulous, darling. Simply fabulous." She leaned against the wall, her arms crossed. She'd helped me with my hair and makeup. For a moment, I'd felt like I was getting ready for the prom. Hopefully tonight would be better than my actual prom, an event that had ended with my date throwing up all over the dress I'd worked hard to purchase myself.

"Thanks."

"And you look nervous." She studied my face a little too closely.

"I get to network. I'm not great at doing that." It was the truth.

"So, this isn't about Garrett?"

"Garrett?" I scoffed. I turned in the mirror for another view of my hair. Holly had done a great job smoothing it out and adding soft curls. "No, it's not about Garrett."

She crossed her arms. "You're attracted to him, aren't you?"

"My relationship with Riley isn't over, even if it feels like it is. I'm not the cheating type."

"That's good. Just stay on guard."

My gaze jerked to her. "What does that mean?"

She shrugged. "Just figure out your relationships before making any big changes."

She was obviously reading more into this than I was.

But she had some good points.

"How'd you get so smart, Holly?"

She blew out an imaginary puff of smoke. "It's elementary, my dear. Elementary."

I couldn't help but laugh.

"I assure you that this meeting is purely professional. He wants to introduce me to someone who might have a job opening in forensics. This is networking, and that's it."

"Well, knock 'em dead, girl."

I sucked in a long breath, smoothed my dress with one hand, and gripped my clutch with the other. "I'll do my best."

Just then, the doorbell rang. Holly rushed downstairs. By the time I got there, the front door was open and the limo driver stood there. Garrett had called an hour ago and explained he had to be at the gala early for sound check. He'd apologized profusely and asked if it was okay to send a limo.

I gripped my purse and stepped outside. The driver opened the door. He seemed pretty nondescript at first— tall, uniform-clad, with a driver's cap over his eyes—until I noticed his goatee and wire-framed glasses.

"Ms. St. Claire." He extended his hand to usher me into the back.

Several people on the sidewalk paused and watched as I got inside. For a moment, I felt like a celebrity. As I slipped inside and the driver shut the door, a rush of excitement fluttered through me. Whenever I felt a touch of my old self return, I treasured it. There were many parts of my old self that I just wanted to disappear. But the spunky part, the sassy part, I was ready for that to return.

My bad luck streak had gone on for too long now. It reminded me of a crime scene Chad and I had cleaned once. A dimwitted burglar had poured motor oil all over the inside of a home and tried to light it on fire after stealing the TVs and other valuables while the family was on vacation. Since the flashpoint was high enough for the oil to ignite, the home ended up with these horrible— mucky—streaks all over the place. The homeowner hadn't wanted to get rid of the carpet because it was expensive and fairly new. So Chad and I had tried everything under the sun to get that oil up, nearly losing our minds in the process.

Though my life often felt like those impossible to remove mucky streaks, talking with Holly and hearing her story had reminded me about how fragile our time here on this earth was. I had to stop feeling sorry for myself, and I had to make the most of each moment.

Besides, I didn't believe in luck. Despite my circumstances and what felt, at times, like misfortune, I believed in God's providence and hard work. I clung to John 9:3—This happened so that the works of God might be displayed in him. Throughout all of this, I had to believe that everything that happened was for a purpose.

We wound through the streets of Cincinnati. I sat back and tried to relax.

Then my cellphone rang. Thanks to Clarice, I knew exactly who the call was from without even looking at my phone. It was "The Happy Working Song" from *Enchanted*. That meant it was Chad.

He bypassed formalities and launched straight into, "How about Dirtbusters?"

"What?"

"Our new name."

I twisted my lips in thought. "I don't love it."

"Alright. It was just a thought."

"Keep thinking. Anything else new? Any updates on the apartments?" I stared outside as the buildings of downtown blurred past.

"Not yet. We'll let you know as soon as we know anything. Okay, I gotta run. Clarice says hi."

We hung up, and a prick of curiosity crept up my spine. I stared out the window. We'd gravitated from the business part of downtown to a rough looking area. An area with graffiti on walls and trash on the streets and groups of people on corners.

Why would Garrett be attending a gala in an area of town like this?

Flashbacks of my last case began pummeling me. I'd almost died. I didn't know if I'd ever get over it.

But I was going to embrace each moment, I reminded myself. None of this dwelling on the past. *I'm moving forward.*

The limo slowed. I peered out the window. There was no light, no stop sign. This couldn't be the hotel and convention center.

The car lurched slightly, as if being put in park.

I was both curious and on edge. What was going on?

I slid toward the front and tapped at the divider window, hoping the driver would open the slider and explain himself.

The next thing I knew, my door opened. I started toward it but before I reached my exit, a man rushed inside the limo.

He wore a mask. I could only see his eyes. They looked cold.

Fear rushed through me, clawing at the sanity I'd just

earlier been determined to grasp. The door shut, and the man's hand pressed into my mouth, squelching any screams before they could escape.

I kicked, flailed. I'd vowed to never go to this place in my life again. This place of terror.

The man seemed experienced, in control. He was no amateur. In one motion, he'd pinned my arms, my legs.

"Don't make this hard," he whispered.

His face was only inches from mine. His eyes were intense. And they were focused on me.

Finally, I stopped struggling. For a moment, at least.

Maybe I'd jinxed myself when I'd mentally declared my imminent fate would have something to do with a car. Because here I was again. In danger. Because of a car.

"There. You might as well make this a little easier," he said approvingly. "Digging up graves will only make a mess of things."

I tried to say something, but it only came out as "Mwah blwa maba, mab boo."

"Promise not to scream?"

I nodded, unsure if I'd keep that promise. However, I had no doubt that he'd make me pay if I didn't.

He lowered his hand.

"You're the man from the phone, aren't you?" I whispered.

"Smart girl."

"Did you follow me here to Cincinnati? Was that you?"

Something flickered in his gaze. "No."

"So, you're working with someone else." The thought wasn't comforting. "How do you know my every move? I don't understand."

"I have my ways. Let's leave it at that."

I tried to pull back, but I couldn't. "Why do you want me off this case so badly?"

"I can't tell you that. But for your safety, stay away."

"Have you threatened every investigator like this? Because there have been a lot."

"Enough questions. I'm sorry I'm having to go to such extreme measures, but you don't like listening. I don't want to hurt you."

With that, he sprayed something in my face. Then everything went black.

CHAPTER 19

"Ma'am? Ma'am? Are you okay?" a deep voice asked.

"Someone call the police!" a shrill sounding woman shouted.

"What happened to her?" someone else mumbled.

I slowly pulled my eyes open, unsure what I was waking up to. I blinked several times until my vision came into focus.

I was sprawled in an alley. A man in a uniform stared at me. Not a police uniform. More like a . . . chef? A couple of other people stood around me, their eyes wide with curiosity.

The catering staff, I realized.

I pressed my hands into the gritty sidewalk beneath me.

My conversation with the man in the limo flashed back to me. My cheeks flushed as everything rushed into my mind. I straightened my dress and tried to collect myself amidst the stares.

"Where am I exactly?" I pushed myself up on my elbows, causing a dull pain to pulse through my head.

"Service entrance behind the convention center," the chef started. "We found you passed out back here."

A few people stopped watching and continued to carry boxes in through the door. The scent of fish and boiling potatoes drifted outside.

"Passed out?" I rubbed my head and stood up. A

stranger grabbed my elbow and helped me balance.

The man from the limo must have dumped me here. How long had I been out? What had he given me?

I did a quick evaluation of myself. Apparently, the crowd was all either waiting to see if I was okay or for a great story to pass on to family and friends over dinner. I really hoped this didn't turn up on YouTube. I didn't appear to be harmed. Just confused.

"Can someone get Garrett Mercer? Please."

One man nodded and hurried into the building.

"We didn't call the police." The chef leaned closer and lowered his voice. "We're trying to be discrete. I'm not sure this gala is the best place for you in your current condition."

"My current condition?" I realized what he was implying and my lips parted in shock. "I'm not *doing* drugs. I *was* drugged."

The kitchen staff glanced at each other. They obviously didn't believe me. Making matters worse was the fact that other people were beginning to peer down the alley to see what all of the commotion was about.

The main chef guy nodded, but I could tell he didn't believe me.

Thankfully, Garrett stepped out from the back door and rushed toward me. Wrinkles of worry stretched across his forehead and his normal jovial expression was nowhere to be found.

"Gabby? What happened?" His gaze jerked to the street. "Where's the car I sent to pick you up?"

I rubbed my neck. "Long story. Really long story."

His arm went to my waist, he thanked the crowd of onlookers, and ushered me inside. "Let's get you a place to sit down and rest for a moment."

"I'll be fine," I insisted, trying to skirt away from his

touch.

As soon as he let go, wooziness engulfed me, and his arm went back to my waist. This time, I couldn't argue.

"I should call the police," he mumbled.

I shook my head, which made everything spin again. "No, I'm fine. Really."

"What happened?"

"It was the Watcher. He was the limo driver. He told me to stay away from this case and then he sprayed something in my face. I woke up behind the convention center, at the service entrance."

He led me to a room behind the stage area and I sunk onto the couch there. Garrett thrust a bottle of water in my hands.

"Maybe you should be checked out?"

I shook my head. "No, I'll be fine. I don't know what he sprayed in my face, but it's wearing off. Just give me a moment."

I leaned back into the couch and closed my eyes. I wished I could sort out my thoughts. I knew one thing: I wasn't going to sit here and feel sorry for myself. The man was not going to ruin this night. I just needed a few more minutes for my head to clear.

"You're very lucky," Garrett mumbled, kneeling in front of me with concern etched across his face.

"Luck has nothing to do with it," I insisted.

***

I finally regained enough of my thinking that I stood. "We should get out there."

"You sure?"

I paused in front of a mirror and fixed my hair. Thankfully, Holly's dress was okay. Thankfully, I was okay.

The whole situation could have ended much worse. Death worse.

"You look beautiful," Garrett told me. He stepped behind me.

I finally got a good look at him in the reflection there. On a good day, he was handsome. Dressed in a tux, he was worthy of making *People* magazine's 100 Most Beautiful People list.

I think I might have blushed. Then I scolded myself for blushing. Garrett Mercer should not make me blush. He had absolutely no effect on me . . . except that he did.

Which was a problem.

"You look quite nice yourself," I finally managed to get out.

He extended his arm. "Let's get going, shall we."

"We shall." My voice came out with a slight British accent. I hoped that Garrett didn't notice and think I was mocking him. Total accident.

He wagged his eyebrows up and down. "You ready for this evening?"

"As ready as a runner for a race. A pregnant woman two weeks past her due date. A snow cloud in December."

Shut up, Gabby. Stop talking.

Perhaps I was trying a little too hard to act like everything was okay, even though I still felt a little lightheaded.

"Nothing ever flusters you, does it?" Garrett asked.

He obviously didn't know me. "Lots of things fluster me."

"Well, I would have never guessed. You always seem ready with a one liner. Or a two liner."

I hoped he wasn't going to be in for a rude awakening this evening. I was Ms. Put My Foot in My Mouth, Speak Before Thinking, and Trip over Imaginary Lint. I don't know where he'd ever gotten the impression that I never got flustered. I really should give him fair warning that shooting from the hip could get me in trouble with a capital T.

"Despite the way the evening began, I'm glad that you'll be joining me tonight."

"Thanks for asking. I look forward to meeting your friends."

"I think you'll really love them."

We walked down a back hallway toward the murmuring of voices in the distance. "So, what are the updates on the case since we spoke yesterday?"

I pulled in a long breath. "I've talked to a lot of people, but I'm not sure I'm any closer to the answers."

I filled him in on my conversation with Marty Mart Alvin and ended with the update on the private investigator in Pittsburgh, including Sebastian's business trip there.

Garrett blanched at the announcement. "P.I. Perkins was shot? Right after you talked to him?"

I nodded. "Yeah, this simple cold case is suddenly seeming complicated." I glanced at Garrett. "Why'd you choose Perkins anyway? How'd you find him?"

"He solved a big case in New Jersey several years ago. Track records like that are important."

"I didn't have a track record."

"Sure you did. You had Milton Jones. Plus that bombing in downtown Norfolk."

"You do your research."

"I didn't get to where I am right now, just because I grew up with a silver spoon in my mouth, Gabby. At least, I'd like to think that was true."

I nodded. "I'd say it was."

Garrett rubbed his chin and let out a long sigh. "The

killer is still at large, Gabby."

"And apparently he has eyes and ears and trigger fingers everywhere."

"I don't like where this is going."

"As I've stated before, I don't like bullies." I shook my head. "Anyway, Marty Mart mentioned something—"

"Who?"

"I meant Marty. Marty mentioned something about a conversation he overheard your dad having with Sebastian Royce."

"He's a strange man, isn't he?"

"Any reason to suspect him?"

Garrett thought about it a moment before shaking his head. "Not really."

"What about Vic Newport? Do you think your dad was having an affair with his best friend's wife?"

"He didn't talk to me about such things."

"Of course he didn't. But did you ever hear any rumors? Did you ever have any suspicions?"

"Very little would surprise me with my dad, Gabby. Very little."

"What's your impression of Mr. Newport then? A killer?"

"He's meticulous. I'll give him that. But I have a hard time thinking about anyone I know as a killer. Besides, why wouldn't he have just targeted my father if this was all about an affair? Why kill the whole family?"

I shook my head. "I have no idea."

We stopped in front of a door. "We'll talk more later. Right now, I've got to mentally prepare myself to wow investors."

Was I really ready for this? As the door opened, I realized I didn't have much choice at this point. I nodded. "Let's go."

***

This was not your grandma's gala. Sure, it was fancy and filled with rich people. But this one was filled with rich people who were trying to make a difference in the world. Everything about the event screamed trendy and hip—and green, of course. Everything looked earthy and simple. A folksy band played in the corner, decorations consisted of pinecones and leaves and scentless candles. Everything seemed so organic and wholesome.

Garrett introduced me to so many people that I couldn't even begin to keep any of them straight. I smiled politely, prayed that the fancy little spinach-topped hors d'oeuvre wasn't stuck in between my front teeth, and did my best to only discuss things that were considered "safe." So far, so good.

"Will you excuse me for a moment?" Garrett asked during a lull in introductions.

"For a fifty cents an hour raise, I'll give you more than a moment. I'll give you two. "I grinned.

"Your generosity never ceases to amaze me."

I gripped my sparkling water and turned to observe the expert schmoozers around me while Garrett disappeared. For a moment, I froze, wondering what to do with myself. The best way to mingle. The smartest way to not put my foot in my mouth.

"Gabby, isn't it?"

I looked up and spotted a man. It took me a moment to realize he was Smith Wimbledon, the CEO of the pharmaceutical company. "Mr. Wimbledon. What a surprise."

He smiled good-naturedly. "Mr. Newport and I are both here. We like to support Garrett whenever we can."

"That's really great."

"Being here is just a small thing we can do to show our encouragement. People who work at Wimbledon become like family. In fact, some of us prefer our coworkers to our actual families." He chuckled. "How's the case going? Any leads?"

I shrugged. "I don't know if I'd call them leads. But I'm definitely not giving up on this."

He nodded. "Good. Someone needs to do time for this crime. All investigators need is one good break in the case."

"I agree." *And I hope I'm the one who finds it.*

The man's hands were stuffed deep into his pockets and he jangled some change there. "I didn't want to say this in the meeting. It didn't seem appropriate, if you know what I mean. But Edward did mention something to me about some tension between himself and Sebastian Royce."

I twisted my head with curiosity. "Is that right?"

"It was probably nothing. But I drove past one of his stores today and it made me think about an off-handed comment Edward made once. He said never loan money to a friend until you know which one you need most. I'm not sure what happened between the two men, but I know Edward made a passing remark about getting in contact with his lawyer."

"Do you know this lawyer's name?"

He shook his head. "He was my lawyer, as well, but I'm afraid he had a heart attack about six years ago." He offered a sad smile. "I suppose that's the challenge of working an old case like this. The leads that don't dry up face the harsh reality of passing time."

"I can't argue that."

He nodded toward someone in the distance. "Anyway,

that probably wasn't worth much. But it had been on my mind. I hadn't expected to run into you, but you were on my list of people to call. I thought it was worth a mention."

"Absolutely." That was the second time the man's name had come up. The love of money may not be the root of *all* evil, but it was definitely the root of *some* evil. A substantial loan like the one Sebastian had taken from Edward would be enough to put anyone in treacherous territory. What I wasn't sure about was whether or not this loan had been on the books. Had legal action ever been pursued even after Edward's death? Certainly investigators had looked into their monetary accounts and noticed such a large transaction.

And Sebastian had been a sharp shooter. Did he utilize those skills to kill the family? I couldn't be sure.

When I had a chance, I'd ask Garrett.

"Hope you didn't miss me too much." Hot breath hit my ear.

I tensed when I realized how close the temporary boss was. Instead of slapping him, I scooted away. "I do think about people other than you. Not to burst your bubble."

Garrett grinned. "But you think about me some. I'll take that."

"Are you always so full of yourself?" I asked. I wished he didn't amuse me so much in the process. It would make my life so much easier.

"I prefer to call it confident." Those sparkling eyes rivaled the evening sky on a clear night. He extended his hand. "Shall we eat?"

"Food sounds good." I cast one more glance over my shoulder and spotted Vic Newport. I smiled. He scowled in return. Interesting.

Garrett led me to a table near the front where two seats were saved. A moment of anxiety hit me at the thought of meeting the group, remembering their names, keeping a smooth conversation going.

"This is Gabby," he introduced me to the people seated at the table.

I nodded hello and tried to keep track of everyone's names, though I knew it was useless.

As the conversation settled around us, I noticed that Garrett had his arm draped on the back of my chair.

He's just being casual, I told myself.

But I also realized that everyone else at the table was a part of a couple.

I also picked up on the fact that several seemed to be investors in Garrett's company.

As people did the general chit-chat, my gaze traveled across the room. One of the catering staff—one who'd seen me passed out in the alley—leaned over Smith Wimbledon, whispering something to him. Then he looked back at me.

Had the man been warning Smith to stay away? That I was a druggie? Maybe he liked humiliating people and was sharing my story with as many people as possible.

Anger—and embarrassment—surged through me.

"So, how did the two of you meet?" the blonde across the table asked, pulling me away from my thoughts.

I looked up at Garrett and saw him grinning. His face was entirely too close. I looked away.

"We met through a case Gabby was investigating back in Norfolk," Garrett answered.

"Uh oh. Don't tell me you were one of the suspects!" a jolly man across the table said.

He chuckled. "Of course not. I'd like to think I helped her catch the bad guy. Right, Gabby?"

I forced a smile, realizing things didn't sound all professional between us. "Of course you did."

"Gabby is like an urban legend back in Norfolk. She's solved several crimes that the police weren't able to crack. She's gotten some notorious criminals off the streets."

The woman across from me nodded. "Impressive."

"Gabby, I forgot to mention that my friend Margo here is the owner of Grayson Technologies. They manufacture—"

"—much of the equipment that is used in crime scene analysis." I smiled. "I've heard of you. I've even utilized many of your products. It's a pleasure to meet you."

Margo was a blonde with a neat bob and a pear shaped figure. She was probably in her fifties and whenever she looked at the program for the evening, she slid some turquoise colored glasses on the end of her nose.

"Same here," she responded with a professional smile. "It sounds like you have a good track record. Any professional experience?"

Did being a crime scene cleaner count? I shrugged. "I worked for the medical examiner for a while."

"What happened?" she asked.

"Budget cuts."

She nodded. "Looking for a new job?"

"A new job might take me out of state, and I'm not quite ready for that. But I'm keeping my options open." I remembered my conversation with Riley. "You never know what doors will open or close."

"We're always looking for representatives for my company. I'll give you my card before I leave. Maybe you'd be interested?"

"I'd definitely love some more information." Maybe this whole I'll scratch your back if you'll scratch mine thing really did work.

Margo grinned. "Perfect."

I looked up at Garrett, about to smile and show my gratitude. Before I could, his lips covered mine. Just for a minute. A brief minute. A millisecond was probably more like it. But still. His lips and my lips connected.

A jolt burst through me. A jolt of guilt or a jolt of pleasure?

I hated that I even had to ask myself that question.

CHAPTER 20

Guilt, I decided. It was guilt that flashed through me.

I did not participate in that kiss. I was innocent. I hadn't cheated, hadn't puckered in return. I was like a bystander in a drive-by smooching.

Garrett just smiled beside me, as if what had happened was nothing unusual. "I think Gabby would be a great asset to your company. Isn't that great news, Love?"

"Great news," I mumbled.

I tried not to look flustered. But I felt flustered. I felt like running from the table.

Which wouldn't be a good impression for Margo across from me.

So I forced a smile.

Garrett rubbed my shoulder. "I think she's amazing."

The rest of the conversation seemed like a blur. All I could think about was that kiss.

Why in the world had the man kissed me? I needed to talk to him, but I wasn't sure when I'd get that opportunity. I had to force my breathing to remain steady. Force my words to remain calm. Force my brain to stop going the places where it wanted to go.

"Could I have this dance, Love?" Garrett asked. He stood, those British eyes smiling as he extended his hand.

"Of course."

I took his hand—only because everyone was watching—and let him pull me to my feet. I kept my mouth closed until we reached the dance floor.

I tried to ignore the tingle I felt when his hand went to my waist. Those feelings should only be reserved for Riley. So why was my body disobeying me?

I was about to launch into my spiel when he tugged at one of my curls. "I think I'll call you Shirleylock. You know, a combination of Shirley Temple and Sherlock. What do you think?"

I ignored him.

"What was that about?" I demanded.

"What was what about?" He swayed to the music, looking totally at ease.

"You know exactly what I'm talking about."

He nonchalantly looked toward the ceiling. "The kiss, you mean? Oh, that was nothing. I was just going with the moment."

"Nothing, huh?"

"I have to say that investors do like a man in a steady relationship."

"But we're not in a relationship."

He raised my hand. "I noticed your ring is gone. Does that mean the engagement is off?"

My cheeks flushed again. "It does, but the ending of my engagement doesn't have anything to do with you."

"So, you're free now? There are no ugly little lines to cross."

"Not exactly. We called off the engagement, but we didn't break up."

"Called off the engagement but not officially broken up? I think you and I both know that's not true. We know how it works, no matter how hard reality might be to handle."

I looked away, determined that his words were false. "You don't know Riley."

"I don't need to. I'm a man. I know how men think. And I think we could be good together, Gabby. As friends. As lovers."

I cringed, and Garrett laughed, low and rumbling.

"I hate that word," I reminded him.

He grinned. "I know."

"You're terrible."

"Only in a good way."

I stared off in the distance, at the other couples swaying happily to the music. I remembered the kiss. I realized I enjoyed Garrett's leathery scent just a little too much. I enjoyed our banter. I enjoyed the attention, for that matter.

But I also couldn't rely on any of these emotions right now. So I was going to go with the logical approach. There were so many reasons I couldn't date Garrett, even if Riley wasn't in the picture. "You seem like a guy who just likes the thrill of the chase."

"I do like the chase. Is there something wrong with that?"

"I'm someone who thinks romance is a lifelong journey, not a flash in the pan sprint. Excuse the mixed metaphor."

He stepped close enough that I could feel his breath on my cheek. "I think when you meet the right one that everything changes."

My throat tightened. I had to forget about these emotions. "My fiancé and I just broke up."

"Maybe the best way to get over one person is to be with another."

The idea was tempting. I hated to admit it. But it was true. Feeling desired had its appeal, especially after being thrown to the curb like a piece of trash.

He took my hand and pulled me toward him. "Gabby,

you'd never have to worry about money with me again. I could take care of you. Give you anything you wanted."

I let myself imagine that for a moment. I'd never been at that place in life before. I'd always lived paycheck to paycheck. The idea of security tempted me more than it should have.

I pushed him back. "I can't. Not now. Maybe not ever. I don't know. I just know that I need time."

He stared at me a moment. The look in his eyes made me want to forget all of my resolutions. Finally, he nodded. "I'm about to say the most unromantic thing ever."

"I've heard some pretty unromantic things."

The intensity in his eyes remained. "I can't promise you that I'll wait."

That *was* pretty unromantic. Not the words fairy tales were made of. But I'd stopped believing in fairy tales. "What's meant to be will be."

"Excuse me? Garrett?"

I swung my head toward the voice. Lyndsey was here. Garrett's "assistant." When had she arrived?

"Yes, Lyndsey?"

"It's time for your speech to begin."

Garrett leaned toward me, his gaze locking with mine. "Let's finish this conversation later."

***

As Garrett was making his way toward the stage, my cellphone cried out from the depths of my tiny little glittery clutch. After casting an apologetic glance toward the podium, I put the phone to my ear and whispered hello.

"Gabby, this is Jamie. Holly told me where you were.

Sorry to interrupt you, but it's important."

I stared at the stage as Garrett took the microphone. Standing here and talking wasn't an option. I hated to miss Garrett's big moment, but I stepped away from the speakers and went out in the lobby. A security guard stood by the door, but the only other people out here were a couple of ladies headed toward the restroom and a man working the front door.

"What's going on, Jamie?"

"You know that website I told you about, the one with the cold cases?"

"Of course." I wanted to check out the website more when I had time.

"We just got a hit."

My adrenaline spiked. "And?"

"You may not dig this. That's why I wanted to call you right away."

If she was calling me here, it was obviously important. "Okay."

"Someone left an anonymous message on the site. They said you should look into Garrett Mercer."

"What?" The words came out louder than I intended. But of all the suspects I expected to hear, Garrett Mercer wasn't one of them.

"The poster said Mr. Rico Suave was actually in town on the night of the murder."

"No . . ." He was at a party. Certainly the police had verified that. Besides, Garrett wouldn't kill his own family. I refused to believe it.

"I'm just relaying the message. This person also said that three other investigators he hired have turned up dead, not including Perkins."

A chill spread through me. "Are you serious?"

"I wish I weren't. This could be nothing, Gabby. I know

that. But just in case it *is* something, I wanted you to know. Especially since . . . well, you know. You're with him now and all."

"I appreciate it. Thank you."

I slid my phone back into my purse and listened to Garrett's voice ringing out in the background. The audience laughed, as he no doubt said something that charmed them.

Charm was deceptive and beauty was fleeting. They were the perfect masks to cover up an ugly heart and devious spirit. Just what were those qualities masking about the real Garrett?

I had to make a decision. Did I take a taxi home and hide? Confront Garrett? Call the police?

I wasn't sure. But I needed to decide and soon.

CHAPTER 21

I leaned against the cool marble wall behind me and let my thoughts simmer for a moment.

I considered Garrett as the killer, along with what his motives, opportunity, and means might be.

Usually one of the first suspects was a family member. Check.

Garrett was in town—possibly—on the night his family died. Check.

Garrett stood to inherit a fortune if everyone in his family died. Check.

He appeared that he wanted to find answers, but other investigators in this case had died. Check.

Garrett was the one who knew I was coming to Cincinnati. He knew a limo was coming to get me. He could have easily arranged for someone to threaten me. Check.

Where I was drawing a blank was when it came to the question of why? Why hire investigators only to kill them? Why threaten me when he could simply take me off the case?

Was he psychotic? Did he get some kind of pleasure out of it? Did he feel like this threw the police off of his trail?

Something else didn't make sense. Someone had shot at Garrett. The bullet would have hit him if I hadn't thrown him out of the way.

The questions were enough to make my head spin.

Applause sounded inside. Was Garrett's talk over? I still hadn't decided what I would do. Just because someone made a claim online didn't mean it was true. The accusation could have been made by the real killer as he tried to derail our investigation.

The door opened beside me, and Garrett stepped out.

"There you are!" Garrett reached for my hand. "I thought you'd left."

"We need to talk," I muttered.

He dropped his hand and frowned. "Well, yes, I was hoping we might talk again and finish our conversation."

"About something else. About the case."

His gaze shifted behind me, to the people who'd wandered out. To ears that could eavesdrop on this conversation.

He looked back at me. "Might we do that later? Not here."

I knew this was his big night, and I hated to rain on his parade. But those accusations were serious. Especially if they were true. "We either talk now or I start screaming."

"Screaming?" His eyes narrowed with confusion. Finally, he nodded. "Let's go somewhere private."

I shook my head. "We talk here. You were in town the night your family died."

He looked around, as if to make sure no one was listening. Was he afraid of tarnishing his image? Here, he was a golden boy. Everyone worshipped him. He'd almost had me fooled for a moment, as well.

He lowered his voice. "Yes, I was."

"You lied to me." My voice started rising.

"I knew how it would look."

"If you were innocent, you would have known you'd be cleared."

He shook his head. "Innocent men go to jail every day,

Gabby."

"Were you there when your family was murdered?" The words tasted bitter as they left my lips.

He grabbed my arm. "Gabby, it's not like that. *I'm* not like that."

"If you lie about one thing, who knows what else you've lied about."

"Nothing, Gabby. I promise you." His eyes begged me to believe him.

"Why are all of these other investigators turning up dead? Can you tell me that?"

"I have no idea."

Another realization hit me. "Is that why you hired me? Did you see me as expendable?" I shrugged out of his grasp. "You couldn't care less if I survived this or not, could you?"

He glanced around again as a couple of people looked our way. "Gabby, I promise you it's not like that."

"Then you better start explaining because I'm about to call the police."

His shoulders sagged as something close to resignation seemed to burden him. "I didn't want you to think poorly of me. That's why I didn't tell you I was here on the night of the murders."

"You didn't think I would uncover that information?

"I'd hoped you wouldn't. The police didn't."

"Then maybe you don't have every confidence in me." I turned to walk away, but he grabbed my arm.

"Gabby, it's not very often that I actually care what a person thinks of me."

"You're telling me I'm different? That you actually want to put your best foot forward and make a good impression?" I didn't believe a word out of his mouth anymore.

"That's exactly what I'm saying." His words resounded with an unmistakable sincerity that threw me off guard.

"Why?"

"Because there's something special about you. You're not like all of the other women I meet. You've got depth and integrity. I like that."

He wasn't going to soften me up that easily. "Why were you here? Why lie about it?"

He sighed, his hands shoved deep into his pockets. "I was meeting a girl, that's why."

"And why was that a secret?"

His gaze latched onto mine. "Her name was Olivia."

"Okay . . ."

"Olivia Newport."

Realization washed over me. "Vic Newport's daughter?"

His lips pulled into a tight line. "That's correct."

"You were dating?"

"More than that. She was pregnant."

My eyes widened. And the plot thickened . . . again. If this plot got any thicker, it would need gastric bypass surgery.

"Why was all of this a secret? I'm still not following."

"Mr. Newport didn't think too highly of me. I was into partying. Flunking out of college. I went through women like someone with the flu goes through tissues."

"Okay."

We scooted out of the way and waited for a small crowd to depart. A few people stopped to chat with Garrett a moment, to thank him for his contributions to the world. If they only knew. As soon as the group passed, Garrett turned back to me, a tortured look in his eyes.

"Before life threw that curveball, Olivia and I were going to break up. We knew it was best for both of us. She wanted to be a fashion model. I didn't want to be tied down."

"And then she found out she was pregnant," I finished. "That could really throw a wrench in your plans."

"Exactly. Her dad would have been furious. I had a moment of clarity. I was going to, for once in my life, do the right thing. I was going to ask her to marry me."

"Wow." That was unexpected.

"We met at a cabin my family owns just across the state line down in Kentucky so we could talk. But her mind was already made up. She said she didn't want to marry me. She wanted to terminate the pregnancy."

My heart ached at his words. "And?"

"She left, and I stayed at the cabin for the rest of the night, trying to figure out what to do next."

"Why didn't you tell the police?"

"Telling the police would mean owning up to the pregnancy. That was the last thing Olivia wanted. Her father would have gone ballistic."

"He's the ballistic type, huh?" I made a mental note of that.

"Some would say. And, of course, staying quiet had its advantages for me, as well. I was at a party the night before. People have faulty memories. They thought I was there longer than I was, and I didn't correct them. I stuck with my story that I'd driven in that next morning. Olivia never corrected it."

"What happened to the baby?"

"She had a miscarriage." He hung his head as if the remembrance pained him.

"I'm sorry."

He frowned. "Me too. No one ever understood that I not only lost my family that night, but I also felt like I'd lost my future."

"You were excited about being a dad."

"I finally had a reason to live for someone other than myself."

"I guess you found your purpose again when you started GCI."

He nodded. "The company saved my life. Literally."

Against my better instincts, I believed him. Still, I had to trust but verify. Any good investigator would. "Where is Olivia now?"

"She's in New York."

"I want her contact information."

"Of course."

I stared at him, contemplating my next move. "If you keep anything else from me, I'm calling the police and telling them you were in town on the night of the murder. And I'm still sending you my bill."

Before he could respond, a commotion sounded inside. The doors burst open, a strange smell leaking out as a crowd of people rushed past.

CHAPTER 22

"What . . .?" I looked at Garrett.

A random stranger must have heard me because he called over his shoulder, "They told us to evacuate. There's a strong chemical smell in there. Like a pool . . . only stronger."

Screams echoed from the room. I stole a glance inside, over the sea of people flooding out, and saw flames.

Had someone knocked over a candle? Or was that fire set deliberately?

"Go outside. Get to safety. Now," Garrett ordered.

"Where are you going?"

"To make sure everyone is okay."

Before I could say anything, he ran inside. I stood there, half tempted to be carried away by the crowds and escape to the sidewalk. I knew I couldn't do that, though. I covered my mouth with my arm and started after Garrett.

The line between dumb and courageous was sometimes very thin.

The overwhelming scent of chlorine filled my senses as soon as I stepped inside. My eyes watered; my lungs tightened. Flames from a tablecloth spread to the floor, just as the sprinkler system came on.

The last few people scrambled out.

I could hardly see, hardly breathe from the moment I stepped into the conference area. Most of the crowd had cleared, but a fire burned at the stage area. Were there people trapped there?

I coughed as vapors filled my lungs, but I kept pressing forward.

Tears streamed from my irritated eyes. I spotted someone passed out on the floor. A table was on top of her. Had it been knocked over in the mad dash for people to evacuate?

I rushed toward the woman.

Margo.

I grabbed the table and tugged. It was wedged on the ground, the edge caught on the stage. It barely budged.

"Someone! I need help over here!" I yelled.

Garrett appeared. Grit was smudged across his cheeks and his jacket was torn. Without asking any questions, he grabbed the table and maneuvered it out of the way.

I glanced at Garrett, saw the determination on his face. Certainly he wasn't a killer. A killer wouldn't rush into a burning building to save virtual strangers . . . would he?

"Grab her, Gabby!"

I grabbed Margo under her arms and tugged. Thankfully, she easily pulled out.

I took one arm, and Garrett took the other. Together, we carried her outside.

Paramedics rushed toward us and took over.

Firefighters dashed inside the building. A paramedic put oxygen masks on us. I gulped in the clean air.

Garrett pulled his mask down for a moment.

"That was brave of you back there," Garrett muttered, leaning against a police car.

"Same for you."

"I think we make a good team."

"I think we still have a lot more to talk about."

"You're probably right." He nodded toward an approaching detective. "It looks like we have someone else to talk to first, though."

***

The tension was thick between Garrett and me as he drove me back to the Paladins' house. I had reservations about riding with him, but the bullet that had been fired at him while at the house was his saving grace at the moment. I just hoped he wasn't devious enough to think up that crazy scheme himself as a way of solidifying his innocence in all of this.

He put the car in park, not at the Paladins' but at a nice little park overlooking the city. I didn't feel scared. Not really, but I did remain on guard.

"What are you thinking, Gabby?"

"I don't think that was an accident, despite what the police said."

There'd been a chlorine leak from the pool, which was below the convention center. The vapors had traveled up and were strong enough that several people had been sent to the hospital.

He sighed. "I'm not convinced it was an accident either."

"I'm thinking you disappeared for a while at the gala tonight. Disappeared backstage." Despite that reasoning, I still didn't think he was a killer. Still, I had to ask the hard questions, or I'd be a fool.

"Gabby, I always take a moment to do some deep breathing at events like this. It helps me stay cool and in control. I wasn't tampering with chlorine."

I shook my head and stared at the lights of the city ahead. I could see the stadiums, the sparkling skyline, the magnificent bridges. "There are things that don't make sense."

"Talk to me about them. Maybe I can help you figure them out."

Where did I even start? "Tell me about these other P.I.s you've hired."

He leaned back in his seat. "I only knew that one of them had died and I assumed it was because of another case he was working on. Not mine. Then today you told me about Bradley. How many others have there been?"

"Three."

"That's unfortunate." His words were tinged with a grim grief. He understood loss. He didn't dismiss their deaths.

I appreciated that. But I still had more questions. "Why not the police? The FBI? Why would someone only target P.I.s?"

"Your guess is as good as mine. Maybe even better. I have no idea."

My thoughts still churned. "Why the chlorine tonight? Why was tonight a threat to someone? This person has already warned me to back off."

"His earlier attempts to quiet you didn't work. But this person is getting desperate."

"But then why in a roomful of people?" It was one thing to shoot at a P.I. It was an entirely different thing to try and send a message with a group of innocent people. "Unless it was because you were there too. Maybe this person wanted to send a message."

He raked a hand through his hair. "You know what? You're fired, Gabby. I want you off this case."

I jerked my head toward him. "You can't fire me."

"I most certainly can."

"Well, I refuse to quit then."

"I'm withholding all of your money until you agree to back off."

"I'll hire a lawyer."

His head dropped as he swung it back and forth, heavier than a pendulum fit for Big Ben. "Come on, Gabby. I wouldn't be able to live with myself if something happened to you."

"You asked how I keep solving cases? What my secret is? I'm stubborn. That's my secret. I don't let things go."

"I see."

"Someone wants to keep their secret covered up. They're willing to take some risks in order to ensure that they're not discovered. The good news is that in their madness, they may just end up giving us more clues. Fear makes people do irrational things, even the most brilliant criminals."

His head popped up. "I think you're pretty brilliant."

I would love to bask in his affection and compliments. Losing myself in someone else would be a nice escape. But it couldn't happen. "Garrett, that kiss shouldn't have happened. Things are not resolved in my relationship with Riley."

"I can respect that. I don't like it. But being faithful is a good quality to have, Gabby."

My throat squeezed. "Thank you."

He cranked the engine. "I guess I should get you back home."

I nodded. "Yeah, I guess you should."

I kept my gaze focused out the window, wondering why I felt like crying. Allergies, I told myself. That was my story and I was sticking to it.

"Do you have any tissues? My eyes are probably burning from the chlorine." Yeah, the chlorine. That was an even better excuse.

"Try the glove compartment."

I opened it and gasped.

Stuffed into the small space were probably ten different cellphones. Cellphones that someone like the Watcher might have used in order not to be traced.

CHAPTER 23

The first thing I did the next morning was to call Olivia, who was now a fashion designer in New York City. I left her a message and three minutes later, she called me back. She sounded terse and suspicious, but that didn't stop me from asking my questions. I needed answers ASAP because I feared the killer had been under my nose this whole time. I would not be played.

"Look, I'm investigating the Mercer family murders. Garrett claims you two were together on the night the crime happened. I just need to confirm whether or not it's true."

There was a long pause.

Finally, she said, "Yes, it is."

"When did you leave the cabin?"

"I don't know. 10:30 or 11." She sounded annoyed.

My back muscles tightened—not because of her bad attitude, but because if what she'd said was true, Garrett would have had enough time to make it back to his house. He may *not* have an alibi.

"You and Garrett were dating back then?"

"We were. That was a long time ago. We've spoken maybe three times since that night."

"Like when you lost your baby?" I kept my voice soft, knowing the subject could be delicate.

"Exactly." She said it like other people talked about getting rid of old clothing. "I told him what had happened, and we could both breathe a little easier and stop fighting about how to handle things."

I already didn't like her. "Olivia, what did you do when you left Garrett that evening? Where did you go?"

"Home. Where are you going with this? I have a meeting with a team of investors. I really don't have a lot of time. I was simply curious about what you could possibly want to speak with me about."

"Just one more question: Did your dad catch you?" I asked.

"My dad wasn't even home when I got there, so you're going to have to take my word for it. Please don't tell me you think I killed the Mercers."

"No, I don't. I'm just fact checking. Did you tell the police that your father wasn't home?"

She snorted. "No, of course I didn't implicate him. We both vouched for each other. The police never took it any further."

I had nothing else to ask her, and I could tell she didn't want to talk, so I said thank you and dropped my phone back on the bed. Olivia and Vic Newport had lied for each other. That left me feeling unsettled. That was the thing about liars—it was hard to believe a word coming from their mouths.

Also, the realization that Vic Newport wasn't home sent up some red flags in my mind. Where would he have been at that time of night?

Perhaps my conversation with Olivia didn't bother me as much as finding those cellphones in Garrett's car last night. He'd insisted he had no idea how they got there. That he'd been set up. After he dropped me off, he'd gone straight to the police station to report what had happened.

I wanted to believe him. I really did. But doubts

lingered in my mind and I knew I needed to put some space between me and Mr. Rico Suave, as Jamie had called him.

I hurried through my morning routines and went downstairs, my head nearly ready to explode from information overload. Just as I hit the bottom step, the doorbell rang and I heard familiar voices downstairs.

"Detective Morrison! What a surprise to see you here," Holly said.

"I was hoping I might speak to that P.I. who's staying with you."

"You mean Gabby? Let me see if—" She twirled around and spotted me as I stepped into the foyer. "There you are!"

I nodded at Morrison. "Good morning, Detective."

He wore a fedora and droplets of rain were sprinkled across the rim. "May I have a moment of your time?"

"More than a moment," I assured him.

Holly extended her arm. "Come on in out of the cold."

He stepped inside and Holly took his jacket, ever the polite hostess. Droplets of water hit the floor, rolling off his coat.

"Sit down for a while and let me get you some coffee," Holly continued. "You need a warm drink on a cold, wet day like today."

While Holly hurried off to the kitchen, the detective and I settled in the living room. Detective Morrison perched in an overstuffed red chair, and I lowered myself onto a cheerful, flowered couch across from him.

"To what do I owe the honor of this visit?" I kept my voice light, trying not to sound pushy. But I couldn't stand it any longer. Why was he here?

His weary eyes rested on me. "I heard about the incident last night."

"How'd you know I was there when it happened? Did word get around town that fast?"

He pointed to the newspaper on the table in front of me. "Everyone knows it."

A picture of Garrett and me with our arms around Margo, leading her from the hotel had made the front page. It was a very heroic picture, if I said so myself.

He cleared his throat. "I realized I wasn't very helpful the first time we spoke. Seeing that picture made me realize how serious you are. How serious this case is. I wanted to offer you any assistance necessary."

"I appreciate that." The man had done a 180. I wasn't going to complain.

Holly set down some coffee on the table beside him, along with a plate of homemade cookies. I seriously didn't know where that woman found the time to bake like that.

He let out a long breath. "To be honest, not solving this case has not only tarnished my reputation, it's affected my psyche. I vowed to solve this crime before I retired, and that never happened. I let the people of this city down."

"You solved a lot of other crimes, got a lot of other bad guys off the street."

He raised a bushy eyebrow. "You been researching me?"

I shook my head. "No, but the department wouldn't have kept you as a detective if you didn't. Besides, I can see that gleam in your eyes. That desire for justice."

I recognized the trait in others because I felt the desire so strongly within myself. When I met other likeminded people, I felt an instant connection with them. Maybe that was why I got along so well with Jamie and Holly.

"I was right about you. You are kind." He took a sip of his coffee. "So, do you have any more questions for me? I want this guy put away just as much as anyone else.

Maybe more."

"Maybe I could talk through the case and share what I've learned so far. I think I've ruled out two of my potential suspects."

"Who were they?" Morrison asked.

"Marty Alvin, Cassidy's boyfriend. His drug use would make people think he could be guilty, but he was in a—"

"In a car accident right before the crime occurred. We looked at him," Morrison confirmed.

"I also have another suspect." I hesitated before announcing the next name. "Garrett Mercer."

The detective recoiled. "The son?"

"Correct. Was he a suspect?"

"Garrett? No, he wasn't in town."

I didn't want to sell anyone out. I really didn't. But . . . "Did you confirm that?"

The detective set his coffee down on the table. "He was at a party and didn't come in until morning. Why are you asking?"

I stared at him a moment, contemplating my words. There was no need to hide things. I wouldn't lie to protect a potentially guilty man. Besides, I'd told Garrett if he lied to me again I would go straight to the police. Detective Morrison was retired which officially made him unofficial.

"Because Garrett was in town. He was having a rendezvous with a pregnant girlfriend at an undisclosed location."

The detective's eyes narrowed before he slowly shook his head. "Three coeds confirmed he was at that party."

"They could have been too drunk to realize what time he left," I argued. "He made an appearance. Garrett verified that."

"Plus, we had camera footage of him at a gas station between the college and his house," Morrison continued, staring off into the distance.

"He must have stopped there after meeting with Olivia Newport. He said he drove around for a while."

"What would Garrett's motivation be?" the detective asked.

"Money. He stood to inherit a lot. That money helped him to start the successful business he has today." The words left a bitter taste in my mouth. Somewhere along the line, Garrett had begun to feel like a friend, I realized. My loyalties felt torn between justice and friendship.

But he had an alibi. Supposedly.

Holly shook her head. "I don't know Garrett, but he doesn't seem like the murdering type."

"A lot of people who kill don't," I told her. "Here's the other thing: Four of the P.I.s that Garrett has hired have died mysterious deaths, and now someone is after me."

I told him about my phone calls with the Watcher, including the cellphones found in Garrett's car.

The detective studied me for a moment. "Maybe we could put a tracer on your phone, see if we can pinpoint where those calls are coming from."

"I thought about that. But this guy calls me from a different number each time. He's using a new phone with each contact and disposing of the old one. Plus, the conversations are short. My gut is telling me he knows that he can't stay on the phone long, just in case."

"You may have a point. Have you considered that maybe someone is setting Garrett up?" The detective's words echoed through the room.

I shook my head, unsure of anything at the moment. "Or maybe he really is guilty."

"He wouldn't have ruined his own gala," Holly argued.

"The chlorine leak happened after he finished talking. He stepped in the hallway to speak with me. Five minutes earlier, and he would have been in the middle of it." I shook my head, battling my own doubts. "I'm not saying he's guilty. But I'm not saying he's innocent either. Which brings me to where I am now. Did you ever investigate Sebastian Royce?"

Morrison squinted. "The name's not ringing a bell."

"He owns Winners, the sports super stores."

Recognition stretched across his features. "That's right. We questioned him. A peculiar man, isn't he? He was never a suspect. Should he have been?"

"He left yesterday for Pennsylvania. Yesterday is when another P.I. on the case was shot."

"Another P.I.? I'm not following," the detective said.

I explained to him the string of deaths associated with the case.

"You're serious?" Detective Morrison said. "How did that get past us?"

"There was no one to connect the dots. Well, no one except Garrett and he pleads cluelessness. Said he had no idea. And, in his defense, their deaths occurred *after* they worked the case, at a point in time when Garrett had already lost contact with them."

Morrison leaned back, a thoughtful look on his face. "How'd they die?"

"One was in a car accident. Another was shot while investigating a different case. The third drowned on vacation, and the fourth was just shot point blank."

"Just shot?" Morrison asked. "As in, it just happened?"

I nodded and explained.

"That's scary." Holly shuddered.

"I know. But I'm trying to make sense of all of it. Why kill the P.I. after I spoke with him? What sense does it make?" I shook my head. "I still don't have any good ideas."

"Maybe whenever people get too close to the answers, they die," Holly offered.

"Then why didn't any police officers or FBI agents die?" I countered. I'd asked Garrett the same question last night, but it was worth raising again. "It's only the people hired by Garrett."

"You raise some interesting points," the detective agreed.

"Plus, there's the fact—maybe I should call it a rumor—that Sebastian borrowed money from the Mercers. A lot of money."

"We never saw any record of that," Morrison said.

"Edward Mercer may have had an offshore account. Some would call it an off-the-books account."

"Now that's interesting." The detective rubbed his chin.

I nodded. "Maybe he was planning something. Or hiding something. Funneling money away to pay someone off maybe?"

"Let's not assume anything. I can talk to some of my friends on the force. It's going to take a lot of time to get information like that. The legal process alone could take weeks." He shook his head. "We could give it a shot, see what we could dig up. Follow the money, as they say."

"Someone's not telling the truth," I said. "We just have to figure out who."

We all exchanged glances. It was because we all knew that figuring out who would be the hardest thing of all.

"What's your next plan of action?" Holly asked.

"Scientific theory would tell us to only test one variable at a time," I mumbled.

"Who's your variable?" the detective asked.

I sucked on my lip for a moment. Unless more implicating evidence turned up, I was going to choose to believe Garrett was innocent. I'd still stay on guard, though.

That left Vic Newport or Sebastian Royce. Both gave me a reason to pause. But Sebastian Royce gave me 10 million reasons.

CHAPTER 24

When the detective left, I turned toward Holly. It was time to start ruling out some suspects, starting with Sebastian Royce.

There was only one person I could think of who could answer my questions. One person other than Sebastian Royce himself, that is.

"Holly, can I have Kevin's number?" I stood, stretched, and refilled my coffee.

"You can have it and you can keep it." She grabbed her purse from the table by the front door and plucked his card out. "Here you go."

Without wasting time, I grabbed my phone and dialed his number. His boss—Sebastian Royce—was supposedly still out of town, so I hoped to catch Kevin while he still felt like talking. Just as I was about to hang up, he answered.

"Kevin here." His voice sounded dull, unenthused.

"Kevin, my name is Gabby St. Claire. I'm a private investigator, and I was hoping to ask you a few questions." I jammed my hip against the kitchen counter and stared at Holly.

"Pertaining to . . ."

"Sebastian Royce."

"I don't think it would be in my best interest to answer those questions. Not if I value my job."

"If you don't answer my questions, I'll simply tip off the police. You'll be subpoenaed. Things can really get ugly then. Your answers will be public record. There's no job security in that."

He paused. "I see how you're playing this game. What do you want to know? My answers are dependent on your questions."

I raised my cup of coffee. "I'm investigating the murder of the Mercer family. You heard of their deaths?"

"Everyone has. What's this have to do with my boss?"

"I discovered he borrowed a substantial amount of money from Edward Mercer. Some people believe Sebastian might have been so desperate for his business to succeed that he took out the whole Mercer family in order to not have to pay the money back."

"That's pretty desperate."

"Ten million dollars desperate. Plus, there's the fact that he's known for his shooting skills."

"There's the fact that he *was* known for his shooting skills," Kevin corrected.

My thoughts ground to a halt. "What do you mean?"

"I mean that Mr. Royce is legally blind. He can't even drive anymore. He has a driver who takes him everywhere."

I set my coffee back on the counter, stupefied. "How long has that been the case?"

"He had early onset of macular degeneration, beginning in his early thirties. It's only gotten worse as the years have gone on."

I did some quick calculations. The man was at least in his fifties now. That meant ten years ago, he was already considered legally blind. Sneaking to the Mercer's house and shooting them with such precision would have nearly been impossible."

Something still wasn't adding up in my mind. "But he plays polo and golf," I argued.

"No, he *watches* polo and golf. With someone. Who gives him commentary the whole time. He may even make unauthorized bets on the games sometimes, just to make his life more interesting. I say that off the record, of course."

"He's a gambler?"

"They don't call him 'Sebastian The *Rolls* Royce' for no reason. Roll being the choice word here."

"Aside from gambling, I saw him checking his phone." I clearly remembered him doing it that day at the country club.

"He's got a special screen that makes the text bigger. Plus, since he's nearsighted he can see things up close a little better."

That was a major hole in my story. "Is someone with Mr. Royce now on his trip to Pennsylvania?"

"Pennsylvania? Why would you think he was there?"

I wanted to scream, "Because you told us!" Instead, I said, "I heard a rumor."

"He is on a trip. But he's having eye surgery. He's just telling people that he's out of town on business because he doesn't like people to feel sorry for him because of his condition. He said it would make others perceive him as weak."

***

Holly and I sat on my bed as if we were two middle school girls at a slumber party. Only, instead of looking at pictures of celebrities in gossip magazines and painting our nails, we pored over crime scene photos. Bloody crime scene photos.

Kevin had given me the name of a hospital and doctor where Sebastian was supposedly having this surgery. I looked up the information, and everything looked legit.

It appeared that Kevin was telling the truth. That meant that Sebastian Royce could be ruled out.

"I guess we can move on to Vic Newport," I muttered. "I just have to figure out a motive."

"Maybe he found out that Olivia was pregnant and went to confront Garrett. Only Garrett wasn't there. Maybe things escalated, she said with a touch of soap opera drama to her voice."

I shook my head. "There's no sign that things escalated. The whole crime scene was pretty cut and dry."

A breeze floated through the room—drafty windows, I'd discovered on my first night here—and I shivered. The chill caused something to click in my mind.

I grabbed the photos and found the ones from Cassidy's room.

It was just a hunch, but . . .

I pulled out my laptop.

"What are you doing?" Holly asked.

"I've got to check something. I promise I'll explain it all in a moment." I found a website that showed the weather in different parts of the country throughout the past several decades. I typed in Cincinnati, OH, November 12, ten years ago.

It was a cold day. Like, a really cold day, even by Ohio standards. Twelve degrees Fahrenheit.

This could be nothing . . . but it could be something. I had to know.

I picked up the phone. "I need to call the detective."

I found his number in my "Recent Calls," and hit SEND. He picked up on the third ring.

"Detective, this is Gabby. I'm looking at some of the crime scene photos from the Mercer family murders. I know it's been ten years, but I have a question about something I'm seeing."

"I'll do my best to remember."

"Cassidy's room." I stared at the picture, trying to put the horrors out of my mind. "Was there any confirmation that the killer got in through her window and that Cassidy died first?"

"When the crime scene was reconstructed, that was the conclusion of the team of investigators."

"Detective, Garrett told me that his sister always liked the room cold. She loved getting bundled up under blankets and with slippers. He said she always cracked the window open, even in the winter. I realize that the order of their deaths was determined by the coroner. She tested their body temperature, rigor mortis, and entomology—the study of bugs."

"I know that, Gabby."

"Sorry. Anyway. It was below freezing that day. If Cassidy's window was open when she died, it would have slowed down the process of rigor mortis. The coroner would have wrongly assumed based on all the given factors that Cassidy Mercer died first."

"You're thinking like a detective. But even if you're right—how does that help us?"

I stared at the crime scene photos, my thoughts percolating. "What if Edward Mercer knew the killer? What if he let them inside? That would explain how the alarm system was bypassed."

I held my breath. Did the former detective hate my theory? Think it was stupid?

"I think you could be on to something, Gabby."

I released my breath. "Really?"

"Yes, really. In fact, here's what I'll do. I'll make a few calls, see what I can find out. I've already talked to someone about those offshore accounts."

"Sounds great."
"Good work, Gabby. I'll be in touch."

CHAPTER 25

After lunch, Jamie stopped by and told me she got another hit on her website. It was from someone claiming to be a good friend of Cassidy Mercer's when they were in high school. Though I truly believed Edward Mercer was the target of this case, I still wanted to meet with this friend of Cassidy's and find out her take on the Mercer family.

Holly and Jamie asked if they could go with me.

"The MOD Squad," Jamie reminded me.

The company—and the additional sets of eyes and ears—sounded like a good idea.

Holly drove us in her Mustang across the river to Kentucky. We pulled to a stop in front of a house that could rival Garrett's childhood home. Everything about it was big, from the porch to the columns to the massive trees in the backyard.

Before we even rang the doorbell, Tess Windsor answered. She was everything I'd imagined her to be—and more. She was pretty, skinny and stuck up—I could tell by the way she assessed us as she opened the door. She must not have approved, because she frowned before inviting us in from the gray, dreary weather outside.

"I'm glad you could come," she muttered.

I'd asked Holly and Jamie to let me do most of the talking. "Thanks for getting in touch."

"I probably won't be much help." She frowned, already

appearing bored and nonchalant.

"You never know," I tried to assure her.

She led us past a massive entryway and into a formal living room. We all sat stiffly on the equally as stiff couch there while Tess sat in a wing-backed chair across from us. Something about the situation felt awkward. Was it Tess's lack of hospitality? Or the fact that three of us had shown up? Both?

"So, you were Cassidy's best friend," I started.

She nodded. "That's right. We were best friends from the time she moved into the area and started going to school with me."

"Did you know Marty?" Marty had an alibi on the night of the murders, but I wanted to get more insight on the relationship. Leave no stone unturned—or uncleaned. That's what I always said.

"Yeah, I knew him."

Uh oh. This was going to be one of those conversations where I had to pull every answer out of Tess. I already felt exhausted.

"What did you think of him?" I prompted.

She shrugged. "He was okay. I thought she could do better, but Cassidy seemed to either love him or hate him."

I tapped my pen on my notepad. "What do you mean?"

"They were either madly in love or they were fighting." She examined her manicured fingernails, appearing not *just* bored but *extravagantly* bored. "They had that kind of relationship, if you know what I mean."

"Do you think Marty would have killed her?" I didn't, but I wanted her take on it.

She snorted. "No way. They may have fought, but Marty really loved her."

"Even if he was drugged up?" Jamie asked. "Drugs make people go wacko. They make wacko people go even more wacko. I know that firsthand."

I wondered what that meant. I'd have to ask later.

Tess shook her head, her smooth hair slapping her cheeks. "Maybe he would have killed her parents so they wouldn't keep them apart. But no way would he hurt Cassidy. No way."

"Maybe Marty resented Cassidy," I said. "After all, she was the one who got him into drugs and look at where he is today. His addictions have ruined his life. I could see Marty thinking that Cassidy, in essence, destroyed him. He lost his scholarship. He's living at home with his parents now and apparently doesn't have a job."

Tess shrugged. "Maybe now he feels that way. But back then, he didn't. Cassidy had him under her spell."

I had the same impression. So I needed to change my approach and explore another possibility.

Before I could, Holly jumped in. "What was Cassidy's home life like?"

She sounded just like a social worker doing a home study. I'd bet she was good at her job. She was calm, caring, and determined.

"Her parents let her do whatever she wanted. They were never around to stop her. I think she wanted their attention. I told her she was lucky—she could get away with a lot."

"I take it you were one of her partying friends." Part of Marty Mart and his funky bunch. In fact, I'd bet Tess was still a partier and that she lived off of her daddy's money. That was the vibe she gave off.

"We liked to have a good time. Why not? There was nothing stopping us. We were young and foolish."

I needed to get this back around to Edward Mercer.

"Did she mention any family problems?"

Tess gave up on examining her nails and now studied the tips of her hair. "Her mom and dad argued quite a bit. I guess her dad was pretty uptight with his new job."

That was the first I'd heard of that. Everyone I'd spoken with had said Edward was a model employee. "Did she say why he was uptight?"

"I'm sure Cassidy didn't know or care. Her dad wasn't the kind to talk about work too much, unless he wanted to gloat about his accomplishments." She scowled at a split end.

"But Cassidy thought something was going on? Otherwise, why did she mention it?" I pressed. I really wished the woman would make eye contact. This only seemed to drive home the point that she was self-absorbed.

"She said he'd been more uptight than usual lately. He was snappy, distracted, always having private phone conversations. Stuff like that."

From the email on the website, I'd had the impression Tess wanted to talk. Speaking with her now, it seemed the opposite. It was time to call her out. "Is there any particular reason you wanted to meet with us, Tess?"

She looked away from her hair and frowned. She let out a long breath and rubbed her lips together. She'd been trying to act aloof, I realized. But her friend's death had affected her more than she probably ever let on to those around her. I wasn't sure why she wanted to maintain an image around us, though.

"I've never forgotten that night," she whispered. "We were all supposed to go to a party. But her parents laid down the law. Any other time, she could come and go as she pleased. But that night, they wanted her home. And for no apparent reason, other than the fact that they wanted to talk to her and Garrett about something."

Maybe we were finally on to something. "Did she have any theories why?"

Tess rubbed her hands on her jeans. "No idea. She thought maybe her parents were going to announce they were getting divorced or maybe that one of them was sick with cancer. She had no idea. She hoped they would say they were moving back to England. She said she liked it when her dad didn't work so much. That hadn't happened since they moved to America."

I stored away the new information. Very interesting.

"Is there anything else you can think of? Anyone who acted strangely around Cassidy?" Sometimes that final, open-ended question brought about the best answers.

She looked to the side in thought. "This is probably nothing. But I know there was this guy who had a crush on her. Sometimes, he kind of gave her the creeps."

My adrenaline started to bubble. "Who was he?"

"His name was . . ." She shook her head. "I can't remember. She called him the Silent One. All I remember is that her family and a couple of families from her dad's work used to take vacations together. Like, extravagant vacations, even by my standards. I think they rented an entire Caribbean island once. One of the guys from those trips was always watching her."

My spine clinched. Watching her? That, of course, made me think of the Watcher. It also made me think of that beach picture I'd seen in Cassidy's room. Was the Silent One in that photo? "What else can you remember?"

"I want to say he wasn't a direct family member, but he was on the fringe somehow. He could have even worked for the vacationing families, for all I know. Something always seemed a little off about him. I remember something about his mom having a disability.

Maybe mental? Maybe she was in a home? I know this is all vague."

"No, it's helpful," I insisted.

That seemed to encourage her, because she kept talking.

"Cassidy used to always say that the Silent One should get together with The Clingy One. It was some girl who liked her brother."

"I guess when you're rich and beautiful, everyone likes you," Jamie muttered.

"That's not always a blessing," Tess whispered. "Everyone wants to use you is more like it."

"If you think of anything else, let us know," I encouraged.

Tess nodded. "I will. I probably wasn't much help. No one really takes me very seriously."

I could give her some advice in that area, starting with: *Stop examining your nails and hair.* But I didn't.

"You were great," I said instead. And she had offered some interesting information. "Thank you."

We walked back to the car. I wanted to rehash everything with the girls, but before I could, my phone cried for my attention. I didn't recognize the number, which always set me on edge.

I hit the speaker button, but before I said anything, the caller spoke. "Hello, Gabby."

The Watcher.

I didn't waste time with formalities. "You were responsible last night, weren't you? That chlorine leak was no accident."

"There were a lot of bad people there. People who only think of themselves. They need to pay. I just wanted to give them a taste of their own medicine. The resulting fire wasn't supposed to happen."

I exchanged glances with Holly and Jamie, who were both riveted on the conversation.

"Why not just shoot me? Why put those other people in danger?"

"That's not the way this works. It wasn't about you last night. It was about making a statement."

I shook my head, trying to figure out what this guy was thinking. "That makes no sense."

"I determine what makes sense."

Maybe it was time to stop playing nicely. "Well, you're delusional. Why do you keep giving me these warnings? What kind of game are you playing?"

"My ways are not yours to question."

"You have a God complex or something?" My words were tinged with anger. I was tired of playing and being played.

"Life and death are in my hands, whether I like it or not."

Something about his statement didn't sit right with me, but I didn't have time to examine it at the moment.

"Why not just leave this be? Why continue the killing? You could have just disappeared, like you have been for the last ten years. But instead you come out now. You put yourself at risk."

"I wish I could stop." His voice seemed to soften.

I decided to take a risk. I remembered what Tess had said about the Silent One from those family trips. She'd mentioned something about his mom suffering some kind of illness. "How's your mom doing?"

He paused for just a millisecond. "My mom? What does she have to do with any of this?"

"I heard that she wasn't well." Maybe if I fished for answers, he'd take the bait. Could this be the same man whom Tess had mentioned? Someone who'd had a crush on Cassidy? Who was somehow connected with Wimbledon Pharmaceuticals?

"Leave my mom out of this," he barked. "You don't know what you're talking about."

My pulse spiked. Could this be what I was looking for? "Did Cassidy reject you? Because, if she did, that wasn't very nice. But you really need to get over it. We all get rejected." Riley's face flashed through my mind.

"You're asking too many questions." His voice rose with emotion. "Don't get me in trouble. Watch your back. I'm not done with you yet, Ms. St. Claire."

The line went dead.

I turned and glanced at Holly and Jamie. Their faces had gone slack, but their eyes certainly reflected mine.

We were on to something and that was enough to get excited about.

"I think you struck a nerve," Jamie muttered.

"Maybe this conversation with Tess was just the turning point we needed. We have to find out who went on those vacations. I'm going to talk to Garrett, see what he remembers."

"You feel comfortable being near him?" Holly asked.

I nodded slowly. "Yeah, I do. I really hope I don't regret trusting him."

"All I know is that phone call was creepy," Holly said.

I agreed with my new friend. But there was something else that bothered me. The Watcher had said he could get in trouble. The only way he could get in trouble was if he was working for someone.

Was this man just another player in a twisted game?

CHAPTER 26

I sat at a coffeehouse in an area of Cincinnati known as Over the Rhine. When it came to rough areas of town, I'd bet this was considered one of the worst. It was just a guess, but the area was located in downtown Cincinnati and felt very inner city poor.

But Holly and Jamie had insisted that the coffeehouse was one of the best in the area, and I had to agree that my caramel macchiato was tasty. The servers all were grungy with piercings, tattoos, and funky hair. The patrons were varied, and the interior was nothing fancy.

I'd wanted to chat with Garrett, but when I'd called Lyndsey answered his phone and informed me that Garrett was in the middle of an important business call. As much as I wanted answers now, I decided to let my theories simmer. I tried to brush off my curiosity about Garrett's meeting and his relationship with Lyndsey, too.

The woman had a certain possessiveness in her gaze that was fine with me. She could have Garrett all to herself.

As we huddled in a corner, Jamie pulled open her laptop. "What do you want me to look up? You name it, I'll do an Internet search for it. They don't call me Twinkle Fingers for nothing."

I wasn't used to having such willing accomplices . . . er, helpers.

"I hardly know where to begin. I really think, at this

point, that the murders are somehow tied in with Wimbledon Pharmaceuticals, in part because those vacations Tess mentioned were with people from the company."

"The Watcher certainly reacted when you mentioned his mom, which would line up with your theory," Jamie said. "If that's the case, the motive would go back to Cassidy instead of Edward, though. Right?"

"Possibly," I said. "My gut is still telling me that Edward was the killer's primary focus. Until I talk to Garrett, I have no way of obtaining any more information on those vacations, including who was there and what happened. Edward is a better one to start with. He was having marital problems and maybe even problems at work also."

"What kind of problems at work?" Holly asked. She batted her eyelashes, truly reminding me of someone from the fifties—innocent and sweet.

"I talked to his coworkers and they gave no indication that anything was wrong." Then again, people lied all the time, especially if it was in their best interest.

"But things aren't always as perfect as they seem," Holly reminded us.

"Then what about his marital problems?" Jamie asked.

"I know the police and the FBI examined Mr. Mercer's love life pretty extensively," I told them. "They found all of his affairs very suspect. But the police questioned all of those women and cleared them." It was why I hadn't questioned any of them.

"Is Garrett like that?" Holly asked. "A womanizer?"

I frowned. "I thought he was. Now I don't know. He confuses me."

"Typical man," Jamie proclaimed.

We all laughed. Her words were too, too true.

I sobered when I remembered the case. I warmed my

hands around my mug and leaned forward. "Let's just imagine for a moment that somehow this murder had something to do with Edward's job. The problem is: How do we prove that? I don't have access to anything at the company, and I have no way to get access. Plus, there's the fact that Vic Newport's daughter was pregnant with Garrett Mercer's child, and the fact that he wasn't home when his daughter arrived there on the evening of the murders."

"Vic Newport, huh?" Jamie mumbled. She tapped away at her computer. A moment later, she turned the screen to us. "Check out this picture. Is it just me or is Vic Newport giving the strangest look to the woman posing with him?"

I leaned closer to the computer and studied the picture. I recognized Vic Newport, and both Reginald Jr. and Smith Wimbledon. There were also three others in the photo. They were accepting some kind of award. The woman wasn't named in the caption.

"She does look familiar." I shook my head, unable to place her. Maybe I'd seen her in the office that day? At the gala?

The woman had short brown hair, a long nose, glasses, and a matronly suit. The date on the picture said it was taken six years ago. The woman looked to be in her mid-twenties, I'd guess.

I looked away. "I'm not sure if this photo helps us. Maybe it was just taken in one of those off moments and the look on Vic Newport's face means nothing. I'm not sure it tells us anything."

Jamie sat up, her eyes bright. "Maybe I could help find some answers about Mr. Newport."

"How do you propose to do that?" Hope tinged my voice.

"Maybe I could say I want to write an article on the

company." She shrugged. "I am a freelance journalist. I've written for some local magazines and newspapers. As I was surfing around online, I saw that Mr. Newport won a leadership award. It's the perfect angle for a human-interest story. Companies love stuff like that."

I was sure Portman from Publicity would jump at the opportunity.

But her suggestion was risky. Intriguing, but risky. "What if they say yes to an interview? What then? Are you going to sneak off and search through their files?"

She shrugged. "I don't know. But something is better than nothing, right?"

I shook my head. "I don't want to put you in harm's way or get you in trouble."

"Girl, I'm putting myself in harm's way and getting myself in trouble. But I'm okay with that. Besides, I've got a good head on my shoulders. I know how to be sly."

I glanced at Holly. She nodded enthusiastically.

"I'd trust her," Holly added. "A girl who has enough self control to lose 100 pounds can handle something like this."

"Really?" I questioned.

Jamie tilted her head. "Girl, I was fat. Went from 260 to 160. Now people can't take enough pictures of me. In fact, I photo bomb people as often as possible. That's how proud I am of this new body."

She ran her hand up and down, as if showcasing herself.

"I'm impressed. Losing that much weight is not an easy task." I didn't even have the willpower to give up coffee. Not that I'd ever tried. I mean, the very idea was ludicrous.

Jamie stared at me, waiting for my response, light dancing in her eyes. "Besides, I might not even get the interview. This is just an idea. I mean, it's not like you can go, Gabby. They've already seen your face there."

She had a point.

"Let's test the waters," I conceded. "I doubt you'll even get in. They seemed pretty stringent."

Jamie still tapped away at the computer. "I'm sending an interview request email now and marking it urgent."

Before I could say anything else, my cellphone started singing, "That's Amore."

My heart sped.

Riley.

CHAPTER 27

I stepped outside—despite a warning from Jamie and Holly that this wasn't a safe area of town—and put the phone to my ear. "Hey, Riley."

"Hey, Gabby. I've missed you."

My heart warmed. Maybe I was reading too much into this and things really were fine between us. "I've missed you, too. How are you? How's therapy going?"

"I think I'm making some progress. I mean, living with my parents isn't ideal. Not at my age. But I think the decision was good."

"I'm glad." I stayed under the ripped awning as water dripped from the nighttime sky.

"How are you, Gabby?"

I looked around me as a police officer chased a man down the street. I remembered being drugged, my tires being slashed, and my every move being watched. "Doing okay. Nothing too exciting here."

"I saw the picture."

I searched my brain for a frame of reference but got nothing. "The picture?"

"The one in the paper. You were rescuing a woman from a hotel in Cincinnati."

Surprise—and maybe guilt?—washed over me. "Oh, that picture. All the way out in D.C., huh?"

"It made national news. You have that many powerful people in one place and it gets attention."

Why hadn't I considered that? So much for keeping this under wraps. On the other hand, I was amazed that Riley had put that together. Again, how his brain worked right now continued to perplex me.

"You would think people had better things to report on, right?" Again, I kept my voice light. As two police cars came blaring my way, I stepped back inside, trading privacy for safety.

"You didn't tell me you accepted the P.I. job." Hurt lined his voice.

"I didn't want to stress you out," I told him honestly. "I was trying to keep things simple."

"You could have told me."

"Things just seem so complicated right now, Riley." Maybe I shouldn't have said the words. Maybe I shouldn't stir things up. But what I'd said was the truth.

I secretly wanted him to correct me. To insist that things were simple. That nothing had changed.

Instead, he said, "You're right. Things do feel complicated."

Silence stretched. I didn't know exactly what to say. So I figured I should say exactly that. "What's this mean for us, Riley?" My throat ached as I said the words.

"My therapist says—"

"No offense, Riley. I'm sure your therapist is very wise. But I really want to know what you have to say." I closed my eyes, waiting for his response, trying to ignore the dread forming in my gut.

"I'm just trying to take it one day at a time, Gabby. You've been my rock."

"I want to be your rock now."

"Gabby . . ." Silence stretched another moment.

I could tell he was trying to find the words. "Yes?"

"I need to go," he finally said. "My head is pounding.

But we'll talk again soon, okay?"

I pressed my lips together, trying not to let my chin quiver. "Okay, let's talk soon."

I hung up and stared at my phone a moment.

Just what did all of that mean? And how was I ever going to come to terms with all the real and potential changes in my life.

***

The next morning I went to church with the Paladins. Part of me had wanted to skip services and continue investigating. I couldn't do that, though. If I did, my life would be out of balance. If God could take time to rest, then certainly I could, too.

Being around the Paladin family fascinated me. Mrs. Paladin always had a big smile stretched across her face, Alex had a dry sense of humor, Ralphie may have been a bigger schmoozer than Garrett, and Holly just sat back, soaking them all in.

They'd moved on from the heartache of losing their dad; yet, they had no idea about Holly. I hoped she told them soon.

It was good to see a family that had pulled through a tragedy and were stronger than before. Tragedy had only torn my family apart. Just as tragedy continued to pull my world apart now. I had to make the uncertainty in my life work to my advantage, work to make me a better person.

After church, we had lunch. I met Alex the Great's fiancé. Holly's "friend" (and Ralphie's campaign manager) Brian had also stopped by. I had the impression that Sunday lunches were important to the family; that they rarely missed them. I also had the impression that the family often included others. Being around them made me miss my friends in Norfolk. I'd see them soon enough, I supposed—provided that I hadn't been evicted from my apartment building under a potential new owner.

Jamie called as lunch wrapped up, and Holly handed the phone to me. "You'll never believe this," Jamie rushed.

"Believe what?"

"Wimbledon Pharmaceuticals emailed me back."

"On a Sunday?" It sounded like other people needed some of that same balance I'd been seeking lately.

"I know. That's what I said. I guess their PR people work around the clock. They agreed to an interview tomorrow."

"No way!"

"It's true. It helped that I gave them a deadline of Tuesday."

"You sure you're okay with doing this?" I still had concerns.

"You know it. They want all of the positive publicity they can get on their employees and their charitable efforts. I might just have to throw in a few questions to throw them off guard, though." She paused. "One other thing. I called Rebecca Newport again."

"And?"

"She said a whole bunch of stuff. Most of it didn't make sense. Honestly, I think the drugs messed up the woman and she still has a few screws loose. But she did say one thing that caught my attention. She said her ex, Vic Newport, had one mean temper."

"Enough of a temper that maybe he snapped and pulled the trigger?"

"That's the question."

When I hung up with Jamie, I called Garrett. I needed to ask him about his vacations. I hoped Lyndsey didn't answer again. She didn't.

"Where's your assistant?" I couldn't stop myself from asking.

"Headed back to Norfolk this morning. You're not jealous I was spending time with her, are you?"

"Don't flatter yourself. I was just worried because of your emergency board meeting."

"Nothing to worry your pretty little head over. Now, what can I do for you, Shirleylock?"

I didn't love the nickname, but I ignored it. It was better than him calling me Love. "I'd like to ask you a few questions and also to get a photo from Cassidy's room."

"You've got me curious now. How about if I meet you at the house in thirty?"

A half an hour later, I pulled up to the Mercer house. No sooner had I put my car in park when that familiar uncomfortable feeling washed over me. The feeling of being watched.

For that reason, I stayed in the car and waited.

I never let my gaze stop roaming the area.

I'd almost been here for a week, and I knew if I didn't wrap this case up soon, I was going to have to leave this unfinished and do the rest of my research back in Norfolk. I didn't want to do that. My best chances were here in Cincinnati, and I did feel like I was getting closer. I had to remember that the police had worked on this for years without any conclusions. Who was I to think I could wrap it up in a week?

I scanned the woods again. Whoever this guy was threatening me, he may not hesitate to put a bullet through the windshield and, in effect, through my head. Especially not after I'd aggravated him yesterday.

Thankfully, Garrett pulled up just then. With two of us here . . . well, what protection was that? Both of us could die now, I supposed.

Garrett looked a little sad as he approached my car. I saw the haunted look in his eyes. This case was beginning to weigh on him. I realized that, with everything that had happened, it was no longer just a cold case; it was now an active investigation. Covering up his mourning with his charm was becoming more difficult.

"Gabby. Good to see you again."

"Thanks for meeting with me." I took his arm and pulled him toward the door. "We're too exposed out here. We've got to get inside."

"You think . . ." His eyes scanned the perimeter of the land, only briefly, and then his steps picked up. "Let's go."

We reached the door, he unlocked it, and we rushed inside.

As soon as we stepped onto the tiled entryway, we froze.

Someone had been here. They'd either been looking for us or trying to send a message. The couch was overturned, pictures were slashed, curtains were ripped.

"I guess it's time to call the police again," Garrett muttered.

I squeezed his arm, seeing the pain in his eyes. I had a feeling that, through this vandalism, he was somehow reliving coming into his house and finding his family. How did someone get over a tragedy like that? They either made themselves better or they let their grief consume them. Consuming grief led to depression, despair, and sometimes even psychotic episodes.

Which one was Garrett? The overcomer everyone thought he was? Or a man with split personalities, a man who set up crime scenes like this to keep people interested in the case?

I shook the thought off, thinking about that bullet that could have hit him.

But then I remembered that he'd lied about being in town on the night of the murders. I thought about him disappearing at the gala, those cellphones in his car, the fact that Garrett had never been with me when the Watcher called.

My thoughts were ridiculous, and I needed to put them to rest. A man who spent his life trying to help the less fortunate in other countries wasn't secretly a mass murderer.

He pulled out his cellphone and dialed 911. "The police are on their way."

"Can I go into Cassidy's room before they get here?" I knew if I didn't get to that information now, I was going to have to wait until the scene cleared. I didn't have that time.

"I thought we shouldn't touch anything?"

"Whoever did this didn't leave any evidence. I think we both know that."

He stared at me a moment and then nodded. "Okay. Let's go."

I was careful not to disturb anything as I followed Garrett upstairs to his sister's bedroom. The inside of this room had also been tussled. Someone had wanted to make a serious statement, or they were looking for something. My bets were on making a statement.

"What do you need to look at?"

I went straight to the pictures on her dresser and grabbed them. I knew I didn't have much time. "How about journals?"

He shook his head. "She wasn't the journaling type."

"Are there any more photo albums or pictures around here?"

He pointed to a basket by the closet. "Check over there."

I slipped some gloves on.

"Gloves?"

"You never know when you might need them."

Garrett raised his eyebrows. "I hear you. You better get moving."

I began riffling through the most promising looking photos, grabbing any I saw from the beach. I wished I could ask Garrett questions as I went, but I knew I had no time.

"What are you looking for?"

"I don't know for sure. But I'll know when I find it."

He paced back toward the door. "The police are here, Gabby. You've got to get downstairs."

I rushed through a few more pictures. My fingers moved more frantically as my heart rate quickened.

"They're at the door. We've got to go."

I grabbed a small album. "I'll give these back. I promise."

I shoved them into my oversized purse, thrust the basket back in place, and went to meet the officers at the door.

CHAPTER 28

I studied the pictures while eating at a rib place overlooking the Ohio. I'd opted out of the messiness factor of world famous, slathered barbecue ribs and had gotten a chicken sandwich instead. If I kept eating on this trip, I was going to gain twenty pounds. My friends would tell me that was okay since I'd lost a considerable amount of weight during the stress of the last few months.

As I inhaled the scents of vinegar and grease and smoky cumin, I picked up a picture album. The photos in front of me showed happy, cocky teens playing volleyball, sunbathing, on each other's shoulders in the pool. I spotted some photos—probably not from vacations—of Tess Windsor and Marty Mart. I searched the other faces for someone familiar.

Garrett slid into the booth across from me. He'd slipped away to talk to Lyndsey for a minute about something that couldn't wait.

"Everything okay?" I asked.

He shrugged. "I wanted to check in about a special project she's working on for me, but she didn't answer."

"Certainly you let your employees have a life outside of work."

"I do. But she's my right hand man—woman, I should say. I pay her well to be available."

I raised my eyebrows.

"In a business capacity," he added. "What kind of a

239

man do you think I am?"

I shook my head. "The two of you just seem close."

"We work well together."

I raised a hand to stop him from saying anything. "You don't have to explain to me. It's none of my business."

And it wasn't. Their interactions just had me curious.

He cast another inquisitive glance my way before leaning toward the sea of photos on the table between us and frowning. "Tell me what you're thinking, Love."

I wiped my hands—salty from my fries—and held up a photo of Garrett and Cassidy posing together on the beach. "Tell me about your vacations growing up. I heard you took some fancy ones. Your family and maybe a couple of other families. From your dad's work."

"Oh, those. Yes, I suppose we did. I tried not to hang too much with the family back then. I thought I was too cool for that. Don't I wish I could go back now?" He took a long sip of his iced tea.

"Hindsight truly is 20/20. Who are these people in the photos?"

He studied a couple of them. "It varies, I suppose. I know the Newports went. Reginald Wimbledon came a couple of times with his family. Smith Wimbledon came also. I think they all used it as a tax write off. The men had business meetings for half of the day while the rest of us partied."

"Was there anyone on those trips who stood out?"

He shrugged and shook his head. "To be honest, Olivia and I were pretty wrapped up in each other. I didn't pay attention to anyone else."

I watched his expression for a tell tale sign of deception. He kept his gaze steady, though. "Who was the Clingy One?"

He tilted his head. "The Clingy One? I haven't heard

that name in a long time. I suppose that would be Jenna Royce—Sebastian's flavor-of-the-month wife. They came with us once. Back then, he was in his mid-forties and she was 21, I think. It was obvious she only married him for his money. That woman hit on every eligible guy on that trip."

"Have you seen Jenna lately?"

"Saw her a couple of years ago. She's happily married now with two kids. Living in New York. Why are you asking?"

I shook my head. "I can probably rule her out then. Do you remember a guy who liked your sister?"

He raised his eyebrows wryly. "Every guy liked my sister."

I stared at the pictures spread between us. "Someone who was kind of on the fringe. Maybe he came on the trips, but he wasn't a direct blood relative with the rest of the family?"

He shook his head. "That doesn't ring any bells. But, like I said, I was pretty self-absorbed back then. Are you going to explain?"

I took a long sip of my Mountain Dew. "Tess Windsor— you remember her?"

Garrett nodded. "My sister's snooty friend."

"I talked to her yesterday and she mentioned something about a guy who liked your sister. Then, when the Watcher called yesterday, I said something to him about those vacations. It shook him up, so I wonder now if I was on to something."

"You very well could be." He rubbed the side of his glass and stared out the window.

"I'm going to keep researching. But, in the meantime, I don't want to close any doors or get too narrow-minded."

"Sounds like a solid principle."

"Tess mentioned maybe this guy's mom was sick. Does

that ring any bells?"

Garrett shook his head. "I really have no idea." He stared out the window again. "Now that I'm thinking about it, I suppose Smith Wimbledon's mom did have cancer."

That was interesting. "Is she still alive?"

"If I remember correctly, she's struggled with the disease on and off for years." Garrett held up a photo and pointed to a young man with blond hair. "That's Smith when he was younger."

"Were you guys friends?"

He shrugged. "He was a little older, a little more studious. I think he preferred hanging out with adults more than he did with the teens."

I pointed to a woman with dark hair standing beside him in one of the photos. "Who's this?"

"His sister, Winnie Wimbledon."

I studied the photo more closely. I couldn't tell enough from that snapshot. I searched through the rest of the pictures until I found a better image of her. In another shot, she stood in a group in front of tropical waters. Except, she kind of stood apart from the group. She didn't match the rest of the gang, who all had self-assured smiles and boisterous mannerisms.

She was the woman in the online photo with Vic Newport, I realized. The one Vic was giving a strange look. The one I'd seen somewhere before.

"What do you know about her?" I asked.

"Last I heard, she was working for the family business. She was always kind of quiet and didn't draw much attention to herself. Honestly, we hardly talked. She seemed to prefer a good book to people. The Wimbledons were kind of like that. Quieter, more intellectual."

I had to chew on that information some more. In the meantime, I had more questions for my temporary boss.

"Garrett, do you have any idea what your dad wanted to talk to you about?" I was pretty sure I'd asked everyone except Garrett that question. "Why he wanted you home that weekend? It's my understanding that your dad didn't demand very much from you or your sister, but that he was serious about everyone being together."

He shrugged. "I've thought about that many times. I'm not really sure. And you're right. He pretty much let us do our own thing. Of course, he expected us to be there for family weddings or funerals or times when we needed to appear cohesive and happy."

His words had a touch of bitterness to them.

"I see."

"My dad did a lot of things right. He was a hard worker. But I learned a lot from him on what *not* to do. When I have my own family one day, they're going to know that they're my priority."

"I didn't know your dad, but you don't seem like him, Garrett." Had I just paid the man a compliment? What had gotten into me?

He smiled sadly. "Thank you." He twisted the watch at his wrist. "This used to be my father's, you know. Probably the only thing I've kept that was his. I mean, in reality I've kept everything. But this is the only thing I really see every day."

"It's nice." I wasn't done with my questions, though. "Your cabin was to the south of your home, yet you were photographed on the night of the murders at a gas station to the west. It was part of the reason the police never suspected you."

His eyes widened. "You do your research."

"That's why you're paying me the big bucks."

"Absolutely. You're right. After Olivia left me, I stayed at the cabin for a while, trying to let everything sink in. I'd told my parents I wasn't making it in that evening because I had to turn in a paper. I didn't want to pull up to the house in the middle of the night. So I started driving around."

"Why didn't you just come clean about being in town that night? Why hide what really happened?" I'd had a day to chew on what he'd told me, and now I had more questions.

He grabbed a toothpick and twirled it in his mouth. "A couple of reasons. First of all, I'd promised Olivia to keep her pregnancy quiet until she figured out what to do."

"Until she figured it out?"

"She wasn't giving me much choice in it. As I was driving away that night, I determined I'd talk to her again, convince her to have the baby. I played with the idea of taking her to court over it."

Surprise filled me. "Really?"

The sparkle that normally graced his eyes was nowhere to be seen. Maybe he was finally letting down some of his walls. "I believe in life, Gabby. Life at conception. I didn't really want to be a father, but the idea was sobering and made me realize I needed to reevaluate my priorities."

My throat burned. I wished it was from the hot sauce, but instead it was from the horrific reality that Garrett had experienced. "Then you discovered your family."

New lines appeared on his face. "I'm not saying I forgot about Olivia. Not by any means. But I had to put that on the back burner for a while. By the time I spoke with Olivia again, she told me that she'd actually miscarried the evening after our talk. All of our arguing was for nothing, I suppose."

"Yet you still didn't tell the police."

He planted his palms on the table. "I knew how it would look, Gabby. And here I had this alibi that I hadn't even tried to get. People from college claiming I'd stayed at the party longer than I had. The gas station. No witnesses to me being at the cabin."

I grabbed a dinner roll from the center of the table and pulled off a piece. I nibbled on it, my thoughts turning. I could feel it in my blood that I was getting closer to the answers. But I wasn't there, yet.

"What are you thinking?" Garrett asked. "I can see those mental wheels turning."

"Olivia said she went home after she met with you that night, Garrett."

"Okay . . ."

"She said her father wasn't there. She also said that she gave him an alibi when the police asked. She claimed they'd both been in all evening."

His eyebrows scrunched together. "Where was he?"

I shook my head. "I have no idea."

"You don't think . . ."

"I think all of this has something to do with your dad's work. I just need to figure out what. There's no way I'm getting into his office to look at his things there. But your dad seemed like someone who'd bring work home with him."

"He most certainly did."

"This cabin you mentioned, the one you and Olivia went to . . ."

"It was my dad's place. He liked to go there when he needed to get away. Of course, he always brought work with him."

"Do you still own it?"

Garrett nodded. "I do."

"Can I see it?"

"Let's go."

CHAPTER 29

As we drove from Cincinnati toward the hills of Kentucky, my mind wandered to Riley. He couldn't drive yet after his brain injury, so I'd been taking him everywhere. Simple places—places we'd gone all the time—he suddenly couldn't remember how to get there. Sometimes he'd forget where we were going in route.

The memories pulled at me. I tried to push away the melancholy that came with the thoughts, but the emotions seemed stronger than my willpower.

My cellphone rang, pulling me from my drowning thoughts.

My heart raced for a moment. The Watcher? Or someone else?

It was Sierra.

"Where are you calling from?" I asked. It wasn't her normal ringtone. Clarice may have been onto something when she programmed my phone for me because I was starting to depend on those digital cues.

"I'm working late on a protest we're planning here at work. But I promised you I'd call as soon as I heard anything."

"About the apartment," I realized with a dull thud of my heart.

"We were informed today that it sold. The 'For Sale' sign disappeared and everything."

"That was quick." Just like that, more pieces of my life

felt like they were slipping away.

"Yeah, tell me about it. I heard the person who bought it paid cash, so that cut the time virtually down to nothing."

"Are we being kicked out?" I hardly wanted to hear her answer. I just wanted things to go back to the way they used to be; yet, that wasn't possible. Change would always be a part of life. I had to somehow come to accept that fact.

"That's what I haven't heard yet. I'm sorry, Gabby. I know it's not what you want to hear."

"Thanks for letting me know."

"Oh, and before we get off the phone, Chad wanted me to tell you 'Partners in Grime.' I told him it was lame."

"Tell him I echo your thoughts on that one. Let's keep thinking."

I hung up and noticed Garrett glanced at me from the driver's seat. "Everything okay?"

I told him about the apartment building being sold. What I didn't tell him was how that building was where I'd met my best friend Sierra. Or how I'd met Riley in the parking lot on his first night as a resident as he tried to get a parrot down from the tree outside his window. Nor did I tell him the horrific things that happened there. The man who'd been murdered in my kitchen. Or how Milton Jones had sneaked in to threaten me in the middle of the night.

"You think the person who bought it will kick you out?"

"I'm preparing myself to look for another place." Away from Sierra and Chad. Away from my crazy, radio talk show host neighbor Bill McCormick. Away from the eccentric writer I called Mrs. Mystery.

Away from Riley's place.

That apartment building had so many memories for me.

Maybe moving would be for the best. That's what I needed to convince myself of, at least.

I'd been saying that life wasn't based on luck, but there were times I felt like the most unlucky girl in the world. No, since I was a crime scene cleaner, maybe I had more *muck* than luck—in more than one way. An image of those impossible to remove streaks of oil flashed back into my mind again.

"I know it will all work out, Gabby," Garrett said.

I wished I felt that sure.

We pulled up to a cabin nestled in the woods along a river. It wasn't nearly as extravagant as the Mercer's mansion, but the place was still a nice size. I stared at it from the passenger's seat.

"Was it weird that your dad had this place?"

Garrett shrugged and cut the engine. "After we moved here, my dad seemed to like time by himself. Money was never an issue, so buying this place wasn't really a big deal. My dad mostly used it, but I came here some."

We climbed out of the car. The sun was setting and the pleasant smears of a fluorescent sunset lit the sky beyond the river. I could see where someone might want to come here to relax.

"Have you been here in a while?"

"I actually do like to come here for personal retreats, to revitalize myself and think about the company."

I'd known Garrett's lifestyle was different than mine, but just the thought of being able to get away and have weekends to clear your head made me realize how far apart our worlds were. I couldn't even entertain the thought of such a luxury.

"Who keeps this place up for you?" I stepped onto the massive wooden porch, longing for a moment to sit on one of those rocking chairs and simply relax.

"I use a management company. They rent a lot of cabins in this area. Of course, I don't rent mine, but this business manages the property. That works for me."

"Sounds expensive."

"Maybe. But there are some things that I just can't get rid of. My mom insured that I didn't ever have to worry about money. I've invested in a few different properties."

He unlocked the door, and we stepped inside. The cabin was cozy and just the kind of place I'd love to go on a quiet vacation or for a romantic getaway. There was a two-story fireplace, a loft, and a wall of windows showing the river behind the property.

"It's chilly in here, isn't it? Maybe I'll start a quick fire to warm it up. I know we won't be here long, but at least we'll be comfortable. Besides, a nice fire always helps me relax and relaxing sounds really good right now."

While he worked on the fire, I wandered around downstairs, looking at pictures of Garrett and his family.

You'd never have to worry about money with me again.

That's what Garrett had told me. For a moment—and just a moment—that idea tempted me beyond what I was prepared for. It would be so nice to not have to worry about paying the bills or where I was going to live or what my future would hold. Not that money or love would answer all of those questions. But stability sounded nice.

I stepped toward the window and stared at the sunset against the river. I wished my heart felt as peaceful as that sunset. The pastor at my church had once said that peace comes with understanding. But maybe peace really just came with accepting—accepting your circumstances, accepting the uncertainties in life, accepting that some things were simply beyond your control.

"The fire's blazing. Hopefully it will warm up in here soon." Garrett's voice sounded close.

Without turning I could sense him behind me. In the briefest flash of desire, I imagined him putting his arms around me and holding me close.

My heart lurched. I loved Riley. So why was I feeling these things?

"You okay?" Garrett asked.

I didn't dare look at him. Instead, I stared out the window and crossed my arms. "Yeah, I'm going to be fine."

"Gabby . . ."

I still didn't turn. I didn't trust myself. That first kiss with Garrett had been all his doing. If we kissed again, I'd have to take responsibility.

I cleared my throat. "Yes?"

His hand went to my shoulder. Heat from his touch seemed to sear through my clothing all the way to my skin. The cabin, the fire, the sunset . . . it was proving to be too much for me.

Before I let myself down in a major way, I decided to remove myself from temptation—kind of like Joseph fleeing from Potiphar's wife. I darted to the other side of the room, my heart pounding in my ears.

"We should stay focused."

Garrett shoved his hands into his pockets. "Of course. What do you want to look at here? I wasn't quite clear."

Great, he probably thought I'd asked to come here as some kind of excuse for a rendezvous.

I shook my head, determined to stay strong. "I don't know. I want to figure out what your dad wanted to talk to you about. If this was his space, then maybe there's a clue."

Garrett nodded slowly, pinching his lips together. "Okay then. Where do you want to start?"

I started pacing. "I'm not really sure. Did your dad have an office here?"

"Right upstairs. I can take you there."

I nodded and followed him, ignoring the urging in my head to run. I'd been called a lot of things in life, but I'd never been called unfaithful. I didn't plan on adding that to my list.

"Did the police come here?"

"The police went everywhere. I'm sure they came here, but I don't remember them finding anything of significance."

"Did your dad have any kind of safe where he might keep valuables?" *Or secrets?*

Garrett shook his head. "You mean, like hiding behind a picture?"

I nodded. "Whatever floats your boat."

"Typical myth about the wealthy. We don't keep safes behind wall art."

I shoved a painting out of the way, just to prove his point. What I saw made me pause. A metal plate. In the wall. With a small door. "Are you sure about that?"

Garrett stepped closer and squinted. "No way . . ."

"Maybe hiding a safe here is so obvious that it's not obvious."

"You've got to be kidding me." He took the picture off the wall and examined the metal box there. A combination lock was nestled in the center. "I'll be darned."

Yeah, me too. I truly hadn't expected anything to be there. But I wasn't complaining, either.

"You know the combination?"

He shook his head. "No, but I'd be willing to try a few things."

He tried a couple of different combinations, his eyebrows thoughtfully knit together as he spun the dial. "What else could it be?"

"Birthdays?"

"I tried those."

"Addresses?" I suggested.

"Tried some of those, too."

"Maybe some kind of code from when you lived in England? Similar to a zip code?"

"It's worth a shot." He spun the numbers around again.

The next moment, the door popped open.

I held my breath as I waited to see what was inside.

CHAPTER 30

Garrett reached inside and his hand emerged with a wad of cash. And then another. And another.

"That's a lot of money," I muttered.

There were blocks and blocks of hundred dollar bills. "There are thousands of dollars in here."

Even Garrett, who had a lot of money, seemed in awe.

"Why would your dad keep money here?" I asked. "Certainly he had accounts."

"Beats me." Garrett pulled out some papers, his eyes widening as he studied the contents. "Offshore accounts. Worth millions. Where did he get this money?"

"Maybe it was your mom's?"

He shook his head. "No, my mom kept a tight rein on her money. It was all in her name, even. She insisted on buying the house and keeping it in her name. She said something about her parents advising her to do that."

"How'd your dad feel about that?"

Garrett shrugged. "Not sure, but I can imagine it wasn't a great premise to have in their marriage."

I nodded toward the safe, resisting the urge to reach into it myself. "There's more."

Garrett pulled out a box and, holding it against his chest, opened it up. Passports were inside, along with awards, resumes, and driver's licenses.

His family's pictures graced the covers, but . . .

"That's not your name," I blurted, pointing to one of

the licenses.

Garrett looked at me. "I have no idea what this means, Gabby. My father has fake driver's licenses, not only for himself, but also for the rest of the family. Passports. Offshore accounts. Tons of cash."

"He was planning to run. Maybe that's what he wanted to talk to you about. I mean, look at the dates on this resume. It says his last job ended the week before he died."

Garrett sunk down on the floor, still staring at the information in the box. "I just don't understand. Why would he run?"

"Did he get himself in trouble? Witness protection? Maybe he had to testify against someone at the drug company who'd done something illegal?"

"I have no idea."

Before I could second guess myself, I slid down onto the floor beside him and squeezed his hand. "I'm sorry, Garrett."

He nodded. "Me too."

I picked up a resume and studied it a moment. "Garrett, according to this resume, your dad's last job wasn't at Wimbledon. It was at a company called Dermott Technologies. I've never even heard of that company."

Garrett took the paper from me. "What? This makes no sense."

"Maybe he was creating a new identity for himself. Maybe he needed to cover up parts of his past."

"Why?"

I shook my head. "I'll do my best to wade through all of this. My next question is: Are you sure you're prepared for the answers?"

***

"We need to call the police."

Garrett shook his head. "Not yet. Please. Just give me a day. Let me try and figure out what was going on."

I stared at him. I saw the pain in the depths of his eyes. I saw the suspicions that somehow his father was betraying his family by keeping secrets—big secrets. I tried to put myself in his shoes.

"A day," I finally told him. The investigation wasn't ongoing, but I didn't want to impede anything.

I knew Garrett worried that this information would somehow make his father look bad, and that he wanted to do his own research first. I really hoped this wasn't his way of trying to cover up something—like his own guilt in this.

We'd moved downstairs in front of the fire, and we'd brought everything from the safe with us. I also pulled out Cassidy's pictures. All the information was spread out on the coffee table. Garrett and I sat beside each other on the couch, each mulling over our thoughts.

"Can we talk this through?" I finally asked.

Garrett nodded, still looking more somber than I'd ever seen him. "Why not?"

"Okay." I crossed my legs and sucked in a deep breath. "I still believe that this is somehow tied in with your family's vacations, which always included people from his work. That means that Wimbledon Pharmaceuticals could somehow be connected."

"Remind me why you think that again? My head feels like it might burst right now."

"That's based on a couple of things, including my conversation with Tess. I also heard hints that your father hadn't been very happy at work. What if your dad was a whistleblower?"

Garrett shook his head. "He wouldn't have run from

something like that."

"Okay. Let's talk about the Watcher then. When I hinted that his involvement in this had something to do with his mom, he sounded like I was right. You said Smith Wimbledon's mom was sick."

Garrett dragged his eyes up to meet mine. "You really think Smith Wimbledon would do this? He was just a teenager when my family was murdered."

"I think that the Watcher is being manipulated by someone. What if Smith is being blackmailed to do this, some way?"

Garrett shook his head again. "I just don't see it."

"What about Vic Newport? His wife battled with drug addiction. She's been in and out of rehab. Could someone have been blackmailing him?"

"I just have trouble seeing any of those people taking the time to follow you around and warn you to stay out of trouble. People at the office would notice if Smith or Vic didn't come to work. Besides, who's the one really pulling the strings?"

"I wish I knew. I have to figure out how the P.I.s somehow tie into this. I mean, why was Bradley Perkins shot now? He's not even on the case anymore." I rested my head in my hands, feeling a headache coming on.

"I'd offer to rub your shoulders," Garrett started.

I shook my head. "Tempting, but better not."

The less he touched me, the better.

"Don't say I didn't offer."

"I hope you didn't hire me to no avail."

He patted my knee. "You've made more progress than anyone I hired. I'd say that was a success."

"Success to me is finding a killer."

Admiration sparkled in his eyes. "And that's just one more reason I hired you. Tenacity. And you're really nice to look at in the process."

"You're a lawsuit waiting to happen."

He shrugged. "Nothing wrong with surrounding myself with beauty."

I remembered everyone at his company. From his receptionist to his assistant, I had no doubt his words were true. "There are not-so-attractive people who could add value to your company."

Before he could respond, my phone screamed. I answered on the first ring, hoping it was Morrison calling with another update. Maybe even hoping it was Riley calling from a different phone number.

"You're a busy girl."

It was the Watcher. I mouthed the words to Garrett. He scooted closer and put his ear to the phone.

"I like to call myself productive," I retorted.

"Ask your friend Garrett how he liked the chlorine at his gala."

I glanced at Garrett, whose eyebrows were knotted together on his forehead.

"What are you talking about?" I questioned.

"He should know. He should remember."

"I thought you just did that to prove to some rich people that they weren't all that." Wasn't that what he'd said when I'd left Tess's house?

"The chlorine was on purpose. But I'd bet you Garrett was too into himself to remember what happened. I, on the other hand, can't forget."

I looked at Garrett again. He shook his head, looking clueless.

"I don't want to hurt you," the Watcher continued.

"Why? Why don't you want to hurt me? I don't understand."

"I have my reasons."

"Why don't you tell me what they are? Help me to understand you."

He was silent before chuckling. "You think you're going to get me that easily? You just want to profile me. Figure out who I am."

"Certainly telling *me* why *I'm* still alive won't reveal too much about *you*."

Silenced stretched a moment. I waited, restraining my tongue, giving him a moment to speak.

"No one else was supposed to be there that night," he finally said. "At least, that's what I heard."

"Edward Mercer was the target, wasn't he?" I asked. I hated to say the words in front of Garrett, but I had to know.

"It wasn't supposed to be like this. It keeps getting bigger. I'm tired of this game, Gabby."

I gripped the phone even tighter. "Then why not end it?"

"For reasons you'll never understand." He almost sounded defeated.

"If you tell me, I will."

"I'm not the one pulling the strings here. None of this is my choice. But now I'm a scapegoat. You need to tell Garrett that no one close to him is safe."

My lungs tightened. I glanced at Garrett and saw his eyebrows furrowed together in worry.

"Why hurt innocent people?" I asked.

"It's complicated. And it doesn't matter. Whatever happens, the police will think everything is my fault."

This guy seemed to be having some kind of break down or crisis of conscience. He sounded like he wanted out but was trapped.

"I can tell them it wasn't."

"It's too late for all of that." Silence stretched again.

"You remind me of my mom, you know. She's the reason I ever got involved. I had to help her."

"Your mom, huh?" I straightened, feeling like we were getting somewhere.

"She has hair like yours. It's red and curly."

"I think it's wise that you're honoring your mom, then." I was oh-so-grateful to have red hair at the moment. It was actually a lifesaver. I never thought I'd think that. "Why target P.I.s and not the police? Can you tell me that?"

While he was opening up, maybe I could get more information out of him.

"For years, no one connected the P.I.s. They were expendable. I had to . . . I had to take care of my mom. If I go to prison, she'll have no one."

"But people would have noticed a pattern if you'd killed the police officers." I nodded. That made sense, in a twisted kind of way, at least. "Why not stay in hiding?"

"My isolation is being threatened. That urged me to action. He keeps trying to pull me back in. I keep telling him I can't do it."

"Who's he?"

"He's—" Something rattled in the background. "What the . . . ?"

"What's going on?" I asked, against my better judgment.

"Hold on a second."

Hold on a second? What kind of psycho mass murderer said things like that?

Over the phone line, I heard something rattle. Then, I heard a clatter, almost as if the phone had dropped to the floor.

"You? You were the one behind this all of this time?" the Watcher mumbled. His voice sounded far off and muted. "What are you doing here?"

Then I clearly heard a gunshot.

The silence afterward had my blood curdling.

CHAPTER 31

Garrett and I were up for most of the night. Thankfully, he had a never-ending supply of coffee at the cabin. We both probably downed ten cups. We were living both on caffeine and adrenaline and the reckless hope that the answers were in our grasp.

After the phone call, we'd alerted both the police and Morrison. Two detectives, three officers, and Detective Morrison had shown up at Garrett's cabin. We'd had no choice but to explain everything, including the fact that someone had been murdered while I heard it all over the phone.

The *Watcher* had been murdered.

This case just continued to get more and more twisted.

Yes, the noose was tightening and the stakes were becoming more deadly by the minute.

Since I hadn't hung up the phone and neither had the Watcher, the police were attempting to trace the call. Maybe we had a chance.

I didn't know what had happened, but I had a feeling the Watcher really was dead.

But who would have killed him? Had there been another person pulling the strings? Working with him? Had this other person decided the Watcher was too much of a risk and expendable?

Nothing made sense at the moment.

At 3 a.m., the detectives thought they'd successfully

traced the number and they were closing in on a location.

By 6 a.m., we got the news that the police had discovered a body.

There was an unsigned suicide note, but I knew this man's death was no suicide. In his supposed note, he'd owned up to the Mercer family murders. Said he was rejected by Cassidy. That didn't match what he'd told me, though. He'd said *he* was a scapegoat.

The police had found his phone. He must have dropped it and it had been kicked under the couch. The killer probably hadn't known it was there.

What the police were still trying to figure out was who the man was. He had no identification on him. His truck was stolen. The house where he'd been wasn't his; he'd broken in while the owners vacationed down in Florida for the winter.

By 8 a.m., one of the lead detectives came back. He held up a picture and showed Garrett and me. "You recognize this man?"

As soon as I saw the picture, I gasped. "That's the caterer. He was at the gala on Friday. He's the one I saw whispering to Smith Wimbledon."

How had I not recognized him? Then I remembered that the driver of the limo had a goatee and glasses, as well as a hat pulled over his eyes. When he'd confronted me in the back of the vehicle, he'd donned a mask, as well. When I'd seen the man in his catering uniform in the alley, he'd changed clothes and ditched the facial hair. He hadn't looked a bit familiar.

I'd thought the man was trying to warn Smith about me and the supposed drugs I'd been doing. But what if the two were just conspiring about the murder?

Garrett peered over my shoulder. "I know him from somewhere else." Suddenly, he squeezed his eyes shut. "I know where now. He was Reginald Jr. Wimbledon's nephew. I think his name was Skip. His mother has been in a mental hospital for years, so this guy would come on vacations with the Wimbledons. He was from Reginald Wimbledon Jr.'s wife's side of the family, and they weren't wealthy. He was treated like a black sheep and always kind of an outsider."

The Silent One. Skip was the Silent One.

The detective jotted down everything. "Anything else you can think of?"

Garrett pinched the skin between his eyes. "How could I have not seen this? One summer, there was a chlorine incident at the indoor pool while we were on vacation. I haven't thought of it in years. We were at a resort, and a woman died from inhaling too much of the chlorine fumes when the tanks were improperly installed. I didn't know the woman; I just remember it was a tragedy. I can't imagine what it would have to do with this case, though."

"Anything else you can remember about Skip?" I asked.

"I'm pretty sure he joined the army after high school. I never saw him again after that."

The detective's jaw hardened. "I hope to have some answers soon. In the meantime, you two are free to go. I'll need you guys to keep this quiet for a while. No media leaks, not until we know more."

"No problem here."

Then I remembered Jamie's meeting at Wimbledon today. We needed to cancel. But if I suggested that, Jamie would know that something was going on.

I knew I should feel relief at the start of a resolution to the case, but I didn't. There was still something I was missing.

Someone had shot that man.

The questions were: Who and why?

***

Garrett dropped me off at the Paladins' and decided to head back to his apartment, just in case the police needed him for anything.

Without saying too much, I'd explained to Holly that there had been a development in the case that I was ordered not to talk about. Before I could call Jamie, she showed up. But from the way she stood with excitement dancing in her eyes, something was up. She charged inside. "My interview was canceled."

Holly and I glanced at each other before following after her. She went straight for the kitchen and began pacing.

"Did they say why it was canceled?" I asked.

"They didn't say anything, but thanks to my police scanner, I know the scoop." A satisfied smile stretched across her face.

I crossed my arms. "What's going on?"

"Smith Wimbledon is missing."

My mouth dropped open. "What?"

She nodded. "It's true. He never showed up at work today and his family said he's been gone since last night."

Had he disappeared to elude police? Or had the same person who'd taken out the Watcher taken out Smith, as well? I really wished I could share more details with Holly and Jamie, but I couldn't.

"The police are looking for him now," Jamie continued. "In the meantime, I decided to do a stakeout yesterday."

"A stakeout?" Had I heard her correctly? This girl was hardcore.

She nodded, as if it were no big deal. "I knew you were all wrapped up in Garrett Mercer."

"Busy *investigating* with him. Wrapped up has a different connotation," I corrected.

"And Holly was resting. So I went by myself."

"Did you find out anything?" I questioned.

"Interestingly enough, Vic Newport went to Smith Wimbledon's place at eleven last night. He looked rather anxious."

I blinked with surprise. "Is that right?"

Jamie nodded. "He left after an hour and then he drove around on some back roads for what felt like hours. A little past midnight, I lost him. I don't know where he went."

"You didn't see him leave with anyone, right? Smith didn't leave with him?" I asked.

"No, Smith didn't leave with him," Jamie said. "But something's going on."

My thoughts exactly. Just what had Vic Newport been doing last night? Had he found Skip and killed him?

Just then, the doorbell rang.

"Someone's supposed to deliver some papers for my mom," Holly explained.

"You look tired," I told her. "I'll answer for you."

When I pulled the door open, I spotted Vic Newport standing on the porch, sweat sprinkling his forehead.

Where was my gun when I needed it?

CHAPTER 32

"Mr. Newport." I took a step back. "What are you doing here?"

"We need to talk." His words sounded clipped, tight.

"This isn't a great time."

"Please. It's important." He stepped inside the house. I tried to push the door closed, but it was no use. His foot was there. His shoulders were wedged in the opening. "I know you're investigating me."

I tried to remain calm. "Why would you think that?"

He suddenly released his hands as if the handle had caught fire. He raised his arms in the air. "Look, I'm not trying to hurt you. I just want to talk. Please."

"How'd you know where I was?"

His face pinched. "I know you followed me last night."

I stared at him, contemplating his sincerity. I didn't trust him in the house, so I shook my head.

"We talk here. You on the porch, me and my girls inside the house." I held up my phone. "With 911 on speed dial."

"Fine." He wiped his brow.

I considered slamming the door and locking it. The other part of me wanted to hear what he had to say. I pulled the door open so that Holly and Jamie could hear— and to let him know that I wasn't alone.

"I didn't kill the Mercer family," Vic Newport started.

"I didn't think you did."

His breathing slowed for a moment. "You didn't?"

I shook my head. "No, I think you possibly hired someone to do the deed for you."

His face reddened again. "You've got to believe me. I'm innocent."

"Prove it. Because right now you've got the motive, the means, and the opportunity."

"It's true that I did think he was having an affair with my wife. But he wasn't. I thought about going to the house that evening. I thought about confronting him and demanding that he tell me the truth."

"Did you?"

He shook his head. "No, I felt like I was coming unhinged. I was trying to get a grip, so I drove around some. I decided to swing by the cabin the Mercers owned. I figured that would be a given rendezvous spot. My wife was out for the night, and I thought she and Edward could be together."

"The cabin?" I questioned.

He nodded. "I pulled up and saw two cars there. I crept closer, hoping to catch them in the act. Instead, I saw my daughter and Garrett Mercer there. They were arguing."

"Because Olivia was pregnant."

He nodded and rubbed his forehead again. "That's right. I thought it would be one bombshell and it was another. I decided to go to my favorite bar and drink away my troubles instead."

I wasn't buying his story that easily. "Did you ever think about confronting Garrett?"

"Absolutely. But then his family died and Olivia lost the baby."

"She told you she lost the baby?" I'd figured she'd kept it all quiet.

He shook his head. "By all definitions, I suppose she

had a miscarriage. But I found her in the bathroom. She'd taken some drugs. A lot of drugs. She's never told me, but I knew she did it to end the pregnancy. I rushed her to the hospital. We never told Garrett that part. There was never a need to. He already had enough going on."

I believed him. But while he was here, I had some other questions for him. "Where'd you go last night?"

"I thought I was going to get fired. I went to talk to Smith. The conversation didn't go well, so I drove around afterward. That's the truth. I promise."

"Fired over what?"

He let out a long breath. "Smith Wimbledon is a figurehead. He knows nothing about business. In a moment of weakness, I told him that. I regretted it afterward. I knew I could get fired, and I didn't want that to happen. I've been at the company for a long time."

Maybe that was the tension I'd felt between the two of them at the meeting that day.

"Who is the woman in this picture?" Jamie shoved her laptop his way. The online photo of him giving the strange look to the woman beside him.

He studied the picture a moment. "Her? That's Winnie Wimbledon. Smith's sister."

"Why are you giving her such a strange look?" I asked.

"She's different. Just kind of off beat. She made some kind of comment before the photo was taken, and I remember thinking about how strange she was. Of course, you have to act like you like her because she's the boss's sister."

"Does she work for Wimbledon Pharmaceuticals?" Holly asked.

"She's in and out. She's been mostly out of town lately. Probably having more plastic surgeries."

"Has she had a lot?" I asked.

He rolled his eyes. "You wouldn't even recognize her. She has a different nose. She's lost weight, has different hair, different style. What does this have to do with anything?"

I shook my head. "I'm not sure yet. If I have any more questions, can I contact you?"

"Please do. I want to find this murderer just as much as anyone else." He started to walk away but stopped. "There is one other thing that could be worth mentioning."

"What's that?"

"Another P.I. called me the other day. It's probably nothing, but it seems a little strange."

"What did he say?"

"His name was Bradley Perkins. He was asking about one of the drugs that we discontinued before it went on the market."

***

I headed over to the penthouse where Garrett was staying, hoping if the two of us put our heads together, we might figure out some answers. Holly and Jamie wanted to come, but I knew Garrett and I couldn't speak freely if they were there. I promised to give them updates as soon as I knew something.

As I drove, I chewed on what Vic Newport had told me. Bradley Perkins had been asking him about a drug they'd almost released at Wimbledon, but pulled off the market at the last minute. I also reflected on Smith Wimbledon's disappearance, Vic Newport's late night trip, and Reginald Wimbledon's nephew being the Watcher. Put all of this together, and what did it mean? I wish I knew.

I picked up some Chinese food. Garrett looked tired

when he met me at the door. Had something else happened?

"What's going on?" I slid past him and set the food on the table.

"No one has talked to Lyndsey since yesterday." He leaned against the breakfast bar, his arms crossed.

"She didn't make it back to Norfolk?"

He let out a sigh. "No one there has seen her. Someone at the company called this morning to say she hadn't come in. I made some calls, and she's gone."

I sucked in a breath as a chill rushed down my spine. "You think the person who killed the Watcher got to Lyndsey, too."

He nodded. "He did say that no one around me was safe."

"Maybe she's just taking some time off. She did work this weekend."

"She's usually very dependable. I'm hoping she's just having an irresponsible moment and that this psycho hasn't somehow gotten ahold of her." He shook his head. "I probably sound paranoid, but there are just too many crazy things happening lately."

"Crazy's one way to put it. Did you call the police?" I started doling out food onto some paper plates I'd picked up at the restaurant.

"I did. A Detective Adams is supposed to be looking into it."

I shoved some plasticware into the mounds of fried rice and pushed a plate toward Garrett. "I know Adams. He's a good guy. If anyone can get to the bottom of this, it's Adams."

"That's reassuring." He let out another sigh before picking up his fork, only to immediately put it back down. "Anything new on your end?"

I gave him an update on my visit with Vic Newport, ending with the information about Perkins calling to inquire about a certain drug.

"Does that drug thing ring any bells?"

"Honestly, I wouldn't know. My dad didn't talk about it. I didn't ask." He finally took a half-hearted bite of his lunch.

"That has to be why Perkins died."

"I can't disagree, but I don't have any answers for you. Your phone call to Perkins must have triggered something in him. He followed up, and . . ." Garrett shook his head. "I don't like where this is all going."

His gaze looked especially heavy. Was it just this case? I decided to ask. "Is something else wrong?"

He shoved his fork into his rice and leaned back. "My problems seem to be mounting. I also found out this morning that one of our competitors is releasing a proprietary coffee flavor that we've worked on developing. They're hitting us a week before our big debut."

"Coffee flavors can be proprietary?" I muttered, before shaking my head. "Never mind. I guess, even for a company that's globally minded, this is a big deal."

"Without good business sense, we can't make as big of an impact with our charities. We've got to make the money in order to spend it on building the wells in third world countries."

I nodded. "I see. How did this happen?"

"Someone got a hand on one of our formulas. They're beating us to the punch."

"But people who like your coffee are still going to buy it. Right?"

He stared at me. "This is a big deal, Gabby. We're going to lose money. A lot of money."

I hardly heard him. My mind started racing. I stood, pacing to keep up with my thoughts.

Garrett stopped talking. That's when I realized that he had still been talking. "What is it, Gabby?"

"I know why your father was killed." I closed my eyes as more facts began coming together. Everything was finally making sense. "And why he had that cash and the passports stored away."

"Please share then."

I kept pacing with my eyes closed, pinching the skin between them as I sorted out my thoughts. I remembered his dad's resume. I remembered my suspicions about the pharmaceutical company being the source of this somehow.

"Gabby, please. The suspense is killing me."

I held up a finger. I just needed one more minute to make sure this made sense before I spouted off my theory.

I had it, I realized. I knew what had happened.

I paused, swallowed and looked at Garrett. "Your dad was a corporate spy."

His eyes widened. "What?"

I nodded. "That would explain why his resume was the way it was. Your dad was desperate to be on top. I'd bet you anything that his former company was paying him, off the books, for him to give them the scoop on what was being developed at this company."

Garrett nodded as he considered my words. "Pharmaceuticals are a highly competitive field. But there are clauses, papers that you sign before you start working there."

"That won't stop some people. Your dad was probably making a lot of money from the deal. Maybe enough that he finally felt like he could compete with the money your mom already had from her upbringing. You said your dad was a proud man. He didn't want his wife to have more money than he did. It took away from his manhood. That's why he worked so hard. It was one of the reasons, at least."

Garrett stood now and looked into the distance. "I suppose that would explain why we moved so suddenly when my dad had seemed so happy at his former company. He also asked us not to talk about that job. I always thought it was because it ended poorly or something. But maybe he just didn't want anyone to know that he'd worked there."

"I think someone figured out what he was doing. I think they confronted him. Wimbledon Pharmaceuticals probably stood to lose millions of dollars."

He shook his head. "But there are patents and processes. I'm not sure how easy it would have been."

"But if one company doesn't dominate the market, then the prices have to be competitive. Garrett, you have to admit that it would be reason enough for some people to murder."

"Then who? Vic Newport?" he asked.

I shook my head. "I don't think so. But it was someone inside the company who was angry with your father. Someone knew he was the traitor. Just like someone at your company is a traitor now. I don't think that is a coincidence, either."

"You think I unknowingly hired a corporate spy?"

"What makes them a spy is the fact that they're so good at what they do. They're slick. They're sly. They're not obvious."

He shook his head. "I can't imagine anyone under me doing this."

"You need to keep thinking then." I sucked in a deep breath as more clues clicked in my mind. "How could I not have seen this before?"

"Seen what?" Garrett asked.

I reached into my purse and pulled out the picture Cassidy had on her dresser. Winnie was in that picture. Winnie was also in that picture with Vic Newport. I showed Garrett. "Imagine Winnie with different hair, thinner, more stylish. Plastic surgery."

He squinted. "Okay."

"Garrett, Winnie Wimbledon is Lyndsey. Your assistant."

His eyes widened. "No . . ."

I nodded. "She's been the one behind this."

Garrett ran a hand over his face. "This is going to take a while to sink in. I just can't believe it."

"This is huge."

"How could Lyndsey do this to me?" He rubbed his temples.

"Some people might have asked the same questions about your father."

He shook his head. "Greed. I always vowed I wouldn't be like my father. I wouldn't let money rule my life. Maybe the love of money is the root of all evil."

"What I don't understand is how she's always a step ahead of us, even while here in Cincinnati. That's what doesn't make any sense to me. Unless . . ."

His brows furrowed together. "Unless what?"

I pointed to his watch. "You never go anywhere without that, do you?"

"No, it was my father's." His face went slack. "I had Lyndsey take it into the shop to be repaired a few months ago. Do you think . . . ?"

"Money can do a lot of things. Like put bugs into watches so the other side can hear every word we're saying."

He pulled off the watch and threw it across the room. "I hate being duped."

"I need to call the police, Garrett." And I had to do it quickly. Because if my theory was right and that watch was bugged then—

The front door burst open.

The first thing I saw was a gun. Pointed right at us.

CHAPTER 33

"Not so fast," Lyndsey muttered.

She closed the door behind her and stepped inside with the grace of a cheetah. A deadly cheetah.

"Lyndsey, why don't you put the gun down? We can talk this through," Garrett started.

The look in her eyes was steady. And lethal. And that was the scariest thing of all.

"I knew it was just a matter of time before you'd put everything together." She stepped closer. "You want to know what happened on the night your family died? Why don't we reenact it, right here, right now."

"Lyndsey?" Garrett started to approach her, then seemed to think twice and stopped. "You were the one behind all of this? How could you?"

She sneered. "I'd hoped it wouldn't come to this. I'd hoped you would just forget about what had happened and move on. That this would be a terrible tragedy. That you'd accept there were no answers."

"One doesn't easily forget about the murders of their family." Garrett's face—slack just a few minutes ago—now looked tight and angry.

Lyndsey shook her head. "In the meantime, I was going to give you what you deserved."

"What did I deserve, Lyndsey?"

I couldn't help but think that might not be the best question. No need to put any more ideas into her head.

She laughed, but it sounded empty. "You didn't even recognize me, Garrett. You hired me without blinking. Oh, I suppose you said I looked vaguely familiar. But suddenly you noticed me. All of those years I tried to get you to even look my way, and you never did."

"Lyndsey, I was a different person back then." He raised his hands, those expressive green eyes coming in handy now as he silently pleaded with her.

"Ha!" The word came out a little too forcefully. "You were shallow. Into the pretty girls. Ignoring the one who'd give up everything to be with you."

She was getting closer to Garrett and the vengeance in her voice was growing. I had to step in.

"Did you kill his family?" I tried to reconcile in my mind teenage Lyndsey as a mass murderer. I had trouble seeing it.

She snorted, swinging the gun toward me. "Are you kidding? I was sixteen when his family died."

"You're picking up where your father left off," I filled in. "Everything was on the line for him. Edward Mercer nearly took down his company. He would have lost everything."

"Exactly! One more way the Mercers could ruin my life. He only intended to kill your father. He had no idea anyone else would be home. Too bad you weren't there." She glared at Garrett.

"So you're fulfilling your father's dying wish?"

She nodded. "I was more than happy to help. Family loyalty means everything."

"Why pull your cousin Skip into this?" I asked.

"He accidentally killed that lady on vacation, didn't he?" Garrett whispered. "He was probably messing with the chlorine tanks. I seem to remember he wanted to be a lifeguard."

Lyndsey smiled. "I'm impressed. I was the only one who saw him do it. I've been holding it over his head for years. Only he never knew it was me. I reminded him that if anyone found out what he'd done, who would take care of his mom? She's still in the mental institution, you know. She's crazy."

"You must have inherited the trait," Garrett mumbled.

Did the man have no idea how to talk to a homicidal, crazy woman? Obviously not!

For once, I was the one reining the conversation in. "Brilliant on your part, Lyndsey," I offered. "You threatened to turn him in. You knew what he'd done. He, in return, became the Watcher. He did your dirty work."

"Then you got a job with me so you could really keep an eye on things," Garrett said.

Great. He was talking again. Not a good thing.

The woman shot daggers at him with her eyes every time he opened his mouth.

"Another brilliant move," I started. "You rented the car for me. You knew my cell number, my basic schedule. You even had someone follow me, didn't you?"

"I was hoping they might scare you off. You're tougher than I thought you'd be."

"We're both tough women." Again, I tried to appeal to her ego, tried to make her feel like we could relate. "How'd you know about Perkins?"

"He called my brother asking some questions about a drug that was taken off the market. I just happened to be in the office when he got the call. Wimbledon Pharmaceuticals developed the drug, but the patent hadn't gone through yet. Then Edward Mercer sold the proprietary formula to another company. My father confronted him about it, and Edward didn't care. My father knew what was going to happen. Edward was about to split with all the money he'd made selling our secrets."

"Then your father snapped," I filled in. "He killed the Mercers. When he realized what he'd done, he took the drug out of production, doctoring the paperwork and convincing the board it wasn't safe. He was afraid the police might make the connection."

"You got it. Thankfully, Pittsburgh was only a five-hour drive away. I convinced Skip to take action."

"Your plan almost worked, except that Skip somehow got his conscience back and started talking too much."

Lyndsey sneered again. "I had to take care of him. Just like I have to take care of you now." She nodded behind her. "You're going to walk calmly to my car. We're going to take a little drive."

A car. Not a car.

I'd seen the writing on the wall with that one. Death by car seemed a little too obvious to me.

"Cars really aren't a great idea. Too many people might see us," I offered.

Garrett's head swerved toward me, an incredulous look in his eyes. I shrugged and mouthed, "Long story."

"What do you suggest, Shirleylock?" She rolled her eyes. "Yes, I had to listen to every disgusting moment of him flirting with you. You're a smart girl for turning him down. It's about time someone said no to the man. He's been handed everything on a silver platter."

And Lyndsey hadn't? I kept my mouth shut on that one.

"I don't suppose going down to the police station is an option right now?" My idea sounded feeble to my own ears.

"At this point, I have no choice. You're both going to die." She raised her gun.

"You always have a choice," I insisted, not that my

voice of reason would do much good right now. But I needed to keep her talking. The more she talked, the less likely she would pull that trigger. And the more opportunity I had to reach my purse and grab my own gun.

Justice, mercy, humility.

How could I bring all three of those things into play right now?

Lyndsey shook her head a little too violently. "It's too late."

If this woman would kill her own flesh and blood, she wouldn't hesitate to end my life or Garrett's life.

I crept closer to my purse.

"Why don't you put the gun down?" Garrett urged. "We can talk about this like two rational people."

Lyndsey laughed, the sound on the verge of madness. "You got your father's gift of business and cleverness. It's gotten you far. You're the type who'll do whatever it takes to get ahead."

"That's not true, Winnie."

She let out a laugh, but it sounded crazy and uneven.

The woman was spiraling into lunacy. "Your father cost the company millions. Millions. My dad had to lay off workers. New drug production was put on the back burner because we couldn't afford it. The company put millions into that drug. And your father stole it."

"He should have gone to jail for doing that, Lyndsey," I started, again trying to get the focus off of Garrett. "You have every right to be upset."

Make her think you're on her side. Don't let her emotions escalate any more.

"All your dad cared about was matching his wife's wealth." Vengeance gleamed in her eyes.

"Some people never seem to have enough. It's called greed," I said, stepping closer to my purse.

She scoffed. "It's more than greed. It's backstabbing. It's disloyalty. It's betrayal."

"My father wasn't right in doing that, Lyndsey," Garrett pleaded, his hands raised. "But two wrongs don't make a right. Isn't that the saying?"

I nodded slowly, calmly and took another shuffle toward my purse. "What happened to Smith?"

The smirk returned. "He's fine. Just locked away at our father's old place. I figured the police would want to talk to him. I didn't want anyone putting the pieces together yet." She stepped closer to Garrett and ran a finger down his chest. "Back when we were teens, you wouldn't give me the time of day, you know." She jabbed him in the chest.

"I had no idea, Lyndsey. I was young."

"You broke my heart. Made me feel not good enough. Not pretty enough. When I came of age, I begged for a nose job. Colored my hair. Had vision-correcting surgery. Hired a personal trainer. I essentially became a new person."

"The changes were . . . impressive," Garrett muttered.

I wanted to roll my eyes. This was no time for Garrett to show his shallow side.

"We all have to pay the consequences for our actions," Lyndsey continued. "And pay for the actions of our families, as well." She raised her gun. "Now, let's get this over with."

I raised a hand to stop her. "Not to sound cliché here, but you're never going to get away with this. You might as well give up now."

"I've gotten away with it already. I have a plan for this one, too. Murder suicide. We might as well do it here in the apartment rather than at the house, although your old house would be more poetic. You've been talking too much and we've been running out of time. You couldn't take the pain of your family's death anymore, Garrett."

"Anyone who knows me won't believe that."

Lyndsey lunged forward and grabbed me. She put the gun to my head with one hand and tossed something to Garrett with the other. "Take those pills or she dies."

Garrett stared at the medication in his hands. "What is this?"

"The drug your father sold us out with. You're going to overdose on them. After you supposedly shoot your little girlfriend."

"There's got to be another way, Lyndsey," Garrett said.

He knew what I did: If he swallowed those pills, neither of us would stand a chance.

"Take it!"

Garrett raised his hands and glanced at me. I saw the agony in his eyes. "Okay. Okay. I just need some water."

"Try anything and I'll shoot her. You know I will."

"I'm going. I'm going." He slowly walked to the kitchen and got a glass of water. Then he opened the packet and raised it. "Should I take them all at once?"

"What do I look like? A life coach? Do whatever you want. Just take them."

"Okay, okay." Garrett swirled his water around before raising his glass. "Here goes."

He popped the pills in his mouth.

If he swallowed that stuff, our fate would be sealed.

"Garrett, no!" I grabbed Lyndsey's arm, bent forward, and pulled her over my shoulder. Her gun sounded, and I heard a cry of agony.

I just wasn't sure whom the sound had come from.

It could have even been me.

CHAPTER 34

Garrett hit the ground, glass shattered, and the front door flew open.

Detective Morrison charged inside, his gun drawn. Officers flooded in behind him and handcuffed Lyndsey Wimbledon.

I pulled myself off the floor and dashed toward Garrett. From across the room, I spotted the blood. On his sleeve, I realized.

Thankfully, the wound wasn't fatal.

I knelt beside him. "Are you okay?"

"I think I'll recover quite nicely, especially if I can hire you to be my nurse." His eyes hadn't lost their sparkle. That was a good thing.

"I'm a terrible nurse. I pass out at the sight of blood."

"Said the crime scene cleaner?"

"Totally different."

"Good work, you two," Morrison said.

I looked up at the retired detective. "How'd you know to come here?"

"We cut through the red tape faster than I thought would be possible. Edward Mercer did have an offshore bank account, where he'd been receiving monthly payments from a company called Ryan Enterprises."

"The company he worked for before coming to Wimbledon?" I mumbled.

"He doctored his resume and made it look like he

worked for a consumer product company," Morrison continued. "That company owns Ryan Enterprises. They were paying him nicely in order to get company secrets from Wimbledon Pharmaceuticals. The account was totally off the books, so there's no way we would have discovered it, if it hadn't been for you, Gabby."

"It was a team effort, on all accounts," I insisted. "What about Sebastian?"

"We're looking into him now, trying to figure out if he did anything illegal."

I watched Lyndsey being led away and shook my head. "She could have had everything, but it wasn't enough."

"Money doesn't buy happiness," Garrett said. "Certainly you know that."

"I'll take justice, humility, and mercy any day."

"Huh?"

I shook my head. "I've just had several reminders about how I need to be sold out for what I believe in. There's a Bible verse that seems to sum that up nicely for me."

The paramedics loaded Garrett onto a stretcher and began wheeling him away.

That's when Holly and Jamie burst into the room.

"What are you doing here?" I asked them.

"Morrison called us and asked where you were," Holly said. "I figured something was going down. We wanted to be here, just in case you needed us."

"The MOD Squad always sticks together," I said.

Holly grinned. "That's what doing life together is all about."

CHAPTER 35

I looked at Holly across the table in her kitchen, gratitude filling me. I was so glad that we'd met. She'd reminded me just how sacred life was and how we couldn't take a moment for granted.

We sipped our tea. Holly had made a lemon pound cake that was to die for, again using one of the recipes from her old cookbooks she'd found at the thrift store that had "the absolutely best recipes ever."

"Did you hear from Garrett today?"

I nodded. "The hospital released him, and he's already on his way back to Norfolk. He said he has to clean up the mess at GCI. He's okay, though."

"I'm glad."

"Me too. They found Smith Wimbledon, as well. He's fine. He was totally clueless and innocent about everything. Lyndsey will be going away for a long time after all she's done, however."

"Justice is now served with a side of humility and closure."

"Thank you for helping me out," I started. "I couldn't have done all of this without you."

"I'm glad I had the chance. I can mark that off my bucket list now. I've officially helped to solve a crime."

My smile faded. "About that bucket list. You plan on saying anything to your family?"

Her lips squeezed together before she shook her head.

"No. Not yet. I will, though. I promise. The timing just has to be right. I want Alex's wedding out of the way and for the election to be past. Then I'll let them know about my diagnosis."

"Holly—"

She raised a hand. "I know it's unconventional. But this is the way I need to do it. For me. I'll be okay. I promise."

Finally, I nodded. "Okay, then. I trust you with your decision."

Just then, my phone rang. It was Chad. We did our general chitchat for a moment, and I updated him on the case.

"You given any more thought to expanding our business?" he asked during a break in our conversation.

"I'm still okay with it."

"Okay, okay. How about Squeaky Clean?"

I shrugged to myself. "Now, that kind of has a nice ring to it."

"You think?" The light returned to his voice.

"I do. How about: Squeaky Clean, a Professional Disaster Clean Up Company?"

"Sounds perfect. We'll talk more when you get back tomorrow. For now, there's something Sierra can't wait to tell you."

"I know who the new owner is." Sierra's voice bubbled over the phone line.

"What? Who?" *Was I going to have to move?* That was really the only question I cared about at the moment. I just couldn't stand any more upheaval in my life.

"This is the crazy part. Get this. Garrett Mercer bought it."

"What?" I nearly fell out of my chair.

"It's true. Our former landlord stopped by today to tell us all the news."

"Garrett Mercer?" I repeated, still in shock.

"The good news is that we can all live there still."

I tried to come out of my dazed state. "That's . . . that's great."

He'd bought the house to help me out, I realized. My heart softened. I couldn't believe he would do that for me.

You'd never have to worry about money with me again.

Was he trying to manipulate me with this move? Or was he truly being kind? I'd ask him about it the next time we spoke.

"That's great news, I guess." Was this the special project he'd been working on when he couldn't take my call?

"I know. I can't believe it."

My next question sobered me. "You seen Riley around?"

Her voice softened. "No, I haven't. You've talked to him, haven't you?"

"A couple of times. Nothing feels the same." Just because I had faith that God was ordaining my future didn't mean I didn't have the emotions that came with pain and disappointment.

"I've been thinking about this a lot, Gabby. Do you remember when your mom got sick? You gave up your education—and essentially your life and your dreams—in order to take care of your father."

"Those were some hard days."

"I think Riley realizes how hard that was for you. He knows that you'd do that for him. And I think he wants to see you bloom. He doesn't want to hold you back. He doesn't want you to resent him like you did your dad."

"But he's different. My dad—"

"I know," Sierra said softly. "Believe me, I know how your dad is. But the more I think about it, the more I realize that Riley is doing this because he loves you, not because he wants to hurt you."

Tears washed into my eyes. Her words made sense. Why hadn't I seen that earlier? Riley knew my history. He knew I would sacrifice everything to be with him . . . and he wasn't going to let me do that.

"Thanks for sharing that, Sierra."

"For the first time, I solved a mystery before you did. The mystery of love," she added with an exaggerated sigh.

I let out a chuckle. "The one type of mystery I'm horrible at solving. Always have been."

With uncanny timing, we both started singing "Love's a Mystery" by The Pretenders before bursting into laugher.

"You know what I've realized throughout all of this?" I asked. "Trying to have it all and do it all is impossible. You have to make decisions. Those decisions will show your priorities. And, at the end of your life one day, you'll figure out if you made the right choice or not."

"What's that mean for you, Gabby?"

"It means I have a lot of thinking to do. And it means I need to go call Riley and talk to him. I need to give our relationship more time and let him know I'm there for him. I really think everything else will fall in place. Maybe not now. But with time."

"I think you're right, Gabby. Everything will fall in place with time."

###

Did you enjoy meeting Holly Anna Paladin and all of her friends? If so, check out *Random Acts of Murder*, Book One in the Holly Anna Paladin Mystery Series.

Keeping reading for an excerpt.

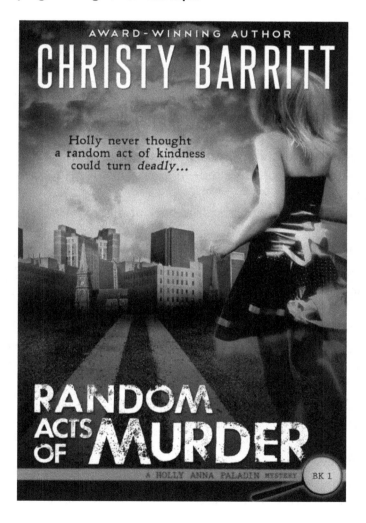

Random Acts of Murder
CHAPTER 1

This had to be my worst idea ever.

Before I lost my courage, I rushed inside the house, turned the locks, and leaned against the door. I tried to steady my breathing and push away the regret that threatened to consume me—regret at my decision to do this.

A dark, silent house stared back at me, almost taunting me.

It was too late to turn back now. I was in. I'd already broken the law. I might as well follow through with the rest of the plan.

"Are you in, Retro Girl?" My friend Jamie's voice sounded through my Bluetooth headset.

"I'm in, Girl Genius." Jamie had picked her code name herself.

"Everything clear?" she asked.

"What's clear is the fact that I'd make a terrible, terrible criminal."

"That's a good thing, Hol—I mean Retro Girl. Be careful."

I nodded. "Roger that."

In the delirium of a restless night, this whole scheme had seemed brilliant. But the fact remained that, in order to execute my plan, I'd just broken into someone's home.

I'd utilized the skills my locksmith father had taught me, though I was certain he'd never dreamed I'd use them this way. I'd become a masked vigilante of good deeds, only without the mask.

My heart slammed at a quick beat into my chest, each thump reverberating all the way down to my bones. I pinched the skin between my eyebrows as I tried to rationalize my actions. This wasn't just a haphazard stranger's home. And I wasn't breaking in for nefarious reasons. That was the good news.

The bad news had generated my new life mantra: engaging in random acts of kindness whenever possible. And not just any ordinary random acts of kindness. *Extreme* random acts of kindness. Life was too short to do anything halfheartedly, after all.

To lay it all out, I'd just broken into the home of Katrina Dawson, one of my former social work clients—but only so I could clean her house and surprise her. I wanted to help. The idea had started innocently enough when I'd sneaked in to clean my brother's house—a drive-by good deed, as I'd called it. He'd been thrilled, especially when he'd found the nice, anonymous note I'd left, explaining I didn't seek recognition but only wanted to make his day brighter.

Cleaning Katrina's house would help her and add a touch of quality to her life. I knew it would. She was a single mom, she couldn't catch a break when it came to getting a decent job, and with a whole gaggle of kids, she barely had time to brush her teeth, let alone clean her home.

A clean residence could do wonders for a person's spirit.

"You still okay, Retro Girl?" Jamie asked in my ear.

"I guess. What's it look like outside?"

"It's all clear. A neighbor three doors down just went

inside. He didn't even look my way. Good thing I'm driving the ghettomobile. It blends right in."

"Here goes nothing, Girl Genius."

I took a deep breath, grabbed my bucket of cleaning supplies, and plunged into the darkness. I planned to focus on the kitchen and bathroom since they usually needed the most attention.

I pushed up the sleeves of my black T-shirt. I'd abandoned my trademark dress in favor of something more sensible. I didn't want to draw any unnecessary attention to myself in the run-down neighborhood. Pulling up in my '64 1/2 powder-blue Mustang—Sally, as I affectionately called her—and stepping out with a vintage frilly dress on just wasn't a smart idea.

I could do this, I told myself, a feeling of false security washing over me. I'd clean, leave a sweet note explaining I was a friend doing a random act of kindness, and then I'd hop in the van and head home. I was making a big deal out of nothing.

That's what I told myself, at least.

I waited until I was away from the front windows before I turned a light on. Before I'd come inside, I'd put my gloves on. I never cleaned without them. Nothing was less appealing than smelling bleach on your hands three days after the fact. Plus, since I was officially breaking in, the gloves just seemed like a good idea.

I set my bucket on the countertop and looked at the mess around me. Dirty dishes in the sink. Junk on every visible surface—everything from schoolbooks to groceries to toys. There was something splattered on the linoleum floor, crayon marks on the wall, and this morning's breakfast—at least, I assumed the food was from today— was still on the little table in the corner.

The house smelled like it hadn't been cleaned in a

while, a mix of trash that desperately needed to be taken out, rotting food on the plates in the sink, and laundry that had been sitting for too long. I'd noticed that on my last visit here. But the main thing I'd noticed had been the look of hopelessness in Katrina's eyes. Hopelessness about changing her life, about getting ahead, about catching any breaks. No one should have to feel like that.

As I picked up my first plate, ready to wash it, I realized that I was breaching an uncountable number of professional standards. The good thing was that, even if I was fired from my job as a social worker, it wouldn't matter.

"Girl, what is that noise?" Jamie asked.

"It's the water running."

"Well, can't you help a sister out and turn it down some? My ears will be ringing for the rest of the night."

Just then, I bristled. Why did I feel like someone was watching me? The thought was crazy. I was the only one here. I'd watched Katrina and her family leave earlier. She worked the graveyard shift and took her kids to a sitter's.

"Girl Genius, something doesn't feel right."

"You broke into someone's house. Maybe that's it."

"But I broke in with good intentions, so that makes it okay, right?"

Jamie chuckled. "You just keep telling yourself that, Retro Girl."

Three months ago, my job and my reputation would have mattered. Three months ago, I'd had a different outlook on life. I'd thought I had forever left.

But sometimes a routine visit to the doctor changed a girl's view and made her realize that she could take chances, that life was too short not to take risks.

My name is Holly Paladin, I'm twenty-eight years old, and I've been given a year to live.

The introduction played over and over again in my mind, much like a broken movie reel. In my head, I also had the same accent as Inigo Montoya from *The Princess Bride*, but that was an entirely different issue.

But this wasn't a movie. This was my life. I only had one year to leave a mark. One year to embrace what I loved. One year to let my loved ones know how much they meant to me.

There was a lot I wouldn't be able to do, so I decided to focus primarily on one task: changing the world. At least, changing one or two people's worlds.

That's why I washed the dishes in the sink.

That's why I collected the trash and placed it by the front door.

That's why I wiped down the counters and the stove and the refrigerator.

When I stepped back, the kitchen looked spotless.

I smiled, feeling satisfied. This *had* been a good idea. I just had to make peace with myself about the implications of my means. I knew my motives were golden.

Now I just had to do the bathroom. I'd clean the whole house, if I could. I'd wipe the windows, scrub the baseboards, and start some laundry. But that would take more time than I had.

I stepped into the hallway, went down two doors, and reached inside the bathroom. Just as my fingers connected with the light switch, I heard a noise.

I froze.

What was that?

I listened but didn't hear anything else. Had that been movement inside the house? But no one was home, despite the eerie feeling I'd had earlier.

Besides, if someone else was here, they would have come out by now. In the very least, they would have called the police.

My heart pounded in my ears.

Bad idea, bad idea, bad idea. The phrase kept repeating in my head.

This *was* a bad idea, no matter how I tried to paint the harebrained plan in a positive light.

I had to clean this bathroom, and then I was getting out of here.

I gulped in one last breath and pushed the light switch up.

I blinked at what I saw there.

It was a man. Lying on the floor. Blood pooled around his chest.

He was dead.

No doubt about it—dead.

If you enjoyed this book, you may also enjoy:

Squeaky Clean Mysteries

Hazardous Duty (Book 1)
On her way to completing a degree in forensic science, Gabby St. Claire drops out of school and starts her own crime-scene cleaning business. When a routine cleaning job uncovers a murder weapon the police overlooked, she realizes that the wrong person is in jail. But the owner of the weapon is a powerful foe . . . and willing to do anything to keep Gabby quiet. With the help of her new neighbor, Riley Thomas, a man whose life and faith fascinate her, Gabby seeks to find the killer before another murder occurs.

Suspicious Minds (Book 2)
In this smart and suspenseful sequel to *Hazardous Duty*, crime-scene cleaner Gabby St. Claire finds herself stuck doing mold remediation to pay the bills. Her first day on the job, she uncovers a surprise in the crawlspace of a dilapidated home: Elvis, dead as a doornail and still wearing his blue-suede shoes. How could she possibly keep her nose out of a case like this?

It Came Upon a Midnight Crime (Book 2.5, a Novella)
Someone is intent on destroying the true meaning of Christmas—at least, destroying anything that hints of it. All around crime-scene cleaner Gabby St. Claire's hometown, anything pointing to Jesus as "the reason for the season" is being sabotaged. The crimes become more twisted as

dismembered body parts are found at the vandalisms. Someone is determined to destroy Christmas . . . but Gabby is just as determined to find the Grinch and let peace on earth and goodwill prevail.

Organized Grime (Book 3)
Gabby St. Claire knows her best friend, Sierra, isn't guilty of killing three people in what appears to be an eco-terrorist attack. But Sierra has disappeared, her only contact a frantic phone call to Gabby proclaiming she's being hunted. Gabby is determined to prove her friend is innocent and to keep Sierra alive. While trying to track down the real perpetrator, Gabby notices a disturbing trend at the crime scenes she's cleaning, one that ties random crimes together—and points to Sierra as the guilty party. Just what has her friend gotten herself involved in?

Dirty Deeds (Book 4)
"Promise me one thing. No snooping. Just for one week." Gabby St. Claire knows that her fiancé's request is a simple one she should be able to honor. After all, Riley's law school reunion and attorneys' conference at a posh resort is a chance for them to get away from the mysteries Gabby often finds herself involved in as a crime-scene cleaner. Then an old friend of Riley's goes missing. Gabby suspects one of Riley's buddies might be behind the disappearance. When the missing woman's mom asks Gabby for help, how can she say no?

The Scum of All Fears (Book 5)
Gabby St. Claire is back to crime-scene cleaning and needs help after a weekend killing spree fills her work docket. A serial killer her fiancé put behind bars has escaped. His last words to Riley were: *I'll get out, and I'll get even.* Pictures

of Gabby are found in the man's prison cell, messages are left for Gabby at crime scenes, someone keeps slipping in and out of her apartment, and her temporary assistant disappears. The search for answers becomes darker when Gabby realizes she's dealing with a criminal who is truly the scum of the earth. He will do anything to make Gabby's and Riley's lives a living nightmare.

To Love, Honor, and Perish (Book 6)

Just when Gabby St. Claire's life is on the right track, the unthinkable happens. Her fiancé, Riley Thomas, is shot and in life-threatening condition only a week before their wedding. Gabby is determined to figure out who pulled the trigger, even if investigating puts her own life at risk. As she digs deeper into the case, she discovers secrets better left alone. Doubts arise in her mind, and the one man with answers lies on death's doorstep. Then an old foe returns and tests everything Gabby is made of—physically, mentally, and spiritually. Will all she's worked for be destroyed?

Mucky Streak (Book 7)

Gabby St. Claire feels her life is smeared with the stain of tragedy. She takes a short-term gig as a private investigator—a cold case that's eluded detectives for ten years. The mass murder of a wealthy family seems impossible to solve, but Gabby brings more clues to light. Add to the mix a flirtatious client, travels to an exciting new city, and some quirky—albeit temporary—new sidekicks, and things get complicated. With every new development, Gabby prays that her "mucky streak" will end and the future will become clear. Yet every answer she uncovers leads her closer to danger—both for her life and for her heart.

Foul Play (Book 8)

Gabby St. Claire is crying "foul play" in every sense of the phrase. When the crime-scene cleaner agrees to go undercover at a local community theater, she discovers more than backstage bickering, atrocious acting, and rotten writing. The female lead is dead, and an old classmate who has staked everything on the musical production's success is about to go under. In her dual role of investigator and star of the show, Gabby finds the stakes rising faster than the opening-night curtain. She must face her past and make monumental decisions, not just about the play but also concerning her future relationships and career. Will Gabby find the killer before the curtain goes down—not only on the play, but also on life as she knows it?

Broom and Gloom (Book 9)

Gabby St. Claire is determined to get back in the saddle again. While in Oklahoma for a forensic conference, she meets her soon-to-be stepbrother, Trace Ryan, an up-and-coming country singer. A woman he was dating has disappeared, and he suspects a crazy fan may be behind it. Gabby agrees to investigate, as she tries to juggle her conference, navigate being alone in a new place, and locate a woman who may not want to be found. She discovers that sometimes taking life by the horns means staring danger in the face, no matter the consequences.

Dust and Obey (Book 10)

When Gabby St. Claire's ex-fiancé, Riley Thomas, asks for her help in investigating a possible murder at a couples retreat, she knows she should say no. She knows she should run far, far away from the danger of both being around Riley and the crime. But her nosy instincts and determination take precedence over her logic. Gabby and Riley must work together to find the killer. In the process, they have to confront demons from their past and deal with their present relationship.

Thrill Squeaker (Book 11)

An abandoned theme park. An unsolved murder. A decision that will change Gabby's life forever. Restoring an old amusement park and turning it into a destination resort seems like a fun idea for former crime-scene cleaner Gabby St. Claire. The side job gives her the chance to spend time with her friends, something she's missed since beginning a new career. The job turns out to be more than Gabby bargained for when she finds a dead body on her first day. Add to the mix legends of Bigfoot, creepy clowns, and ghostlike remnants of happier times at the park, and her stay begins to feel like a rollercoaster ride. Someone doesn't want the decrepit Mythical Falls to open again, but just how far is this person willing to go to ensure this venture fails? As the stakes rise and danger creeps closer, will Gabby be able to restore things in her own life that time has destroyed—including broken relationships? Or is her future closer to the fate of the doomed Mythical Falls?

Swept Away, a Honeymoon Novella (Book 11.5)

Finding the perfect place for a honeymoon, away from any potential danger or mystery, is challenging. But Gabby's longtime love and newly minted husband, Riley Thomas, has done it. He has found a location with a nonexistent crime rate, a mostly retired population, and plenty of opportunities for relaxation in the warm sun. Within minutes of the newlyweds' arrival, a convoy of vehicles pulls up to a nearby house, and their honeymoon oasis is

destroyed like a sandcastle in a storm. Despite Gabby's
and Riley's determination to keep to themselves, trouble
comes knocking at their door—literally—when a neighbor
is abducted from the beach directly outside their rental.
Will Gabby and Riley be swept away with each other
during their honeymoon . . . or will a tide of danger and
mayhem pull them under?

Cunning Attractions (Book 12)
Coming soon

While You Were Sweeping, a Riley Thomas Novella
Riley Thomas is trying to come to terms with life after a
traumatic brain injury turned his world upside down. Away
from everything familiar—including his crime-scene-
cleaning former fiancée and his career as a social-rights
attorney—he's determined to prove himself and regain his
old life. But when he claims he witnessed his neighbor
shoot and kill someone, everyone thinks he's crazy. When
all evidence of the crime disappears, even Riley has to
wonder if he's losing his mind.

Note: *While You Were Sweeping* is a spin-off mystery
written in conjunction with the Squeaky Clean series
featuring crime-scene cleaner Gabby St. Claire.

The Sierra Files

Pounced (Book 1)

Animal-rights activist Sierra Nakamura never expected to stumble upon the dead body of a coworker while filming a project nor get involved in the investigation. But when someone threatens to kill her cats unless she hands over the "information," she becomes more bristly than an angry feline. Making matters worse is the fact that her cats—and the investigation—are driving a wedge between her and her boyfriend, Chad. With every answer she uncovers, old hurts rise to the surface and test her beliefs. Saving her cats might mean ruining everything else in her life. In the fight for survival, one thing is certain: either pounce or be pounced.

Hunted (Book 2)

Who knew a stray dog could cause so much trouble? Newlywed animal-rights activist Sierra Nakamura Davis must face her worst nightmare: breaking the news she eloped with Chad to her ultra-opinionated tiger mom. Her perfectionist parents have planned a vow-renewal ceremony at Sierra's lush childhood home, but a neighborhood dog ruins the rehearsal dinner when it shows up toting what appears to be a fresh human bone. While dealing with the dog, a nosy neighbor, and an old flame turning up at the wrong times, Sierra hunts for answers. Her journey of discovery leads to more than just who committed the crime.

Pranced (Book 2.5, a Christmas novella)

Sierra Nakamura Davis thinks spending Christmas with her husband's relatives will be a real Yuletide treat. But when the animal-rights activist learns his family has a reindeer farm, she begins to feel more like the Grinch. Even worse, when Sierra arrives, she discovers the reindeer are missing. Sierra fears the animals might be suffering a worse fate than being used for entertainment purposes. Can Sierra set aside her dogmatic opinions to help get the reindeer home in time for the holidays? Or will secrets tear the family apart and ruin Sierra's dream of the perfect Christmas?

Rattled (Book 3)

"What do you mean a thirteen-foot lavender albino ball python is missing?" Tough-as-nails Sierra Nakamura Davis isn't one to get flustered. But trying to balance being a wife and a new mom with her crusade to help animals is proving harder than she imagined. Add a missing python, a high maintenance intern, and a dead body to the mix, and Sierra becomes the definition of rattled. Can she balance it all—and solve a possible murder—without losing her mind?

Holly Anna Paladin Mysteries

Random Acts of Murder (Book 1)
When Holly Anna Paladin is given a year to live, she embraces her final days doing what she loves most—random acts of kindness. But one of her extreme good deeds goes horribly wrong, implicating her in a string of murders. Holly is suddenly thrust into a different kind of fight for her life. Could it also be random that the detective assigned to the case is her old high school crush and present-day nemesis? Will Holly find the killer before he ruins what is left of her life? Or will she spend her final days alone and behind bars?

Random Acts of Deceit (Book 2)
"Break up with Chase Dexter, or I'll kill him." Holly Anna Paladin never expected such a gut-wrenching ultimatum. With home invasions, hidden cameras, and bomb threats, Holly must make some serious choices. Whatever she decides, the consequences will either break her heart or break her soul. She tries to match wits with the Shadow Man, but the more she fights, the deeper she's drawn into the perilous situation. With her sister's wedding problems and the riots in the city, Holly has nearly reached her breaking point. She must stop this mystery man before someone she loves dies. But the deceit is threatening to pull her under . . . six feet under.

Random Acts of Murder (Book 3)
When Holly Anna Paladin's boyfriend, police detective Chase Dexter, says he's leaving for two weeks and can't give any details, she wants to trust him. But when she discovers Chase may be involved in some unwise and

dangerous pursuits, she's compelled to intervene. Holly gets a run for her money as she's swept into the world of horseracing. The stakes turn deadly when a dead body surfaces and suspicion is cast on Chase. At every turn, more trouble emerges, making Holly question what she holds true about her relationship and her future. Just when she thinks she's on the homestretch, a dark horse arises. Holly might lose everything in a nail-biting fight to the finish.

Random Acts of Scrooge (Book 3.5)

Christmas is supposed to be the most wonderful time of the year, but a real-life Scrooge is threatening to ruin the season's good will. Holly Anna Paladin can't wait to celebrate Christmas with family and friends. She loves everything about the season—celebrating the birth of Jesus, singing carols, and baking Christmas treats, just to name a few. But when a local family needs help, how can she say no? Holly's community has come together to help raise funds to save the home of Greg and Babette Sullivan, but a Bah-Humburgler has snatched the canisters of cash. Holly and her boyfriend, police detective Chase Dexter, team up to catch the Christmas crook. Will they succeed in collecting enough cash to cover the Sullivans' overdue bills? Or will someone succeed in ruining Christmas for all those involved?

Random Acts of Guilt (Book 4)

Coming soon

Carolina Moon Series

Home Before Dark (Book 1)
Nothing good ever happens after dark. Country singer
Daleigh McDermott's father often repeated those words.
Now, her father is dead. As she's about to flee back to
Nashville, she finds his hidden journal with hints that his
death was no accident. Mechanic Ryan Shields is the only
one who seems to believe Daleigh. Her father trusted the
man, but her attraction to Ryan scares her. She knows her
life and career are back in Nashville and her time in the
sleepy North Carolina town is only temporary. As Daleigh
and Ryan work to unravel the mystery, it becomes obvious
that someone wants them dead. They must rely on each
other—and on God—if they hope to make it home before
the darkness swallows them.

Gone By Dark (Book 2)
Ten years ago, Charity White's best friend, Andrea, was
abducted as they walked home from school. A decade
later, when Charity receives a mysterious letter that
promises answers, she returns to North Carolina in search
of closure. With the help of her new neighbor, Police
Officer Joshua Haven, Charity begins to track down
mysterious clues concerning her friend's abduction. They
soon discover that they must work together or both of
them will be swallowed by the looming darkness.

Wait Until Dark (Book 3)
*A woman grieving broken dreams. A man struggling to
regain memories. A secret entrenched in folklore dating
back two centuries.* Antiquarian Felicity French has no clue
the trouble she's inviting in when she rescues a man

outside her grandma's old plantation house during a treacherous snowstorm. All she wants is to nurse her battered heart and wounded ego, as well as come to terms with her past. Now she's stuck inside with a stranger sporting an old bullet wound and forgotten hours. Coast Guardsman Brody Joyner can't remember why he was out in such perilous weather, how he injured his head, or how a strange key got into his pocket. He also has no idea why his pint-sized savior has such a huge chip on her shoulder. He has no choice but to make the best of things until the storm passes. Brody and Felicity's rocky start goes from tense to worse when danger closes in. Who else wants the mysterious key that somehow ended up in Brody's pocket? Why? The unlikely duo quickly becomes entrenched in an adventure of a lifetime, one that could have ties to local folklore and Felicity's ancestors. But sometimes the past leads to darkness . . . darkness that doesn't wait for anyone.

Cape Thomas Series:

Dubiosity (Book 1)
Savannah Harris vowed to leave behind her old life as an investigative reporter. But when two migrant workers go missing, her curiosity spikes. As more eerie incidents begin afflicting the area, each works to draw Savannah out of her seclusion and raise the stakes—for her and the surrounding community. Even as Savannah's new boarder, Clive Miller, makes her feel things she thought long forgotten, she suspects he's hiding something too, and he's not the only one. As secrets emerge and danger closes in, Savannah must choose between faith and uncertainty. One wrong decision might spell the end . . . not just for her but for everyone around her. Will she unravel the mystery in time, or will doubt get the best of her?

Disillusioned (Book 2) *coming soon*
Nikki Wright is desperate to help her brother, Bobby, who hasn't been the same since escaping from a detainment camp run by terrorists in Colombia. Rumor has it that he betrayed his navy brothers and conspired with those who held him hostage, and both the press and the military are hounding him for answers. All Nikki wants is to shield her brother so he has time to recover and heal. But soon they realize the paparazzi are the least of their worries. When a group of men try to abduct Nikki and her brother, Bobby insists that Kade Wheaton, another former SEAL, can keep them out of harm's way. But can Nikki trust Kade? After all, the man who broke her heart eight years ago is anything but safe...Hiding out in a farmhouse on the Chesapeake Bay, Nikki finds her loyalties—and the

remnants of her long-held faith—tested as she and Kade put aside their differences to keep Bobby's increasingly erratic behavior under wraps. But when Bobby disappears, Nikki will have to trust Kade completely if she wants to uncover the truth about a rumored conspiracy. Nikki's life—and the fate of the nation—depends on it.

Standalones

The Good Girl

Tara Lancaster can sing "Amazing Grace" in three harmonies, two languages, and interpret it for the hearing impaired. She can list the Bible canon backward, forward, and alphabetized. The only time she ever missed church was when she had pneumonia and her mom made her stay home. Then her life shatters and her reputation is left in ruins. She flees halfway across the country to dog-sit, but the quiet anonymity she needs isn't waiting at her sister's house. Instead, she finds a knife with a threatening message, a fame-hungry friend, a too-hunky neighbor, and evidence of . . . a ghost? Following all the rules has gotten her nowhere. And nothing she learned in Sunday School can tell her where to go from there.

Death of the Couch Potato's Wife (Suburban Sleuth Mysteries)

You haven't seen desperate until you've met Laura Berry, a career-oriented city slicker turned suburbanite housewife. Well-trained in the big-city commandment, "mind your own business," Laura is persuaded by her spunky seventy-year-old neighbor, Babe, to check on another neighbor who hasn't been seen in days. She finds Candace Flynn, wife of the infamous "Couch King," dead, and at last has a reason to get up in the morning. Someone is determined to stop her from digging deeper into the death of her neighbor, but Laura is just as determined to figure out who is behind the death-by-poisoned-pork-rinds.

Imperfect

Since the death of her fiancé two years ago, novelist

Morgan Blake's life has been in a holding pattern. She has a major case of writer's block, and a book signing in the mountain town of Perfect sounds as perfect as its name. Her trip takes a wrong turn when she's involved in a hit-and-run: She hit a man, and he ran from the scene. Before fleeing, he mouthed the word "Help." First she must find him. In Perfect, she finds a small town that offers all she ever wanted. But is something sinister going on behind its cheery exterior? Was she invited as a guest of honor simply to do a book signing? Or was she lured to town for another purpose—a deadly purpose?

The Gabby St. Claire Diaries (a tween mystery series)

The Curtain Call Caper (Book 1)

Is a ghost haunting the Oceanside Middle School auditorium? What else could explain the disasters surrounding the play—everything from missing scripts to a falling spotlight and damaged props? Seventh-grader Gabby St. Claire has dreamed about being part of her school's musical, but a series of unfortunate events threatens to shut down the production. While trying to uncover the culprit and save her fifteen minutes of fame, she also has to manage impossible teachers, cliques, her dysfunctional family, and a secret she can't tell even her best friend. Will Gabby figure out who or what is sabotaging the show . . . or will it be curtains for her and the rest of the cast?

The Disappearing Dog Dilemma (Book 2)

Why are dogs disappearing around town? When two friends ask seventh-grader Gabby St. Claire for her help in finding their missing canines, Gabby decides to unleash her sleuthing skills to sniff out whoever is behind the act. But time management and relationships get tricky as worrisome weather, a part-time job, and a new crush interfere with Gabby's investigation. Will her determination crack the case? Or will shadowy villains, a penchant for overcommitting, and even her own heart put her in the doghouse?

The Bungled Bike Burglaries (Book 3)

Stolen bikes and a long-forgotten time capsule leave one amateur sleuth baffled and busy. Seventh-grader Gabby

St. Claire is determined to bring a bike burglar to justice—
and not just because mean girl Donabell Bullock is strong-
arming her. But each new clue brings its own set of
trouble. As if that's not enough, Gabby finds evidence of a
decades-old murder within the contents of the time
capsule, but no one seems to take her seriously. As her
investigation heats up, will Gabby's knack for being in the
wrong place at the wrong time with the wrong people
crack the case? Or will it prove hazardous to her health?

Complete Book List

Squeaky Clean Mysteries:
#1 Hazardous Duty
#2 Suspicious Minds
#2.5 It Came Upon a Midnight Crime (a novella)
#3 Organized Grime
#4 Dirty Deeds
#5 The Scum of All Fears
#6 To Love, Honor, and Perish
#7 Mucky Streak
#8 Foul Play
#9 Broom and Gloom
#10 Dust and Obey
#11 Thrill Squeaker
#11.5 Swept Away (a novella)
#12 Cunning Attractions (coming soon)

Squeaky Clean Companion Novella:
While You Were Sweeping

The Sierra Files:
#1 Pounced
#2 Hunted
#2.5 Pranced (a Christmas novella)
#3 Rattled

The Gabby St. Claire Diaries (a Tween Mystery series):
#1 The Curtain Call Caper
#2 The Disappearing Dog Dilemma
#3 The Bungled Bike Burglaries

Holly Anna Paladin Mysteries:

#1 Random Acts of Murder
#2 Random Acts of Deceit
#3 Random Acts of Malice
#3.5 Random Acts of Scrooge
#4 Random Acts of Guilt (coming soon)

Carolina Moon Series:
Home Before Dark
Gone By Dark
Wait Until Dark

Suburban Sleuth Mysteries:
#1 Death of the Couch Potato's Wife

Stand-alone Romantic-Suspense:
Keeping Guard
The Last Target
Race Against Time
Ricochet
Key Witness
Lifeline
High-Stakes Holiday Reunion
Desperate Measures
Hidden Agenda
Mountain Hideaway
Dark Harbor
Shadow of Suspicion (coming soon)

Cape Thomas Series:
Dubiosity
Disillusioned (coming soon)

Standalone Romantic Mystery:
The Good Girl

Suspense:
Imperfect

Nonfiction:
Changed: True Stories of Finding God through Christian
Music
The Novel in Me: The Beginner's Guide to Writing and
Publishing a Novel

About the Author:

USA Today has called Christy Barritt's books "scary, funny, passionate, and quirky."

Christy writes both mystery and romantic suspense novels that are clean with underlying messages of faith. Her books have won the Daphne du Maurier Award for Excellence in Suspense and Mystery, have been twice nominated for the Romantic Times Reviewers' Choice Award, and have finaled for both a Carol Award and Foreword Magazine's Book of the Year.

She is married to her Prince Charming, a man who thinks she's hilarious—but only when she's not trying to be. Christy is a self-proclaimed klutz, an avid music lover who's known for spontaneously bursting into song, and a road trip aficionado.

When she's not working or spending time with her family, she enjoys singing, playing the guitar, and exploring small, unsuspecting towns where people have no idea how accident-prone she is.

Find Christy online at:
www.christybarritt.com
www.facebook.com/christybarritt
www.twitter.com/cbarritt

Sign up for Christy's newsletter to get information on all of her latest releases here: **www.christybarritt.com/newsletter-sign-up/**

If you enjoyed this book, please consider leaving a review.